THE CARAVAN

A "JOHNNY BOY" STORY

By.

Kevin D. Bell

Edited
By
Anja Hebert Ceaser

For my brother Eric Michael Bell

CHAPTER 1
THE BOY

1

The first month of spring was always a pleasant time on the roads in the western part of the land. The sun cut away the thick rain clouds of earlier months allowing the beautiful blue of the sky to shine through. The green grass along the old, cracked, concrete road stretched and grew as they awakened from a long winter sleep. The flowers began to blossom; the sunflowers, the iris, and angel's tears all filling large spreads of green in the land with color and aroma. It was the sort of scenery that people fell in love in, that children played in, and artist wrote about. It was the type of scenery that Miranda loved.

Miranda woke from a pleasant and uneventful sleep with rays of warm sunshine streaming in through the blinds of her small window. The tiny trailer rocked slightly as it was pulled along with the rest of the caravan. She sat up and stretched her thin arms, raising them to the ceiling as her tiny hands and fingers pointed out. Her short, curly brown hair fell over her round face and deep brown eyes. Her skin, lightly tanned from a life in the sun, trembled slightly from the sudden blast of cold air that hit her as her thick blanket slipped off her shoulders. She picked it up and began to fold it. She knew the seasons well, better than was normal for most people, and she wasn't going to need a blanket this thick anymore; not for months. After she changed out of her long baby blue nightgown she would pack the blankets in the storage trailer and get the thinner ones. Before she did though, she pulled back the blinds and looked outside letting the warm light fully into her tiny little room.

It was difficult to tell where they were. There were no sign posts or anything that hinted they were anywhere near a town, but that didn't matter to Miranda. The beautiful sea of colors that stretched out around the caravan was a sight she had missed through winter. It never snowed in this part of the world but the flowers stopped blooming and the sky became gray. Now the color was back and she felt engulfed by it.

She strained with the window for a moment before it finally opened, letting in a gentle breeze and the wonderful aroma of a valley full of flowers. She closed her eyes and took a deep breath, letting the aroma fill her nostrils. If the caravan stopped, as she was hoping it would, she could walk barefoot through the valley. She could feel the grass beneath her feet and run across the valley like she was six instead of sixteen. She would sing a song and...

"Shut that goddamn window!"

Miranda turned to face the opposite end of the room. The voice had come from the person in the small bed that sat against the opposite wall. The person in it was buried underneath the large bundled clump of blanket. If not for the long, darkly tanned, calves and slender feet sticking out of the bottom and the mass of unkempt auburn hair sticking out the top, the bed would've looked empty.

"And I swear to God," the voice continued in an irritated grumble, "if you start singing I'm gonna kill you." She had probably been woken up by the sudden light when Miranda opened the window.

"How can you wake up in such a bad mood Isabelle?" Miranda asked in a much more cheerful tone, "Spring is finally here and we're in a part of the world where we can really enjoy it." She stepped away from the window and sat on the edge of Isabelle's bed.

"Oh Joy," Isabelle said, not sounding the least bit joyous, "in other words we're out in the middle of nowhere with nothing but flowers as far as the eye can see."

"Exactly! It's so beautiful."

"The ocean is beautiful." Isabelle slowly sat up, her hair falling to the small of her back. The strap of her short sleeveless shirt falling off her shoulder a little. "People are beautiful, this place is a lot of grass." She leaned back and stretched her long, lightly glowing, frame in the sunlight.

Isabelle's figure was more curvy than Miranda's; with fuller hips, larger breast, and a slight hint of muscle tone in her arms, legs, and flat stomach. Miranda looked back out the window to avoid comparing her body to Isabelle's. She didn't like feeling self-conscious and that was how Isabelle always seemed to make her feel when she woke up. Even with her hair tangled and in desperate need of some type of shampoo, Isabelle seemed on a different plane from Miranda.

Isabelle finally got out of bed, the old worn-out pants she was wearing

2

swinging out from under the blanket. She was taller than Miranda too. Not by much, maybe half an inch, but it was noticeable. Once Miranda had thought maybe she just hadn't developed like Isabelle because Isabelle was two years older but she was coming to realize it was just luck of the draw. She just wasn't built like her.

"Where are we going anyway?" Isabelle asked, scratching her head and yawning. Miranda shrugged.

"The suns rising on our right side," she said as Isabelle walked toward the small closet in the back of the tiny trailer, pulling her shirt over her head as she went. "So we must be heading North."

"That's good. Then we're probably headed to Frisco. At least the audiences there will have money."

Miranda turned to her, letting the beautiful view leave her mind for a moment.

"Since when do you care about them having money?" Miranda asked, "What happened to 'dancing just for the sake of dancing'?" For a moment Isabella didn't respond, she was too focused on pulling the much too tight pair of black jeans up her left leg while balancing on her right.

"My love for dance won't pay for food," Isabelle said as she nearly fell over, "and it won't pay for our renting this trailer."

"So we pay by working in the carnival for Andy." Miranda said matter-of-factly, "we've done it before."

"I don't like jumping through hoops."

"You don't like being paired with Nathan."

"I **hate** that."

"Whatever we have to do to eat. Isn't that what you're always saying? Besides if it means we can keep doing what we love to do what difference does it make?"

Isabelle stood up, zipped up the jeans, and slipped her feet into a pair of black sandals. Then she pulled a dusty brown shirt out of the closet and began buttoning it up.

"Still a while before we get there." Miranda said. She stuck her hand out the window letting cold air flow through her fingers, "Probably another two months."

Isabelle walked to the door opposite the closet. "I'm gonna get some breakfast." she said and then left, closing the door behind her. Miranda waited for a moment and then pulled the window shut. She had to get dressed.

3

The massive caravan was brought to the side of the road. It's enormous front carriage pulled along twenty trailers of various sizes, all linked together by large steel platforms strong enough to walk on from one trailer to another. It's hulking size and shape made it look like an enormous train mixed with a tank. It's grayish paint was covered in bright, colorful banners that read:

PEN'S GRAND CARAVAN AND STUNT SHOW

The Caravan was run by Andy Che Pen, a tall and very muscular man with a thick, short cut beard and a short cut head of graying hair. His face had the hardened expression of a man who had seen the worst and fought past it. His enemies and admirers knew him as Bloody Pen. His friends, family, and comrades knew him as Andy.

Andy Pen was more than happy to stop the caravan for a bit. The caravan had been running for days and everyone, passenger and employee alike, wanted to stretch their legs and relax in the pleasant weather. Though he was known for being a man of few smiles, even he could appreciate the landscape.

He climbed down from the main carriage slowly, he had various injuries over his body from the years on the roads and he didn't want any of them flaring up. His boots hit the grass with a heavy thud and he glanced across the valley. It was about twelve more weeks until they hit Frisco and there was no need to hurry. They could linger for a bit, maybe do some hunting. The forest was visible barely a few hours walk from where he stood. It would give his more restless crew members something to do. The stunt fighters, Nathan especially, were getting a bit too rowdy and they were making the passengers a little uneasy. Getting them away from the caravan for a while would be good for everyone.

"Isn't it beautiful Andy?" Miranda said from his right. He turned to the sound of her voice. She was a few feet away standing barefoot in the grass. Her long yellow sun dress flapping lightly in the breeze.

"It certainly is." He said, "How did you sleep?"

"Just fine." She smiled and bent down to pick a flower. She had been traveling in the caravan for about five years at that point. She was found by a passenger, hiding in one of the storage trailers. She never spoke of what had led to her stowing away on the caravan, but for the first several months she had woken up at night screaming for her parents. She had changed much since then; she was more vocal, she smiled more, and she didn't seem to tremble whenever someone talked to her anymore. She was becoming a young woman. A young woman he would've been proud to call his daughter.

She started to walk further out, her steps turning into strides. In a few more moments she would begin to blend with the yellow flowers. He didn't normally like her wandering off, it wasn't always as safe on the road as it looked. But the valley was wide and the grass wasn't tall enough for someone to hide in.

"Don't wander too far!" he called out. She didn't respond or look back. Her attention seemed to have been drawn to something in the grass. She bent low and picked something up. Andy couldn't tell what it was from that distance but it caught light and reflected in his eye. She ran toward him, her face now looking fear stricken. He jogged toward her and met her halfway in the grass.

"What is it?" He asked. She was gasping for breath, she was thin but not very athletic. She held out what she had found.

It was a key. A very old, very scratched, very small key. It was gray and looked no more impressive than a key used for an old chest or closet door. Why Miranda had come running was obvious though. The key was covered in blood. He took the key and looked closely at it.

"Get back inside," he took a few steps further in looking toward the forest, "and tell Nathan and the boys to meet me out here."

"There's little patches of blood all over," Miranda said as she moved toward the caravan, "leading to the forest." Andy nodded without looking at her. It looked like they would definitely be doing some hunting. The blood on the key was still runny, it hadn't been there very long. If they moved fast they might make it in time to save someone. If not? No one's body should just be left to rot in the woods. Everyone deserves a proper burial.

3

Isabelle was sulking her way through breakfast, still annoyed at being out in the middle of nowhere. She missed the beach; the sand in her toes, the feeling of water on her body, the cool ocean air. She missed all of it.

Now she was in a place where she wouldn't be able to swim at all. It also meant there was no way for her to avoid Nathan.

The self-proclaimed "Master Warrior Nathan Feldmen" was scared of the ocean. She had no idea why, and she didn't really care. It kept him away from her and that had been enough.

"Can't use that anymore," she thought to herself as she idly stirred her lukewarm oatmeal, *"he'll be coming on to you within the hour."* She had no sooner finished the thought when the large double doors of the dining trailer opened, and Nathan walked in. He looked across the rows of benches and tables, caught sight of her, and headed straight for her. She suppressed a moan, negative signs just made him more persistent.

Physically she had no problem with Nathan. In fact he had a fantastic body in her opinion. He was tall, muscular, with a full head of short black hair, and the barest hint of a beard. She usually liked men with that appearance. She had fallen for men like that, hell she had slept with men like that. It wasn't his looks that made her despise him. It was the way he looked at her.

It wasn't that he looked at her with lust in his eyes. He wasn't the first to look at her that way and he wouldn't be the last. It was that lust was all there was. He didn't see her as an equal or even as a person. It was obvious in how he spoke to her, and acted around her. He saw her as some type of toy or pet that was just being stubborn.

"There you are Isabelle," he said as he approached, "I was wonderin where you were." He stood next to the table and leaned in toward her. He kept leaning in until she pulled away. She didn't like doing anything that he might see as a retreat, but he was just too damn close. He put his hand on top of hers and she immediately pulled it away. "When are ya gonna stop playing like you're innocent?" He reach out and gripped her hand, "you know you want ta'."

"Let go of me Nathan," she said her free hand forming a fist. Her blood was heating up. She wanted him away from her before she hit him. She was way behind on her share of the rent on the trailer and she didn't want to punch one of Andy's most valued employees. Still, she wasn't going to let him think she was okay with this. "Let me go before I break something on you." His smile widened, and a chill ran up her back. He let go of her hand and moved away from her. His smile didn't fade.

"You're blushin." He said. Her face was red, but from pent up fury rather than any latent desire. He turned and made for the door. The fury in her face began to fade. She watched him walk off, wishing she had something sharper than a spoon in her hand.

She began to turn away just as Miranda appeared in her field of vision and began talking to Nathan. When Miranda finished talking Nathan ran off, apparently excited about something. Maybe Andy had something for the pig to shoot.

4

Andy kept the hunting party small. After inspecting the field, Andy had found that the "little patches" of blood Miranda had seem were only the beginning. The patches got larger and became more consistent until it looked like a trail leading into the forest.   Andy followed the trail with Nathan and two other hunters in tow; Curtis Rengrave and Ramon Turno.

Curtis was about fifty years old, four years younger then Andy, and had spent his entire life in some form of physical labor. He was a quiet man, known for having a photographic memory and the best aim out of any of the hunters or stunt fighters. Andy trusted him more than anyone and felt that his quiet nature would help to temper the testosterone crazed Nathan.

Ramon was the youngest of Andy's stunt performers, he had just turned seventeen. He was short and rather bony, his hair a thick tangle of black. He wore a pendant that looked like a bird feather around his neck and treasured it like a rare jewel. When Andy first picked him up Ramon had said it was a gift from his mother, and said nothing else about it. He was a decent performer and a fair hunter but he had a lot to learn and this was as good a training session as any Andy could think of. He held his simple hunting rifle a little too tight, clearly nervous. He was going to be leaning on Nathan through out this whole thing.

Although hunting for food was not the goal, Nathan clearly intended to catch something. He had slung a hunting rifle over his shoulder, two huge revolvers on hip holsters, and an enormous hunting knife tied to his ankle. The others just carried a single hunting rifle each.

They cut across the valley in single file, none of them saying anything but noticing everything. After an hour they were nearing the forest. Its tall oak trees green with the fresh strong leaves of good spring weather. Andy slowed as they neared the trees and the others did the same. Nathan crept around to the front pushing pass the others.

"There aren't any birds chirping," Nathan said pulling the rifle off his

7

shoulder. His eyes bright, "somethings got 'em scared."

"Put that away." Andy said without looking up from the trail of blood, "I don't want you shooting the guy we came here to rescue by accident." Nathan frowned and shouldered his rifle again as Andy picked up the pace and headed into the forest.

It was quiet, abnormally so, and the ground around the trail of blood was clear, like the fallen leaves and broken branches had been swept out of the way to make room for it. Andy stopped. This was very wrong. This wasn't the trail of someone who had been wounded and wandered into the forest, this was someone making an overly obvious path to something. He was getting ready to drop the search and turn back when Nathan suddenly ran past him.

"Nathan!" Andy hissed sharply but Nathan ignored him. Rifle at the ready, Nathan ran along the trail deeper into the forest. He was fast, faster than Andy had thought he was, and he was already fading into the distance. He couldn't afford to lose Nathan. He needed him for the Stunt Show as well as for hunting.

Cursing under his breath, Andy and the others ran after Nathan a chill running up Andy's back the whole way.

5

Nathan didn't know why he was running. His mind had been studying the forest, wondering what the trail led to, wondering who had left it for them to follow, when a single command suddenly popped into his mind.

Come here.

Next thing he knew he had unslung his rifle and was running through the forest as fast as his legs could carry him. His face turned down of its own accord and his eyes became fixed on the blood. The trail was growing, filling the path and starting to swerve from left to right.

Stop!

Nathan ground to a halt just as the trail swerved right. He looked to his right, his eyes following the trail as it began to curve first up and then to the left. It came back around to its starting point forming a perfect circle. Behind him Nathan could hear Andy and the others running after him. He tuned them out and looked to the center of the circle.

Just like the path through the forest, the area around and inside the circle had been cleared of all fallen leaves and twigs. The brown area of dirt in the center was covered in blood. The blood in the center wasn't like the blood forming the circle, the blood in the center was dull and dry. It had dried into the dirt a long time ago. It followed no path and was splattered everywhere. As Nathan stepped into the circle he saw something else, there was a body in the center. Bloody and bruised. Nathan stepped toward it.

It was a young man, maybe two years younger than Nathan. He was fat, dressed in a thick gray wool sweater that made him look like a small gray bear. He was black with skin that was a deep brown that seemed to match the bark of the trees. His hair was like a big poofy black ball of cotton on his head. There was a gash over the boys left eyebrow and from the darkened blood it had been there for a while, and his arms were both broken in two places. Still, despite all the damage to his body this boy was alive and breathing steadily.

Nathan moved closer to him.

The sound of Andy's footsteps growing louder but still very far off. He glanced over his shoulder for a second looking back at the trail of blood. How had he gotten so far ahead?

He looked away from the sleeping boy and noticed something. The circle and trail of blood had disappeared.

6

The still breathing boy proved to be something of a problem to move. His weight matched his shape. Curtis and Andy both commented that it was indeed like trying to move a small bear. Eventually they got the boy up, Curtis under his left arm and Andy on his right, and then began the long trek back.

They made their way back through the forest and across the valley in silence. At one point Ramon commented on the sudden disappearance of the trail but nobody responded at first.

"That's weird ain't it?" Ramon said his voice a little scratchy and shifting; the voice of a boy still in the throws of puberty. His body was done growing but his voice was a few years behind. "I mean for it to just disappear like that, its almost like ma.."

"Shut up!" Nathan hissed. Ramon fell silent. The others were all thinking that exact word though. Magic.

Most people in the major cities of the world snorted laughter at the mention of magic. They called it a ridiculous idea told in stories used to mystify and scare children. Stories about witches, werewolves, ghosts, and the like. The farmers, performers, travelers, and peasants of the world knew better though. Magic was very real. It was real and nothing good ever came from it.

As the sun began to set and the little hunting party reached the caravan, Andy glanced at the bruised unconscious boy. The magic behind the blood had been used to lead them to this boy. Which meant that nothing good would come of him. Still, it was bad karma to leave a man stranded when you could help. Andy knew that rule well, and Karma was something he took very seriously.

Andy only had two places he could put the boy. He could either put him in the one empty trailer, and sacrifice a potential rental, or he could room the boy in the extra room in the back of Cook's kitchen..

Cook was a large, very viscous old woman. She stood at about six feet tall and weighed about two hundred and fifty pounds. Her skin had a mild sickly gray tint to it and her nose was comically long. While the boy looked like a small bear, Cook was like a large rabid elephant. Andy had found her about two years after he started the Caravan and Carnival. She had been trying to kill the owner of a café in a small town. He had loved her cooking but not her attitude. Andy had managed to talk her into joining his caravan by agreeing to giving her the freedom to choose her own kitchen helper's, total run of the kitchen trailer, and the room connected to the kitchen was hers to use as she saw fit. She had ultimately chosen two kitchen helpers; both girls, both about sixteen years old, and both absolutely terrified of her. She was a great cook but had absolutely no love for people and would probably try to kill Andy if he put the boy in her extra room. Since he was sure she would succeed if she tried to kill him, he put the boy in the empty trailer.

The boy was very popular among the crew members, and passengers. Everyone wondered who he was and what had happened to him. Andy instructed Nathan and the others not to mention the circle. Talk of magic made people nervous and he didn't need to deal with any panic stricken passengers. It became the common belief that the boy had tried to travel on foot, been attacked by bandits, and left for dead. For all they knew that might not have been too far from the truth.

One of the paying passengers, a short woman with wide hips and a head of silver hair tied in a bun, was a nurse from a small town that the Caravan had passed through a few weeks before. She offered to check on the boy. "I've worked as a nurse for longer than I care to remember," she told Andy, "and I ain't forgotten none of what I learned," she chuckled, "not yet anyway." She asked Isabelle and Miranda to assist her. Neither was really sure what they could do, but they both agreed.

9

The old nurse stood over the boy in the tiny trailer with Miranda to her left and Isabelle to her right. Miranda looked at the boy's arms, twisting in unnatural angles, and felt she was going to faint just from the image of how they might have broken. Isabelle felt the same and kept her attention on the boys sleeping face.

"Miranda sweetie?" the old nurse said. Miranda jumped suddenly as she was pulled out her nightmarish daydream of having her own arms broken, "Could you go and bring me some water darlin? This poor boys all dried up." Miranda ran out of the room, grateful for an exit. "All right then," the old nurse continued, "let's do this before the dainty lil thing comes back."

She motioned for Isabella to stand over the boy's head. "Press down on his shoulders little one." Isabelle did as she was told. The boy was pudgy but his shoulders were broad and firm. Isabelle imagined there was probably some muscle underneath his body fat.

"Why am I doing this?" Isabelle asked.

"You gotta hold him down if he wakes up from the pain." The old nurse replied as she took the boys left arm in her hands.

"Pain from wh-" Isabelle began, then stopped. The old woman took the boys arms and popped the broken bones back into place. One after the other in a series of unsettling quick motions; POP! POP! POP! POP! The boy didn't flinch but Isabelle felt a few sympathy shivers trailing up her arms. She shook them off and waited a moment longer before lifting her hands off the boy's shoulders. The nurse pulled a large black bag off the floor and propped it on the edge of the boy's bed. She pulled out two long pieces of wood and a huge roll of bandages.

"Help me make the splints sweetheart." The old nurse said. By the time Miranda returned with a jug of water and a small, dented, tin cup, Isabelle and the nurse had tied the boy's arms in splints and were wiping the blood off his face. Soon there was nothing more to do but wait for the boy to wake up. The old nurse got up to leave.

"Check on him every few hours girls," she said to them, "if something happens you come and find me. I'm in trailer number 5." Miranda nodded, a little more stable now that the boy didn't look so viscously beaten. Isabelle nodded and again moaned to herself about how far she was from the beach.

10

Isabelle and Miranda did as they were told. Each day they took turns tending to the boy. It was very boring work, all there was to do was slip a little water between his lips and listen to him sleep. He was breathing normally and his eyelids fluttered a bit from time to time but he never woke up. Whenever they left the trailer, after an hour or so, they would be approached by Andy, Curtis, Ramon, Nathan, the old nurse, or another member of the caravan. All of them with the same question.

"Any change?"

About five days after she and Miranda began these little "check ins", Isabelle was sitting outside the caravan at night. She sat barefoot in the low cut grass in a simple green shirt and short black skirt. The caravan had pulled over for the night and she was looking up at the star filled skies. The grass tickled her bare thighs and the breeze cooled her whole body through the clothing. It was a pleasant night, in a little while she would have to go check on the boy, but for now she was going to enjoy the stars. She was content to enjoy the feeling of the gentle wind in her hair. She was content to enjoy the peace and quiet of the-

"There you are!" Nathan more or less screamed as he appeared on her right side from the other end of the caravan. Isabelle mind focused on one word: "damn." What she wouldn't give to be able to kill him with her mind.

"Just one thought and he could be out of my hair for good."

He came and stood in front of her, blocking the moon from her sight.

His eyes trailed from the swell of her breast under the shirt and then moved down to her tanned legs. She suddenly wished she was wearing jeans. "Cold out here isn't it." That smile was creeping into his face again.

"I like it actually," she said in a tone that she hoped sounded calm but warning, "its pleasant and peaceful."

"You shouldn't be all by yourself though," he rebutted, "ain't safe out here in the middle of nowhere like this. Ya' don't wanna end up like fatty in there." He jerked his head in the direction of the sleeping boy's trailer. "You should have *someone* watchin out for ya."

His eyes were somewhere around her lips, which was closer than he had gotten to her eyes in a long time. Then his eyes began to trail down her neck and she felt her skin crawling. She stood up quickly and he backed away a bit. She brushed the blades of grass off her dress.

"You know," she said hoping that she didn't sound as angry as she was getting, "now that you mention it I think its time for me to check on him." Nathan opened his mouth to offer to go with her, but she turned and stomped off toward the trailer without another word or a look back.

She swung the trailer door open so hard that it flung fully out and bounced off the wall. She grabbed it as she stepped in and slammed it shut behind her. God! She couldn't stand him! She paced back and forth in the trailer, paying no mind to the boy, cursing under her breath. She couldn't understand why she was so angry. She had met a lot of pigs over the years though, they all annoyed her but not like Nathan did. He made her absolutely furious. She couldn't figure out why.

She turned to keep pacing and stopped short as she looked at the boy. The boys face was no longer facing up to the ceiling. It was leaning to the right facing her. His eyes were open revealing themselves to be jet black. His expression was calm.

The boy was finally awake.

11

For a moment Isabelle simply stared wide eyed at the boy. The boy simply looked back at her. He seemed a little bored; as if he routinely woke up in strange places with both his arms broken, and pissed off girls pacing around in front of him. Isabelle calmed after a moment, shaking off the shock that had come from seeing him. She didn't think he had made a sound when he woke up, but maybe that was just because she had been so distracted by her own thoughts.

"You're awake huh?" she said, her voice still sounded a bit startled, but it was calming down, "How're ya feelin'? Aside from your arms?" The boy blinked and his calm expression fell into one of confusion. "What's wrong? Something on my face?" The boy's confused expression stayed. Isabelle's face mirrored his confusion for a moment, then fell in mild annoyance as she understood. "You don't understand a word I'm saying do you?"

"Se-kuropshino," the boy muttered, his voice scratchy. Isabelle's expression went back to confusion. What the hell kind of language was that?

"Re-sudenshim," he continued, *"an-eshitekuhram."* Isabelle shrugged and shook her head. Both her and the boy let out long sighs at the same time.

"Okay," Isabelle said. She said it more to herself than to the boy, "let's at least get a name before I get Andy." She looked the boy in the eyes. She suddenly thought she was falling, sinking into the two pools of black ink. It was terrifying and wonderful at the same time. She felt like she could stay in that darkness forever.

She had to force her eyes away from his and the feeling faded away immediately. She shook the feeling off and turned her attention to his forehead. She pressed her palm against her chest and patted it. "Isabelle." He simply stared at her for a moment and she patted her chest again. "Is-a-belle." The boys eyes widen in understanding and he nodded. He attempted to clear his throat and then spoke:

"Jaw-nee."

"Johnny," Isabelle said with a nod. Then she left to wake up Andy and the old nurse. Johnny watched her go his expression calm and, once again, bored.

CHAPTER 2
JOHNNY BOY

1

The boy's language was unlike anything Andy, or anyone else in the caravan, had ever heard. Add that to the fact that the boy, who everyone was calling "Johnny Boy", couldn't understand them and asking him questions was impossible. Andy didn't like the idea of letting someone stay in the caravan without working or paying, but he couldn't get the idea of payment across to "Johnny Boy" and he couldn't put him to work with two broken arms. As such Johnny just sat around in silence muttering to himself in that strange language.

Miranda and Isabelle came to feed him twice a day. Usually it was Miranda rather than Isabelle, she didn't seem to like Johnny Boy. The old nurse came to check on him every other day. He was doing well in her opinion, too well actually. His arms seemed to be healing very fast. In about another weeks time, he would be able to bend them without any real pain. A week after that, he would be able to feed and tend to himself.

2

Jawnee wasn't particularly comfortable in this strange place. He didn't really mind the company of the two girls who were caring for him, or the old woman who checked on him every other day but everyone else made him uneasy. People had been sticking their heads into the tiny room for several days, all of them asking him questions in that bizarre language of theirs. Where the hell was he?

He had been traveling, he remembered that. He had left behind his sister, his unwanted fiancée, and that old hag Rita. That was back in the Oasis though, past the wastelands, and in the middle of winter. He had no clue where he was now but it wasn't the wastelands of the Oasis and from what he saw through the rooms one window, it wasn't winter.

"At least my arms are almost mended," he thought as he sat in the bed,

"soon I'll be able to move around and figure out where the hell I am."

"Bet ya weren't plannin on comin back!" Rita's voice shot into his head.

"Shut up." He muttered, not realizing he was talking out loud, "I was just making a delivery. A delivery you wanted me to make!"

"Running like a coward." she laughed.

"Shut up!"

"Deals a deal boy. Ya cain't run foreva."

"Shut up!"

The trailer door cracked open and Rita's voice vanished. Isabelle walked in with a bowl of soup. He was always pleased when it was her, the other girl seemed sweet enough but he preferred to see Isabelle. Although, she didn't seem to enjoy being around him. She never seemed to meet his eyes. Still she was a beautiful girl, and he wanted to learn to talk to her, if only to find out why she seemed so uncomfortable around him. For now though, just a simple greeting.

"Isabelle," he said with a smile and slight bow of the head. She gave him a half smirk and a quick nod, but didn't say anything. She didn't take to feeding him, and in truth he didn't like the situation either. It felt humiliating having to be tended to like an infant. He wanted his arms healed even more whenever it came time for Isabelle or that other girl (he thought her name was Miranda but wasn't sure) to feed him. They would heal fast enough if he did what Rita told him. At least what she had taught him was useful. For the next week however, he was going to have to swallow his pride and let himself be fed.

Isabelle grabbed a small stool on the wall, brought it over to the bed, and sat down. The soup today was a brownish broth with something that looked like meat and bits of carrots floating in it. Jawnee was happy to see that they had put meat in it. The last several bowls had been nothing but broth. Isabelle lifted a spoonful of soup to his mouth and he gulped it down. She fed him in silence, never meeting his eyes, and when he was done she got up and left without another word. He watched her leave, wishing he could ask why she was so uncomfortable.

After she left, Jawnee leaned his head against the wall and began muttering the same things he had been muttering for the last several days. If he wanted to use his arms again, he had to do this just right. He had to do it just like Rita taught him.

16

About a week later, Jawnee was able to move his arms again. Not perfectly, but it was enough to feed himself and move around without someone having to help him with this day to day task. He also assumed this meant he could leave the trailer as he pleased, and travel around without people watching him. He was right about the first part.

He noticed three things very quickly when he stepped out of the trailer for the first time. One, he was somewhere in the western part of the country. It was a beautiful place full of green grass and flowers that reminded him of the long valleys back home in the Oasis. Two, he was traveling inside a caravan like the ones he had sometimes seen in the Oasis, though this one was much bigger. It was a lot less friendly looking than the ones Jawnee had seen. It looked like more of a military weapon than a transport. Three, the other people in the caravan watched him wherever he went. Given the interest everyone seemed to have in him, he figured the trip must've been very boring for them.

Everyone came up and asked him questions at some point, even though they knew he couldn't speak the language. Even if he could have understood them, they asked the question so fast and so randomly that he was sure he wouldn't have been able to answer them anyway. He did learn names though and managed to match them to the right faces; Andy, Curtis, Ramon, Isabelle, Cook (the huge monster woman who made the food), Sandy and Jessie (the girls who were Cook's kitchen helpers), Miranda, and Nathan. He liked everyone he met pretty well. Everyone except for Nathan.

Nathan made him uneasy, but he couldn't say exactly why. He imagined that his sister Suruo would've described it as Nathan's "vibe" being off.

"Throws things outta whack, a guy like that." She would've said if she were there to meet Nathan. It was Nathan's walk that Jawnee found himself not liking though, the long arrogant strides he took. Nathan was a threat, Jawnee knew that. He just didn't know what Nathan was a threat to.

His first confrontation with Nathan happened in the dining trailer, about two days after Jawnee started exploring the caravan. Nathan was looming over Isabelle who sat at one of the benches eating a salad, and looking very annoyed. Jawnee recognized it as the look she had had on her face when he woke up. Whatever Nathan was saying as he grinned down at her she clearly didn't like. Jawnee watched from the door for a moment, and then walked toward them. On the way he tried to figure out what he was going to do. As he neared them Nathan looked up and met Jawnee's eyes with a look full of annoyance, then shock, and then fear. Nathan said something to him in a tone that sounded confident but Jawnee was certain he heard fear in it as well. Why Nathan would be afraid of him was beyond Jawneee however. Nathan repeated whatever he said, this time much louder, and when Jawnee still didn't respond he stormed off.

Isabelle watched Nathan leave and a smirk crossed her lips. She glanced over at Jawnee and spoke to him. It was only one word but he understood the meaning and intention instantly.

"Thanks."

It was the first word of the language Jawnee put to memory.

4

The caravan pulled along a line of berry bushes that were part of a small farm. The farm was owned by a couple that had met, and eventually married on Andy's caravan several years ago. They spent the first few years of marriage on the caravan before finally buying and settling on this pleasant little spot of land. The farm was too small to offer anyone in the caravan much in the way of boarding but Andy was welcome to pick as much fruit as he wanted from the berry bushes in front and the apple trees in the back. He asked Miranda to pick berries and Isabelle to get apples. Cook sent her kitchen helper Sandy out to pick berries with Miranda. Sandy agreed without hesitation, "don't piss off the monster" was the first rule in the kitchen. She muttered curses at Cook under her breath for most of the day though. Cook wanted Jessie to prepare lunch for everyone while Sandy was gone.

Jessie, a full figured girl with long red hair and blue eyes, had simply nodded and smiled. Jessie was mute, so most of her day to day conversations involved her simply nodding or shaking her head. She wasn't stupid but she didn't like spending all of her time trying to get across an occasional thought when she didn't have to. She simply went where she had to and did what was needed. So Jessie cooked and Sandy went to get berries.

Sandy was a beautiful young woman; trim, with light cream skin and short golden hair she looked like a princess out of a fairy tale. Her eyes were a sparkling shade of ice blue. Even though her face was constantly covered in grease from being in the tight confines of the kitchen all day she was still considered the second most beautiful on the caravan. Second only to Isabelle. She had been part of the caravan for about three years now, and was considered a friend by both Jessie and Miranda. She smiled, laughed, and talked with them both regularly but she didn't consider either of them a friend. They were a way to kill time since there was no one worth talking to on the caravan. Isabelle saw through her easily and the two of them were always arguing. Always one wrong look or smart-ass comment away from attacking each other.

Sandy and Miranda spent the early afternoon bent over the berry bushes in jeans and green shirts, picking berries and dropping them into a large wicker basket that sat between them. Occasionally they would eat a berry and enjoy the sweet taste, but mostly they talked. They talked about a lot of things but the main topic was Johnny Boy.

"Do ya' think he really is a witch?" Miranda asked in a low whisper. "You really think its true?"

"He healed two broken arms in like a month." Sandy said, her eyes lit up at the prospect of their being a real witch in the caravan. "Wonder if he has any cool powers or spells. I heard witches can hypnotize someone just from making eye contact. Wonder if he's hypnotized anyone." Sandy turned to face Miranda and noticed that she wasn't listening anymore. She was looking at something off to the right. Sandy leaned over a bit to look over Miranda's shoulder. Johnny Boy was standing a few feet away looking toward the farm house. He never glanced at them, simply walked by toward the house and the apple trees behind it.

5

Jawnee wandered past the small wooden house, only giving it a pacing glance for a moment. He took in the red paint that was beginning to peel in some places and the cute little drapes that hung on the inside of the windows but otherwise gave it no notice. Once he was around the back he saw three apple trees, all in full bloom, with large red apples all over them. At the one closest to him, Isabelle was at the top of a tall ladder pulling apples out of the tree and dropping them into the wicker basket on the ground. There wasn't anyone holding the ladder for her.

He had come around looking for her, wanting to at least try to talk to her. See if maybe some of the words he had put to memory could form a cohesive sentence. But now that he was standing beneath her and looking up at the long dark hair that fell down to her back he couldn't think of a thing to say. Now he was wondering what had been going through his head to make him even try. She was going to think he was stalking her. In fact, now that he thought about it, he was simply staring up at her backside while she worked, making no attempt to make his presence known. Stalking might be the perfect word for it.

"Now would be a good time to say something," his other sister Becca said into his head, *"you don't want her to turn around and see you staring do you? She's nervous enough around you as is."* Jawnee took a breath.

"Is-" he began.

"THERE YOU ARE!" Nathan's voice rang out. It was so sharp and sudden that Isabelle faltered. The ladder swayed to its side and began to tip. Jawnee leaped out to catch hold of it, but he was too far away. His hand was going to come up just an inch short.

The ladder stopped in mid-fall and lifted back up, placing itself in Jawnee's hand. He gripped it tightly his eyes wide with shock. He was sure that it wouldn't matter, that Isabelle would fall off anyway, but she caught hold of one of the thicker branches in the tree and held steady. She looked down when she realized that someone was holding the ladder and her eyes widen when she saw him.

"So much for not making her any more uncomfortable." He thought as he let go of the ladder and stepped back. She began to climb down. She glanced over at Nathan who was coming toward them at a quick pace and she stopped moving. Ramon was a few feet behind and slowing his pace so that he wouldn't pass Nathan. Isabelle turned back to Jawnee and their eyes locked. Her eyes fluttered and drooped almost as if she was about to fall asleep. She shook her head and turned away from him. Jawnee remembered his fiancée use to get the same droopy look in her eyes whenever she looked at him. His sister and Rita had told him that was a good thing. He remembered that because it was the only time he could remember either of his sisters ever agreeing with Rita. None of them ever explained why it was a good thing though, or why it only seemed to happen with certain people.

Nathan didn't look particularly happy to see Jawnee with Isabelle.

Jawnee figured that he must not like competition, although Jawnee didn't think he had anymore chance with Isabelle than Nathan did.

6

From Nathan's view of things it looked like Isabelle was as nervous and uncomfortable around Johnny Boy as he was. That was good to know since it meant he didn't have to look at Johnny Boy as any real competition for Isabelle. Still, he didn't like the way the witch boy kept following her around. He had heard all the rumors about what witches could do. How they healed, how they talked to the dead, how they controlled wild animals, and how they hypnotized people. Johnny Boy was a threat in more ways than one and he just had to wait until Andy gave him the okay to deal with him.

He walked past Johnny Boy and came up to Isabelle. She turned and went back up the ladder, not giving him any notice.

"Go away," She said as she started dropping apples into the basket again, "ALL of you." She turned her attention to Johnny Boy, Nathan, and then Ramon. There was a very cold look in her eyes. "I'm trying to finish this so I can get to work on the next tree."

"We just wanted to help Izzy." Ramon said, his voice soft and his eyes turned away from her. Quiet as he was around the guys, Ramon got even worse around Isabelle, and even worse still around Miranda or Jessie.

"Thanks Ramon," she said with a slightly more gentle tone, "But I'm fine. Go help someone else."

"No...Help?" Johnny Boy asked. Nathan felt his jaw fall open and his eyes widen. "You...Sure?" It was slow and stilted but it was understandable.

"No." Isabelle said slowly. She could feel her heart pounding in her chest. "I'm okay. No help." Johnny Boy nodded and then walked away. He walked away slowly, glancing back at Isabelle a few times as he did. He didn't pay any attention to Nathan or Ramon. As he got farther away Ramon walked up to Nathan.

"How'd he learn so fast?" Ramon asked in a choked whisper. "I mean do you think he used magic?"

"Don't matter," Nathan said hoping his voice sounded better than he felt, "lets just tell Andy." The two of them walked back toward the caravan, watching Johnny Boy a few feet ahead of them. Nathan wished

21

there was a way to get rid of this guy. He just couldn't think of anything to do.

7

Jawnee was nearly back to the trailer when he noticed someone loading large baskets of berries into the kitchen's back door. It was one of the girls who worked in the kitchen. The one who never talked. Jawnee was pretty sure her name was Jessie. She had her hair tied back in a pony tail, and was trying to lift two huge baskets at the same time. She lifted them, staggered, and dropped them back down. When they hit the ground she winced and looked into the baskets to see if any of the berries had been crushed, throwing out the onces that had. Then she looked to her left and caught sight of Jawnee.

She stared at him for a moment and then jerked her head at the baskets. He blinked, not sure what that motion meant. She frowned, sighed, and jerked her head at the baskets again. When Jawnee still didn't move she pointed at him and then pointed to the baskets. Then he understood. He ran over to her and grabbed one of the baskets. She picked up the other and Jawnee followed her into the kitchen.

The kitchen was large. Two enormous stoves and a large refrigerator that ran along the wall by the back door. A counter ran opposite the stoves and a small opening in the wall over them led into the dinning room. A large sink on the far wall was full of soapy water and dirty dishes. A smaller empty sink was next to that sink. All throughout the kitchen was Cook, moving around preparing food.

"What took you so damn long!" Cook barked at Jessie. "Put those damn things in the fridge and clean out those goddamn dishes!" Then Cook's face turned to Jawnne. "What the hell do you want? Either help or get out!"

Jessie motioned for Jawnee to stick his basket next to hers on the large bottom shelf of the refrigerator and then pushed him toward the sink.

He spent the rest of the day cleaning the stack of dishes, which never seemed to stop coming. No sooner would he finish cleaning dishes than another stack would come in from the dinning room. By the time he went back to his trailer, his hand were wrinkled and dish panned.

8

Andy made Isabelle, Nathan, and Ramon keep quiet about Johnny Boy's newfound understanding of the language. He wanted to ask the boy some questions before everyone else in the caravan did. He knew the boy wouldn't be able to give him any details, he couldn't have learned that much of the language, but maybe a little information. They were nearly at Frisco, the tall buildings that made up the Queen's Towers were visible on the horizon, and in the next three days the grand bridge would be too. Andy wanted to know who this boy was before they got there.

He had Isabelle bring Johnny Boy to his main trailer and office.

9

Isabelle knocked on Andy's trailer door hard. Johnny Boy stood behind her, she could feel his eyes burning into the back of her head.

He wasn't looking her over or anything. She had never caught him staring at her chest or her ass since he'd been here. His attention was always on her eyes, and she did everything she could to avoid meeting his. She knew that if she turned around he would lock eyes again and she would begin to fall asleep again. She knocked on the door harder.

"Isabelle?"

She turned to face Johnny Boy and focused on his forehead.

"Scared of me?" Johnny Boy asked, tilting his head to try and meet her eyes. She looked over his shoulder at nothing.

"No," she said, "I'm not scared of you?"

"Lie." He said. "Why?"

Isabelle sighed, turned away from him and knocked again. What was taking Andy so goddamn long? This was getting embarrassing, the way she was trembling over a guy who seemed about as dangerous as a kitten. He hadn't done anything to her, or anyone else it seemed, he was a gentleman and kind to her. She wasn't going to keep doing this. She turned and met Johnny Boy's eyes.

She was immediately sleepy, like she was laying her head on a big soft pillow after a very long day. It wasn't a bad feeling. It was comfortable, pleasant, and welcoming. She fought it back as best she could.

"Johnny Boy, is it true what everyone is saying?" she asked, "Are you a witch?"

"Witch?" He asked, giving her the confused look he had on his face when they first met. "What is witch?"

The door opened and Andy stepped out. He was dressed in an old gray army uniform, freshly cleaned and polished. His beard was well maintained and his hair was perfectly orderly. His expression was dark and cold, the expression that Miranda and other members of the caravan crew called "Military Mode." Isabelle got the point of it, Andy wasn't going to waste time playing the gentle father figure with Johnny Boy. He was making the point of who was in charge clear without using any words. She glanced over at Johnny Boy, he was standing up a little straighter than before and his face had gone from confused to serious. He clearly got the message.

"Thank you Isabelle." Andy said, his voice was as emotionless as his face. "You can go back to bed now." She nodded and turned to leave. She started to avoid Johnny Boy's eyes at first and then thought again. She met his eyes, that sleepy feeling hit again but she pushed it back a little easier this time. He smiled at her and she smiled back. Whatever his smile meant, she was giving him an apology. After a moment she turned and walked back to her trailer.

"Goodnight Isabelle." Johnny Boy called out to her. She didn't turn to face him but held up her hand and waved.

10

Andy led Johnny Boy inside the main trailer. It doubled as the control room and Andy's bedroom so it was nearly three times the size of any other trailer. The control room and bedroom were separated by a large metal wall with a steel door. The control room had a large steering wheel mounted in front of the large window with numerous gears and controls all around it. The bedroom had a huge bed against one wall and several chairs in a circle all attached to the floor with a small table between them. On the wooden table was the small key that Miranda had found two months ago.

Andy motioned Johnny Boy into one of the chairs and then sat in the one opposite him. Johnny Boy looked a little uneasy, his eyes were shifting all over the room. Andy watched him for a minute and then leaned in, staring hard into Johnny Boy's eyes. He didn't feel any different, no sudden drowsiness or anything else.

"I have questions." Andy said slowly, "Understand?" Johnny Boy nodded. Andy reached down to the table and picked up the small key. He held it up to Johnny Boy. For a minute there was no response, and then Johnny Boy's eyes widen in recognition. He reached out for the key and Andy pulled it back.

"Yours?"

Johnny Boy nodded.

"What is it for?"

"Chest."

"What chest?"

"My," Johnny Boy paused trying to find the right word, "my life is in chest." Andy assumed this to mean Johnny Boy's personal things. He moved on with the questioning.

"Where is the chest?"

Johnny Boy's face screwed up trying to remember. "Lost."

"Where are you from?"

"Home."

"Where is home Johnny Boy?"

Johnny Boy threw his arms out and shrugged. "Don't know," he said, "don't know where I am."

Andy knew that was all he was going to get in that direction, so he decided to drive forward and ask the big question.

"Are you a witch Johnny Boy?"

"What is witch?" Johnny Boy looked more interested now. .

"A person who uses magic" Andy answered. An *evil* person he almost said, but that would've probably scared Johnny Boy if he knew what that word meant. If he didn't he would just start asking what it meant and they would get off topic.

Johnny Boy's face fell into confusion.

"What is magic?"

CHAPTER 3
SANDY

1

Sandy watched Isabelle talk to Andy as the sun was setting. An hour later she was following Isabelle down to Johnny Boy's trailer. She watched the smart-assed bitch knock on his door and talk to him for a minute. A moment later he nodded and the two were walking toward the front of the caravan. She followed after them and hid behind a trailer whenever Johnny Boy glanced behind them. He glanced back a lot, almost like he heard her. That couldn't be it though, Sandy knew how to sneak around. After all, this wasn't her first time following someone.

A few minutes later they were outside Andy's trailer. Isabelle knocked, Johnny Boy said something, Isabelle avoided looking at him, and Johnny Boy said something else. Sandy wondered if maybe Isabelle had a thing for the fat little weirdo. That was different, usually she and Isabelle went for the same type of guy. Usually Isabelle was the one that got them though. The guys just preferred the easier girls.

She hated Isabelle. Cook wouldn't let her anywhere near Isabelle since they nearly tore each other apart in the dining car a year ago. Sandy didn't really remember why they fought, but she was sure that it was something Isabelle had done. It was always something Isabelle had done. If Cook got mad at her it was because Isabelle had complained. If Nathan kicked her out of bed, something he was doing a lot lately, it was because he wanted to get Isabelle in bed instead. Ever since the day they met, whenever something went wrong for Sandy it was because of Isabelle.

She watched Andy open the door, say something, and then send Isabelle away. She ducked behind a trailer and watched Isabelle walk away. She whispered a few curses at Isabelle and then turned back toward Andy's trailer. Once Johnny Boy stepped in, she snuck up to one of the trailer's windows and sat under it. She listened to every word, praying that she would hear something of interest, something she could make useful.

After nearly two hours Johnny Boy left the trailer and headed back to the other end of the caravan. Sandy sat underneath the window, pouting and horribly unsatisfied. Two hours of sitting in the freezing night air and the only thing she discovered was that Johnny Boy was a moron who didn't know his own ass from a hole in the ground.

What is witch?!

"You're a witch idiot!" she hissed at him as he walked away. He was so far away that she was sure he wouldn't hear her, but he turned around and she had to dive underneath the trailer before he saw her. After a minute he walked on, and once he was out of sight she followed. She had originally planned to go back to her own trailer after listening in, think over what she heard and then plan a way out of this God forsaken caravan. But that plan was shot to hell since she hadn't learned anything of use. So she decided to make a stop off at a different trailer and get satisfaction in another way. She stopped about halfway down the caravan and climbed up to Nathan's trailer. She knocked lightly, not wanting any of the stunt performers in the other trailers to hear her. It was enough, Nathan opened the door and stood before her in nothing but a pair of gray shorts. That alone put her in a better mood.

"Hi," she said to him, her smile spreading slowly from ear to ear, "I didn't wake you did I?" His smile was wide too, looking more like a wolf baring its fangs than a man welcoming a lover. That was part of why she liked him though, animals were fun. They were passionate, they didn't think, and most of all they could be trained.

"No you didn't." He said, and stepped back to let her in. She stepped in and felt the smell of wood and gun powder fill her nostrils. He had been part of the caravan for a long time, and he was a big part of the carnival, so he was one of the few people who got their own trailer. It was a long room with a bed against one wall. Every other part of the room had a gun rack, knife stand, or sword collection on it. They were all of various ages and types but they were all useful and well kept.

Nathan sat down on the edge of the bed as Sandy closed the door behind her. She walked slowly over to him, swaying her hips and letting her eyes trail down his bare chest.

"What're ya' doing up so late anyway?" He asked. She straddled his hips and wrapped her hands around his neck. She stuck her fingers into his hair gripping it tight, pulling it hard.

"I was just walking around." She kissed him hard, forcing her tongue into his mouth. She felt what she wanted pressing into her thigh. She slipped a hand between them and gripped it firmly.

"What were ya' walking around for?" He asked, his voice very hoarse suddenly. She smiled wider, it was always nice to know you had an effect on someone. His hands crept up her shirt and started fondling her breast. Her head lulled back and she moaned.

"Nothing important. Just listening in on Andy's questioning of Johnny Boy." Nathan's face went from lustful to deadly serious immediately. Before Sandy realized the mistake she had made, she was being thrown to the ground as Nathan stood up. He looked like he had completely forgotten about the girl whose breast he was just massaging.

"What did he ask him?"

2

Question, after question, after goddamn question came out of Nathan's mouth before Sandy finally got sick of answering them. She got up to leave, slapped Nathan when he tried to stop her, and stormed out of the trailer. She stomped across the caravan furious and completely unsatisfied. She had wasted the entire night as well, she only had about three hours to sleep before Cook would kick her awake and make her start making breakfast.

She reached her trailer and climbed in, the smell of fruit juice, fried meat, and milk filled her nostrils. On the small bed to the right was Jenny, curled into a ball with her face toward the door. Opposite from her was Sandy's bed, empty and clean. At the back of the room, in a bed about twice the size of the other beds, was Cook. She was laying with her back to the door, her massive back looking like a beached whale. Her snoring was so loud that Sandy couldn't believe that she managed to sleep through that each night.

Sandy laid down in bed and looked up at the ceiling. She couldn't sleep, she was too annoyed. She didn't deserve this life, she was from better than this.

3

Sandy was born Sandy Lucille Delgana, the first daughter of the royal counsel member Martin Delgana. She was raised as a member of the royal court in the King's Towers in the city of York. She grew up alongside five other young girls and three young boys, all of whom she had doing her homework for her by the time she was six. When a group of peasants decided to rebel against the King, the families of those children (and a few of the children themselves) were killed in the struggle. Sandy survived though and she grew into a beautiful young woman.

When she was seventeen years old she became one of five potential brides for the King's first son. She was never more dedicated to anything than she was to getting this engagement. She followed the Prince day in and day out. She spread rumors about her competition. She kissed up to the King earning his praise, even getting him to call her daughter. Within five months she was sure she had set up the rest of her life. Then something happened that she hadn't predicted; The Prince fell in love with one of the other girls.

Sandy couldn't remember the girls name and didn't really care, she was some stupid farm girl whose parents had become nouveau rich and earned her a spot in the court. The girl had given the Prince that "solid moral" crap that Sandy knew how to fake and the moron had fallen for her immediately. He cast aside Sandy and the other girls immediately.

Sandy took her revenge on the girl immediately. One day after the Prince had cast her aside, the farm girl was in an unfortunate 'accident' involving a runaway cart. Sandy scared the horses of a local farmer and sent them charging down a public road where the girl and the Prince had been on a stroll. The Prince was pulled out of the way by one of his bodyguards, the girl was crushed underneath the cart and trampled by the hooves of the horses. In the few seconds that the cart was on top of her the girl was so brutally mangled that she would need to have a closed casket. No one ever found out that Sandy was the one who caused it. The horses charged on for another several minutes, killing three more people before they were finally stopped. The farmer who owned them was punished for it; the grief stricken Prince had him executed.

Sandy was certain that the Prince would begin looking for a new bride eventually. While she waited for him to get over his grief she made sure that the other three girls had similarly gruesome 'accidents'. Between these little projects she played the part of sympathetic ear to the Prince.

Tried to anyway but he never seemed to confide in her. Then one day as Sandy was wondering what type of wedding dress she would wear at the inevitable wedding, the Prince leaped off the top of one of the King's Towers.

There wasn't anything left of Sandy's future but a large red spot in the street.

After that another revolution was waged. This time the King gave no attempt to fight it off, and the royal family of the eastern land was crushed. The royal court disbanded, her family was killed, and Sandy found herself lost on the roads. Two months later she was picked up by Andy's caravan and put under Cook as her kitchen helper. She had been there now for two years, two years of back breaking, sweat stained, hell.

Now she laid awake in bed, staring up at the ceiling listening to the light breathing of the mute to her left, and the loud snoring of the beast behind her. She thought of her life, and of everything she had lost. She wanted her life back, and she had thought that having a witch on her side might have proven useful. She had wanted to get some information she could use but nothing good came from listening to the interrogation. Still, something told her that Johnny Boy was her ticket out of the caravan.

She decided that she would watch Johnny Boy a little longer. He had something she could use and she would find it. She would get out of the caravan even if it meant she would have to kill everyone on it.

Especially if it meant she would have to kill everyone on it.

4

The next morning Cook woke Sandy with a sharp kick to the bed, as she did every morning. She kicked it with enough force to make the bed lift off the ground slightly. Sandy jerked awake, looked around the room wide-eyed for a moment, saw Cook's angry face, and sighed.

"Breakfast," Cook said, "eat. Then start cooking some for everyone else." Then she turned and lumbered out of the trailer. Sandy looked across the room to the other bed, Jenny had already gotten up and made her bed like a good little girl. Sandy dressed in her simple brown work clothes and headed for the dinning trailer, cursing Cook to the grave as she went.

On the way, Sandy passed by Isabelle and Miranda next to one of the trailers. Isabelle was stretching, getting ready to practice her dance routines, while Miranda sat on a wooden box and blew a few notes into an old wooden flute. Miranda seemed lost in thought, but Isabelle was very focused on what she was doing. Sandy wasn't surprised, she knew that Isabelle was already several months behind her rent on the trailer she shared with Miranda. Andy was being tolerant because Isabelle could work in his circus, but she refused to do that regularly so she was going to have to pay or go once they were in Frisco. She would be desperately trying to scrape up cash for her rent. Andy would let Miranda stay on (he treated her like she was *his* damn kid) but not Isabelle. Isabelle would be left behind in Frisco.

It didn't really matter to Sandy though. Still, one less girl to compete with in any situation was always a good thing. Maybe Frisco would be the last time she would ever have to see Isabelle.

5

About four hours after she started in the kitchen Sandy saw Johnny Boy sitting at one of the tables at the far end of the dinning trailer. He had a plastic cup full of what she guessed was juice. His eyes were distant, like he was off in another world.

6

How long had he been away from the Oasis? That was one of the two questions that rang through Jawnee's head. The other one was, "Where is the chest?" The leader, Andy, had said that he'd been traveling with them for nearly two months. But that was only how long it had been since they found him, he had no way of knowing how long he had actually been unconscious. It also didn't tell him where his chest was.

He had forgotten about it. That scared him a bit. His chest had his "life" in it, something too valuable for words and until Andy had shown him the key he had forgotten about it entirely. How was that even possible? Now, if he didn't keep the key on him at all times it began to slip from his mind again. When he had first gotten back to his room after his talk with Andy, he had laid the key down on the bed and the memory of the chest began to blur until he couldn't remember what he had been thinking about. When he picked the key up, the memory came back crystal clear. It also brought back the memory of the day he had left.

He had been talking to Surou right before he left. She had tried yet again to talk him into staying, to talk him into going through with the wedding. "She's a good girl," she had said to him, "sweet, smart, cute, and you'll be receiving a great amount of land as well."

"I know, I know," he had said, 'it is a perfectly sensible thing to do. She's very kind and I enjoy my time around her well enough. It just doesn't feel right." He had paused. "It feels...off." He had finished loading the chest, locked it, and put the key into his pocket. The whole time his sister sat on the edge of his bed and watched him. He remembered looking in her dark brown eyes and seeing that she was still trying to think of something to say to keep him from going. Her long, curly, black hair fell in front of her dark face like a veil and she had brushed it behind her ears.

"Even if you don't want to marry her," she began again, "why take a job from Rita?"

"I'm delivering a pendant is all." He had said, "I won't be doing anything more for her after this. Besides, she agreed to end my teaching once I did this and I thought that was what you wanted more than anything."

"I am happy that you won't be spending anymore time with that old hag. Becca, Mikale, and Shauwn wouldn't want you anywhere near her at all. Spirits rest them. Doesn't mean I want you to disappear into the wastelands. Or even worse go past them, don't you know what's out there? Haven't I told you enough times about those savage people?"

Jawnee began tuning her out at that point. He somehow doubted the stories of the evil creatures outside the wastelands that hid among the people. It was something used to keep curious young people from wandering out of the Oasis. He didn't doubt that it would be dangerous but it was either this or marriage and the young farm girl from down the road was not the woman he wanted to marry. He hadn't met the woman he wanted to marry yet.

So he had left the Oasis with the clothes on his back, a ruby pendant in an old wooden chest with his "life" inside it. He had bought passage on a small carriage that sometimes traveled through the wasteland. The carriage had only three other passengers; a young woman, her son who was about four years old, and an older man in a very expensive looking blue silk shirt with gold patterns on it. Three days later he was several miles from home and watching the first snow flakes of the winter fall around him. One night he went to sleep and the next thing he knew he was in a trailer with Isabelle pacing around in front of him.

Now, as he sat on a bench in the back of the dinning trailer, thinking back on his faded memories, he realized he didn't have the pendant anymore either. Like the chest, he hadn't even thought about it over the last two months.

Jawnee pulled the key out of his pocket, it was very light in his hand. He held out the hand and looked at the key as it rested in his palm. He stared at it for a long minute, thinking about everything and nothing at the same time, trying to understand how he could've just forgotten about the chest.

The key moved in his hand.

It was a slight motion just turning a bit so that the actual key pointed a little to the right. Jawnee's eyes widen and he looked around quickly, no one was paying any attention to him (which was a shock in and of itself). His attention turned back to the key which was now spinning in a slow circle. It spun a little faster each time it finished a rotation until it was spinning so fast it looked like a gray circle. Suddenly it stopped and pointed to the left his eyes followed it pointing out the door.

"What's wrong with you Boy!" Rita's voices shrieked in his ear, *"You can't do that!"*

"Stop it quick!" Suruo's voice screamed in his ear. He stuffed the key back into his pocket and left the trailer as fast as he could without running.

7

Jawnee sat outside a few days later with the key in his hand and watched it spin. It stopped again and now that he was outside he saw that it was pointing to the city they were headed toward. He heard people call it Frisco. He didn't fully understand what it meant but he had suspicions. He suspected that his chest was inside that city, and his "life" along with it.

CHAPTER 4
ERRANDS

1

The city of Frisco, otherwise known as "The Queen's Towers," is a large city. The Queen's Towers are several high building that stand several hundred feet high and are scattered all around the city. The largest ones are near the center and used mainly as the Queen's Palace. The smaller ones are used to store the queen's jewelry or house her servants. The next set of buildings housed bankers, lawyers, and bill collectors. The even smaller buildings housed factory workers, and performers. Outside the city and on the other side of the bridge, were the farmers, vagrants, and peasants.

The Queen, Abigaile Roland, was not a cruel woman or a kind woman. She was neither greedy nor generous. She was a woman who did exactly what she needed to do to ensure that she kept her station. She was as kind to the people as she felt was needed. She wasn't a beautiful woman, nor was she ugly. Her hair was brown, long, and tied through a very elaborate crown of gold and jewels. Her face was attractive enough but full of stress. The stress of a woman who knew that her people were close to revolting despite her best attempts. That stress caused wrinkles that made her look fifty-five rather than thirty-five.

One week before the Caravan of Andy Che Pen would reach the Great Bridge that led to her City, Queen Roland stood at the large window of her bedroom, looking out over the city to the huge expanse of ocean water. It was a beautiful view, but she wasn't really thinking of it. She thought of the old wooden chest that sat in the center of her room.

She had sent a pair of messengers across the country to the King's Towers a few weeks ago. Since the citizens there had revolted she routinely sent communications to the new rulers, just to make sure they weren't planning on coming to the west. The last thing she needed was a group of militant rebels coming to her kingdom when things were so tense.

Her most recent pair of messengers returned with no real news. The new rulers (the council of citizens) were so busy fighting over who got what power and territory that nothing had really changed in the land. Not that surprising to Queen Abigaile, people always hated those in power until they were in power themselves. What had surprised her was the old wooden chest the messengers brought back with them.

It was a simple chest, the wood was worn and unpolished with a small key hole in it. The weathered look of it told Queen Abigaile that it had been out in really harsh weather for a very long time. There was nothing special to it, though. When she asked the messengers why they had bothered to carry it back they simply told her they *felt* they should. She usually would've demanded a better answer than that but something in their faces told her there wouldn't be one.

She'd called in the best locksmith in the city, and old man with long fingers and no hair, but he couldn't get it open. He went through every single key he had and then tried picking the lock. He tried for hours and eventually got so sick of the lock that he slammed his fist down on the chest. His fingers broke on the wood like he had slammed them on steel. He was led out crying at the top of his lungs.

After several other locksmiths tried and produced the same results and injuries, she called in one of her guards to simply break it open. The guard, a large man with a sword on his hip and a shotgun slung around his back, pulled his sword from its sheath and swung it down hard on the wood. The blade broke off on contact, sailed through the air and landed in the guard's shoulder. He was led out crying at the top of his lungs.

Eventually Queen Abigaile had the chest put in one of her treasuries, afraid that eventually someone would die trying to get it open.

For the next several nights Queen Abigaile couldn't sleep. She found herself constantly traveling to her treasury and staring at the chest. When she was around it, she felt nothing but once she was away from it she couldn't think of anything else. Something told her there was something in it, something important. Not dangerous, or powerful, or extremely valuable, but important just the same. After a week, she had the chest brought to her bedroom. She didn't try to open it, she just wanted it near her so she wouldn't obsess over it anymore.

Whenever she left her room though her mind became focused on the chest. She paid little attention to the words of her advisors, council members, or the peasants who came to voice their grievances. Her mind was entirely on the chest. She wanted it open, she needed to open it. She had to get whatever was inside it out so that it would leave her mind. She needed to be free of it.

As she stood at her window, looking out over the ocean she thought about the chest. About the hold it had on her, about the way it consumed her. She wondered if she would ever get it open. If not, how else could she ever be free of it. She wondered if she would ever be free.

2

Isabelle went through her dance routines over and over, letting the motions of her hips match the slow melody of Miranda's flute. She let her thoughts fade away and fall into the music.

Isabelle had been part of the caravan for about four years, and it had always been a shaky situation. She originally had her own trailer but she constantly missed her rent payments. Dancers only made so much money in most towns unless they were willing to privately "entertain" men of stature. Since Isabelle wasn't willing, money was unstable for her. Andy had been ready to kick her off the caravan in one city when Miranda had convinced him to let them bunk together. That was how her friendship with Miranda had started, as well as having Miranda play the flute during her performances.

Andy had also offered Isabelle a place in the stunt performers. It wasn't dancing but it had a certain adrenaline rush that Isabelle did enjoy. The only problem was that Nathan was always paired with her during performances, and his hands had a habit of wandering when he lifted her or caught her. She couldn't do that for a living, so she refused the offer only working when she had no other way to earn her keep. But money had gotten slim again, and Andy wasn't doing her anymore favors. Either she made her rent this time, joined the stunt performers for good, or she would be getting off in Frisco.

It was unlikely that she would get the money for her rent dancing, even in Frisco. Even if she did there was no guarantee that she would have it the next time it was due. She was already trying to come up with a plan for how she was going to live in Frisco. It was a tough city if you didn't know what to do and where to do it.

Miranda stopped playing and Isabelle was pulled out of her wandering.

"What is it?" Isabelle asked, straightening up. Miranda was looking at her with a concerned expression that made Isabelle uncomfortable.

"You should just join the team Isabelle." She said, her voice was flat, emotionless, a voice that said there wasn't really any choice in the matter. Isabelle frowned and turned away from her.

"Keep playing."

"Just ask Andy not to pair you with Nathan."

"I tried that, Nathan's the only one that can keep up with me to do the routine. I tried other people remember? Curtis is too old to keep up, and Ramon was so nervous he kept dropping me."

"Well..." Miranda trailed off, not sure what to say.

"I wouldn't mind if there was another way Miranda but there isn't."

"I don't want you to leave."

Isabelle looked at Miranda, but Miranda turned her face away. Isabelle was sure she was crying, Miranda cried a lot when the subject of Isabelle leaving came up. Isabelle felt like it a little too, Miranda was annoying, way too cheerful, but she was her friend. The only real one she still had, and she didn't want to leave her behind (or would it be Miranda leaving her behind). Isabelle didn't cry though, it wasn't who she was. Still.

"Maybe if Andy had a different routine." She said. It wasn't likely, Andy had a perfect set of routines for his stunt performers and he didn't really like change. The stunts were all well choreographed, pretty, stylish, and above all else entertaining. Why mess with perfection?

"I have an idea for one that he said we could try!" Miranda said, her voice hopeful, "I've been working on it for the last few months."

"You've never said anything."

"I didn't want to til I had it worked out. If it works and he puts it in the show, then you could stay!" Miranda face was going from hopeful to joyous, like it was already a done deal. "What do you think?"

Isabelle could feel a smile coming up in her but she wasn't going to get her hopes up yet. She kept her face straight and her voice calm. "I guess, if it's a good routine." Miranda's face beamed at her and Isabelle felt the smile creep onto her face.

Jawnee stretched his arms. They were perfectly fine now, the muscles strong. It had taken two months for them to heal fully, not nearly as quick as it should have been. Rita was right it seemed, he hadn't practiced her techniques often enough. He could practice again though and he could maybe start helping out around the caravan.

His understanding of the language was much better now. He had listened to so many people over the last two months. The constant questions from the children and their parents. The older passengers who always told him their life stories. He knew his vocabulary was probably small, but he understood the basics and that would be enough for a while. If he didn't understand a word now he could just ask. Also he could start a conversation now, and he was going to do just that. He was going to talk to Isabelle, a real conversation for once.

He was heading toward her, watching her dance while Miranda played her flute, when he heard Andy to his left. He turned and saw Andy standing next to Ramon, talking to him in a low tone that was meant for their ears only. Jawnee could hear them though, he could hear them perfectly well.

"...need you to go ahead and deliver the forms to the theater." Andy was saying.

"What about the rehearsal?" Ramon replied. He looked disappointed.

"You'll be back in time for the second rehearsal," Andy said, "or more like the third. But I want the theater reserved before we get into the city so we can get to work the second we're in town and a ATV moves faster than the caravan."

Ramon frowned but nodded. Jawnee stared at them for a moment and thought about something his sister Becca had told him.

He had borrowed something from a girl in the Oasis, he couldn't remember what (a toy or something) and had broken it. The girl had said it was okay but Becca made him replace it.

"Debt throws off your vibe," she had told him, "bad vibes make it hard to get anything done." He had thought about that for the two months he'd spent eating Andy's food and sleeping in his trailer and how he had done nothing to repay him. Helping load a few boxes and wash some dishes wasn't enough. He wasn't sure if he believed in the concept of a 'bad vibe' but he didn't like being in debt. He would save his conversation with Isabelle for later. Hell, he'd waited this long.

He walked over to Andy, who turned to face him. His eyebrow raised a bit, wondering. Jawnee stood a few feet away from him and looked him in the eye.

"I want to work." Jawnee said. Andy didn't say anything for a moment. Then he nodded.

"Good." Andy said, "Cook needs someone for heavy lifting."

Jawnee nodded, although he really wasn't sure he wanted to work underneath Cook again. She seemed... vicious.

4

Andy regretted giving Johnny Boy to Cook the instant she said she was sending him to Frisco. She wanted supplies and she wanted them before the caravan settled into the theater for the next three months. She gave Johnny Boy a list, and money. Andy could list all the reasons this was a stupid idea but he had to be very careful when he corrected her. She tended to get defensive.

"Just because he can speak doesn't mean he can read." Andy told her. "Never mind that he probably doesn't know how money works."

"That's why he's goin with Ramon." She said, "Ramon can explain everything to him. He gonna need to do it soon or later anyway." Andy argued with her for a while but nothing he said had any impact.

Ramon didn't respond very well to the idea of being alone with Johnny Boy for a day but he did what he was told. He took the large ATV out of the very last trailer and fueled it. The next morning Ramon and Johnny Boy rode off toward the Great Bridge.

5

Jawnee wasn't sure exactly how he was supposed to do this job for Cook. He had spent the last two months learning to speak but he hadn't even begun learning how to read. He was going to ask Ramon for help, but he couldn't get Ramon to look at him. Ramon was so nervous that he swerved whenever Jawnee said anything to him. The sudden motion of the machine made Jawnee sick so he stopped trying to talk to him. He simply focused on the huge bridge ahead of them.

It was a magnificent sight, huge beams of steel and wire that stretched across the huge expanse of water beneath them. The concrete roads on the bridge were as cracked as the roads everywhere else but the bridge was freshly painted, a bright orange that seemed to radiate in the early morning sunlight.

The bridge was mostly deserted but there were still a few travelers on it. Men and women in carriages, a few in small ATVs like the one they were in, and several more simply traveling on foot with a bag slung over their shoulders. Jawnee watched all of them pass by, a few turned and looked back at him. Some of the women who made eye contact with him seemed to drift off to sleep for a moment and then suddenly shake the feeling off. They would walk even faster, avoiding his eyes.

After several minutes of silence Jawnee decided it was worth the unpleasant swerving of the machine to try and set up a plan.

"Ramon," another swerve of the machine, "I can't read. You have to talk. If not, I cannot get Cook's stuff and she scares me."

Ramon kept glancing over at him, he nearly hit two people walking along the side of the road, and then finally nodded.

"Okay." Ramon said very slowly, "So...how do you like the caravan?"

"Everyone good people," Jawnee said, "not Nathan."

"Nathan's a good guy!" Ramon said, but something in his face told Jawnee that was an instinctive response. Not a heartfelt one. Jawnee figured it might be a good idea not to talk about Nathan with any of the stunt performers again.

"What do stunt performers do?" Jawnee asked, "In show."

"We're stunt performers. We do high diving, trapeze, stunt shows, and sometimes we do theater if we can find a few extra actors and actresses in the city that want to perform for free." Ramon didn't seem as nervous when he talked about the show. His voice took on a much more confident tone than what Jawnee had been hearing over the last two months. He wondered if it was because they were talking about the show or because they were away from everyone else. Maybe just because they were away from Nathan.

"Isabelle part of stunt performers?" Jawnee asked. Ramon glanced at him for a second, a smirk playing on the corners of his mouth. "What?"

"Nothing. No Isabelle isn't one of the performers. Not really, she could be and she sometimes works on the shows but usually she dances at the local art houses if the city we're in has one."

"Art houses?"

"Where the hell are you from? Art houses are halls in major cities for dancers and poets and such. People go to watch them and sometime give donations to the artist and the house. That's where most of Isabelle's money used to come from."

"I heard people say she not have money to stay. What happen when caravan move into city?" Jawnee pointed at the huge towers that stood at the other end of the bridge.

Ramon shrugged.

"If she doesn't make enough money to pay another seasons rent plus the rent from the last season that she owes then she'll be left behind in Frisco."

"You don't care?"

Ramon shrugged again.

"It's the way things work. If you can't pay your way then you leave, whether you want to or not. I've been a part of the caravan for five years, a lot of people pack up and go because they can't pay. If you aren't a good worker you'll have to go to."

Jawnee didn't respond. He glanced at the list of grocery items. He was going to need to learn how to read, and very fast. He wouldn't always have someone with him to read the list for him.

The towers were closer now, rising up over him and blocking the sun and casting the two of them into a shadow. As the ATV moved into the city streets, the small key in Jawnee's pocket pulsed and gently pulled toward the towers.

6

The open air theater is an enormous building that is missing the back. From the street it looks like a five story building but once inside a person sees that the back end is open to an enormous crater. The crater has been filled with cement and turned into a large stage. Several rows of benches sit on the floor of the crater and the five stories of the building have been remodeled into balcony seating. It sits empty during the winter, an enormous tarp drawn over the open stage to keep it from filling with snow and water. During the spring it is usually cleaned to allow for renting and during the summer it is usually the housing place for "Andy Che Pen's Stunt Performers." In the off season however it was the property of Queen Abigaile and until permission was given no show would be allowed to set up inside.

The main legal office of the city of Frisco sits further toward the center of the city, among the homes of the lawyer, bankers, and tax-collectors. It doesn't look any different from the dozens of other buildings surrounding it except for the carved stone sign placed in front that reads:
LEGAL

Behind the building is a small concrete parking lot, a few cars and bikes are parked inside it. Ramon pulled the ATV into this parking lot and shut off the engine. He then proceeded to remove a wire from the engine and stick it in his pocket. Jawnee jumped down and stared wide eyed at the buildings around him. He then turned back to Ramon.

"Why take wire?" He asked.

"It won't start without this," Ramon said holding the wire up for Jawnee to see before sticking it back in his pocket, "this way it'll still be here when we get back."

Ramon started toward the Legal Building and Jawnee followed.

"Once we finish here, we'll go to the market and get the supplies for cook." Ramon said. Jawnee nodded and attempted to ignore the pulse and pull of the key in his pocket. It was stronger the closer to the larger towers he got.

Ramon led Jawnee into the large building, its large marble wall and polished floors glowing in the sunlight that streamed in from the windows. People of various classes were walking around, filling out forms at one of the several tables in the center of the room, or waiting in line at one of the windows that lined the back wall. Ramon walked toward one of the lines and Johnny Boy followed. After waiting in line for a few moments Ramon pulled out a small form from his pocket. Jawnee looked over his shoulder to stare at the letters and ink splotches all over the paper.

They waited in line for nearly a half hour, moving a few inches toward the window every few minutes. Ramon was silent, reading over the form in his hand. Jawnee stuck his hands into his pocket and felt the pull of the key as he clutched it in his hand. The strange pulsing feeling turned into a sound in Jawnee's head. *Thump-Thump Thump-Thump*. It was a light sound though and Jawnee could stand it, not sure what it even meant. The key had never done this before.

They finally reached the front of the line and Jawnee saw that there was a plump older woman behind the window. A small hole was cut in the center of the window and a slot was cut in the bottom of it. Ramon stepped up to the window.

"I need to turn in the forms for renting the grand theater." Ramon said without looking up from the form he was reading. He stuck it through the slot and the woman took it. She began reading and glanced up at Jawnee when she felt his eyes on her. She smiled at him but Jawnee was pretty sure it was out of habit rather than any kind of attraction or affection. He had seen that false smile on a few people in the caravan and he was seeing it on even more people in the city. These people seemed very disconnected, Jawnee couldn't imagine why.

The woman stamped the form with a huge gray stamp and then pulled out another form from under her side of the window. She pulled the pen from her ear and filled the form out quickly. When she finished she stamped it and handed the new form to Ramon.

"You're done." She said, and Jawnee was again struck by how disconnected and uninterested she sounded.

"Right." Ramon said in the same uninterested tone as he turned to leave. Jawnee smiled at the woman again but she had already moved on to the person who had been waiting behind them and paid Jawnee absolutely no mind.

"Come on," Ramon said, "the markets a long way from the Legal District." Jawnee followed after Ramon, stealing one last look over the buildings huge open interior.

When they got back to the parking lot Ramon replaced the wire in the ATV and the two started off toward the market area. It was a long way, a good hour from the Legal Building. Jawnee watched all the people they passed by and he could see the slow and steady drop in social status. The buildings got older, the paint on the buildings more peeled, the little patches in grass around the buildings grew duller then brown, and the people's clothing grew more worn and less flamboyant. These people also seemed more connected then the woman in the Legal Building. The were smiling at each other and a few stopped to talk as they walked past someone they recognized. Jawnee watched as a woman with a little boy holding her hand stopped to talk to another woman holding a little girl's hand. The two talked, the kids played, everyone seemed happy. For a moment Jawnee's main thought was *"I could live here."* He wondered why he was even having that thought and then realized that he wasn't really sure what he planned to do. Was he going to stay on the caravan even after he found the chest? Was he really that concerned with the chest? He seemed to forget about it entirely sometimes even with the key in his hand the chest didn't seem that important. It felt far away and unnecessary. He clearly didn't need it to survive so what difference did it make?

The buildings got smaller the further they drove and soon they were nearing the ocean on the other side of the city. The smell of ocean water had wafted through the whole city but once they were in the market the smell became even stronger. It was a good smell and Jawnee loved the market the instant he set eyes on it.

The streets trailed around the edge of the coast, a guard rail separating the travelers from the slight drop that led into the ocean waters. On these streets were several rows of street vendors and shops selling everything from food and clothing, to jewelry and perfumes. People window shopped, bought food, and laughed with friends as they made their way through the shops toward the far end of the street. The smell of ocean air was now mingled with the smell of fresh fruits, cooked meats, and perfumes.

Ramon parked the ATV amongst several other vehicles on the side of the road and removed the wire again. He jumped down and held out his hand to Jawnee.

"Let me see the list." He said. Jawnee handed it to him and then jumped down himself. Ramon started up the market street and Jawnee chased after him.

"Help find," Jawnee called after him, "not find for me."

7

It wasn't that hard to do what had to get done. Once Ramon read off whatever item they had come to on the list Jawnee found it with little trouble. Ramon would then take care of the haggling over price, though he retreated back to the more timid tone of voice that Jawnee always heard him use around Andy and Nathan. Seems Ramon was a pretty tough guy until you put him around other tough people. When they came to the butcher, a huge man with a lot of muscle and a long handlebar mustache, Ramon's voice went so low that it was practically a whisper. They didn't manage to haggle the butcher down at all and Jawnee knew they spent a lot more money then they needed to for the meat. Once they were away from the butcher Ramon's tone got more forceful, he must've assumed

Jawnee was timid since he was asking Ramon for help so much during this trip. Jawnee found that annoying.

They finished getting all the food and supplies they needed and made there way back to the ATV, each with a bag of groceries in one hand. As they neared it Jawnee noticed a small piece of paper that was wafting through the wind toward him. The edge of it were tattered and it was missing a section in the middle. He reached out and caught it without thinking and flipped it over. Something was written on it, but the ink was smeared and only one word was legible. Jawnee stared at it for a moment.

"Ramon." Ramon turned and walked back toward him. Jawnee held out the paper, "What does this say?"

Ramon looked at the paper, apparently put off by its ragged and dirty state.

"Revolution." He said.

8

Queen Abigaile stared out over the city streets, watching the citizens far below. They looked like ants, it was a comforting sight to her. It reminded her of how they ranked, of what their purpose was. It helped the fear of revolution slip away from her mind. After a few moments of it she was back to looking at the chest. It had moved again.

This morning it started to give off a strange pulse. It didn't actually send out a physical force but she could feel it. A sort of throb in her head that got stronger whenever she got near it. It pulsed for several hours and then it slid about an inch across the room, toward the window that overlooked the city. She nearly screamed but suppressed it. The guards would've come running in and rumors would've spread that she was going mad. She could practically hear the whispers already.

The Queen is unsettled. Seeing things. Might be time for her to step down.

She wouldn't have that. She would not allow anyone to see her like this. Instead of screaming she called for one of her hands and gave orders that she was not to be disturbed. Since then she went to the window and stared at her citizens. The chest had continued pulsing and moving toward the window, about a quarter of an inch every hour.

She couldn't decide what to do with it. She knew there was no one to summon that could help her, and besides she no longer wanted help. This

45

chest was brought to her, this chest was now in her chambers, this chest was her property. Whatever was in it, whatever it was that consumed her thoughts and made it impossible for her to be away from the chest for long, it belonged to her. No one else would ever have it.

This chest was her life.

9

By the time they were heading back across the bridge Ramon had already settled back into the submissive tone of voice and demeanor that he always seemed to have. Jawnee didn't say anything to Ramon about this, he was pretty sure Ramon wasn't even aware he was doing it. Instead he thought about the chest again. His thoughts focusing a bit more on it now that he was no longer enraptured by the feel of the market.

He knew it was in the city, but he had known that even before he set foot in it. He wanted to find it but he didn't know where in the city to even begin looking. It was too big and he had no way of knowing how long it would take to find it.

The key wasn't pulsing as strongly anymore, and by the time they crossed the bridge and returned to the farm land where the caravan sat, it had stopped completely.

CHAPTER 5
ON THE TOWN

1

The caravan drove through the city streets and parked behind the huge open stage of the theater. The passengers who had paid to come to Frisco left, most without a word of gratitude or farewell, while others rented out rooms in the local hotels, not wanting to spend three months behind the theater stage. Andy had Johnny Boy and a few other stage performers hang a huge tarp over the back of the stage blocking the caravan from sight. They then laid another huge tarp in front of the stage and set up stage lights all over the theater. An enormous spotlight was placed over the top of the building that served as balcony seating and aimed at the stage.

Andy kept Johnny Boy very busy, just in case the boy was planning on staying in Frisco he wanted to make sure the two months of free room and board had been paid in full. He kept him with the more experienced stage performers, hoping Johnny Boy would learn by doing. It turned out that he did just that and as the performers rehearsed, Johnny Boy quickly became a truly efficient stage hand during the day and a kitchen helper at night.

The work was good for Johnny Boy in a lot of other ways as well. His understanding of the language had grown from simple greeting and basic questions and now he was adding cursing to his vocabulary. Once, while unloading one of the larger boxes, Johnny Boy dropped one on his foot. He let out a scream of profanity so sharp and savage that everyone who heard him was taken aback. Cook, the stunt performers, and the stage crew all grew much fonder of Johnny Boy after that. Andy often found him with the other stunt performers during dinner, laughing at the top of there lungs as they exchanged stories about the various girls they had encountered in their travels. Johnny Boy laughed along with them, sometimes laughing so hard that tears were in his eyes, but he never shared any stories of his own. Everyone asked him at one point or another but his skill in the language would take a convenient nose-dive when it came time for him to share.

While the other stunt performers prepared the standard performances of the show, Isabelle and Miranda prepared their new performance. It was originally an elaborate set up that Miranda presented to Andy, a lot of flips, spins, and twirls. Andy made a few suggestions and it was toned down. Soon it was a dance instead of a stunt performance, but it was beautiful and Andy thought it would make a good opening act.

After Miranda finished pitching the idea to him in his office one night he gave her the okay.

"We go on in about three weeks," he told her, "you and Isabelle show me the performance before then. Once I've seen it, then I'll decide." Miranda had squealed with delight and hugged him tightly around the throat. Since then the two practiced endlessly day and night paying no mind to anything but the routine.

While everything was being set up for the performance, Andy prepared things for opening night.

It was customary for the royal head of whatever city they were performing in to attend on opening night. Queen Abigaile had already sent word that she would be attending as she always did but she had a request this time. She wanted an entire floor in the balconies left open for an item she would be bringing with her. Her messenger didn't specify what she was bringing, just that it was of "great value" and she wanted it nearby at all times during the show. Andy reworked his original seating plans to allow her three floors of the balcony seating instead of the usual two. Whatever her item was she would have it directly beneath her for the entire duration of the performance.

2

He liked being called Johnny Boy. It had a certain warmth to it especially when Miranda, Isabelle, or one of the other girls in the caravan (though there weren't many left since the travelers were all gone) called him that. It had a warmth when the other stage performers said it too, all except for Nathan whose fear and distaste of him was obvious. He wasn't sure why they called him that but he didn't see the point in asking. Why spoil something pleasant by digging for a reason behind it?

Andy kept him busy but he couldn't complain, he was enjoying his work; he learned to cook, he learned all kinds of interesting things about the different stunts, and all the heavy lifting was causing him to lose weight. His body size hadn't changed much but it was beginning to show more muscle than fat. Best of all his understanding of the language had grown. Now that he could understand and be understood by those around him, life on the caravan suited him. Johnny Boy was happier than he could remember being in a long time. The only downside was that he never got to speak to Isabelle.

Isabelle was completely absorbed in her rehearsals, and what little attention she had given Johnny Boy before had completely faded away. Except for an occasional greeting when they walked past each other during the day, or a thank you when he brought dinner to her table at night, they never spoke to each other. He usually got a bit more conversation out of Miranda but not much. Her "hello" was usually "Hi, how are you? How is everything?" but that was just the way she was. It didn't seem like genuine interest, just standard kindness that she showed to everyone around her.

3

About two days before opening night Isabelle and Miranda showed their performance to Andy. He approved it and Isabelle felt relieved and calm for the first time since they left the beach. She could stay in the caravan for good, she never had to worry about her money, and best of all she wouldn't have to be worried about being paired with Nathan.

He hadn't been too happy when he heard that she was going to be doing an opening performance for the show rather than being his partner in the more basic stunts, but he didn't complain. Mainly because he knew that there was nothing he could do about it one way or the other. He was upset though and it showed in how he shuffled around, muttering in a low groan. He rarely spent anytime with the other stunt performers and pushed Sandy away from him whenever she tried to talk to him. His mood was at an all time low and Isabelle's quickly rose to an all time high. She wanted to celebrate.

She went into the market and found a small liquor store called Besin's Tap and bought a huge bottle of flavored rum. The owner, a thirty-something man with a short beard looked her over more than once as she searched through the shelves. She didn't complain and even flirted with him a bit. As she had expected it had gotten her a nice little discount on the bottle.

When she returned she went to the dining trailer to ask for a few glasses. Sandy was the only one at the kitchen window and Isabelle knew even before asking that Sandy was going to be a bitch and not give her any glasses. Still, there was no harm in giving it a try.

"Hi Sandy." She said. She held the bottle low and out of sight of the small window Sandy was glaring at her through. If Sandy saw it she might start hinting at wanting to join and the only person Isabelle felt like drinking with that night was Miranda.

"Hi Isabelle." Sandy's voice was so full of venom that Isabelle was sure she was going to reach through the window and grab her by her hair. Her face was smiling but the smile was way too wide to be real. It was like a crocodile smile to Isabelle, she suddenly wanted to take a few steps away from the window but she wasn't going to let Sandy know that. "What can I do for you?"

"Well," Isabelle said, "I just wanted to borrow two glasses."

"Oh sorry," Sandy said, "But we just finished cleaning up for the night and you know how Cook is." Isabelle glanced over Sandy's shoulder into the kitchen. Jessie and Johnny Boy were still scraping the uneaten food off plates and building a pile next to the two huge steel sinks. Isabelle looked back at Sandy. Sandy gave her another fake smile. Isabelle was suddenly very tempted to shatter her bottle of rum across Sandy's face.

"Here."

Johnny Boy laid two clean glasses on the counter in front of Isabelle.

"We're about to start cleaning so just keep them until the morning okay?" He asked. "Slip them onto your breakfast tray or something." Isabelle smiled and Sandy stormed off toward the benches to pick up the rest of the dirty dishes. Isabelle leaned over and picked up the glasses. She looked into Johnny Boy's eyes, felt the familiar feeling of drowsiness she was now used to, and gave him a smile.

"Thanks Johnny Boy," she said, "you're a sweetheart." Later on she would be struck by the slightly flirting way she had said that. It was surprising to her but she simply wasn't scared of him anymore, in fact after the bout of cursing he had done after nearly crushing his foot, she was growing pretty fond of him. Strange as it seemed, hearing him talk like that had humanized him a bit. He didn't seem as…otherworldly to her.

"You're welcome." He said. For a moment he seemed ready to say something else but then he turned away and went back to cleaning. She watched him for a few seconds, considered asking him to join her but brushed the thought away, and left with the bottle of rum in one hand and the two glasses held in the fingers of the other. As she reached the door she turned to Sandy, waited until she looked up, and gave her a big fake smile. Sandy looked like she wanted to slit Isabelle's throat.

Isabelle left feeling very happy.

She was making her way down the caravan to her trailer when she caught sight of Miranda and Nathan. Miranda was facing away from her with her arms wrapped around herself. She kept shifting her weight from her left foot to her right foot like she was getting ready to run. Miranda tended to do that whenever she was nervous or uncertain, whenever life dealt her something she just didn't know how to handle.

Nathan's face was focused and cold. It was the look he had whenever he was getting ready to hunt. A look of emotionless, and heartless concentration. Isabelle had seen that look on Nathan's face before but it had never been aimed at her. Still, just seeing it in general was unsettling. It was no wonder Miranda seemed scared, Nathan's look was just for her.

"Miranda!" Isabelle called out. Miranda spun around, Nathan looked up, and Isabelle waved. She kept her face pleasant and calm, pretending not to notice Nathan bullying her roommate. Miranda waved back and immediately walked toward her, trying not to run. Isabelle looked into her face as she reached her and could see gratitude in Miranda's eyes. She looked over at Nathan who walked away without giving Isabelle his usual leer or piggish comments. "Come on," Isabelle said wrapping the arm with the rum in it around Miranda's back and leading her toward their trailer, "let's go."

Miranda moved quickly getting ahead of Isabelle and slipping into the trailer. Isabelle followed and shut the door behind her. Miranda sat on her bed, wrapped her thin summer blankets around herself, and simply sat with tears standing on the edges of her eyes.

"He wants us to drop the act." Miranda said, "said I should just go back to playing the background music for the stunts." Miranda shuddered under the blanket. Isabelle grabbed her blanket of her bed and then climbed onto Miranda's bed. She sat next to her and wrapped her blanket around herself. The bottle of rum and the two glasses were still in her hands.

"He doesn't usually try to force me to do things. So I told him no, and to leave me alone." Miranda's voice cracked a little and she cleared her throat, "but he's being even worse than usual. He was scary Izzy."

Isabelle didn't say anything.

"I'm not talking about stopping or anything," Miranda went on, batting at the tears in her eyes before they could fall, "I'm not gonna let him bully me. I want this to work."

Isabelle smiled. She pulled out the bottle of rum, undid the screw top and filled up both glasses, balancing them in one hand. Miranda smirked, took one from her, took a huge gulp, and then gagged.

"Couldn't you have picked something sweeter?" Miranda asked.

"Its sweet," Isabelle said gulping her glass down more quickly, "it's a tropical fruit juice blend." Miranda gulped down more, gagged again, and then held out her glass. Isabelle filled it for her.

"Next time just get fruit juice." Miranda said and took another large gulp.

"You can't get drunk on fruit juice." Isabelle said. They both laughed. Isabelle gulped down her glass and refilled it.

"How'd you convince Sandy to give you glasses?"

"I didn't. Johnny Boy gave them to me."

"Oh. That was sweet. He's a sweet guy isn't he?"

"Yeah, I guess so. He speaks a whole lot better now. But I don't think he's told anyone where he's from yet."

"Do you think he ever will?"

Isabelle shrugged. She didn't feel like talking about Johnny Boy. Hell he was all anyone had talked about for the last two months. It was time to change the damn subject for once.

"We should go into the city for the day tomorrow." Isabelle said after refilling her glass again. They were going through the bottle a lot faster than she thought they would. "Once the show starts we won't have much free time. We should take in the sights, go to a diner or something. Have fun for the day."

"Sounds like fun." Miranda said. She gave of a sharp little hiccup and Isabelle could already see that her cheeks were getting a little red. "Can anyone come with us?"

"Like who?" Isabelle said, a teasing smile playing on the sides of her lips, "Ramon? Or maybe Johnny Boy?" Miranda took a huge swallow of rum and held out her glass.

"I was just asking." Miranda said, her cheeks were very red now and Isabelle was sure that had little to nothing to do with the rum. "Besides Johnny Boy is into you."

Isabelle shrugged again, that was true. There was no doubt about Johnny Boy's crush but she didn't know him well enough one way or the other to even care about how she felt about him.

"We can ask Ramon to come along, but you know that means that other people will tag along too. Jessie will wanna come, which is fine I like her. But Sandy will demand to come too and you know there's a chance that I'll hurt her. Hell, its bound to happen. And if they all come..."

"Then Nathan'll come too." Miranda finished. She shuddered slightly and took a quick sip of her rum. "Let's just do the two of us then."

Isabelle held out her glass and Miranda clicked her glass against it. They spent most of the night laughing and drinking before finally falling asleep next to each other in Miranda's bed. The next morning both of them woke up with slight headaches, but nothing severe, and Isabelle left the glasses with her dirty plates at the end of breakfast.

4

Johnny Boy wasn't really sure what to do the day before opening night. Andy had Cook, Curtis, and a few more of the older members of his caravan in his office holding some sort of meeting for most of the night. This left Johnny Boy, Jessie, Sandy, Isabelle, Ramon, Nathan, and a few of the younger stage hands and stunt performers on their own for the day. They were free to do what they wanted provided they didn't get drunk, hurt, or killed before the show opened.

"Once the show is done you can go ahead and get drunk or dead if you want," Cook had told Johnny Boy that morning, "I can find a replacement afterwards but not right now."

What a pleasant woman.

Most everyone disappeared before he realized they were gone. The stunt performers and stage hands disappeared into the city early in the morning. Isabelle and Miranda had moved slower, they seemed to have headaches, but they did leave and after a brief discussion took Jessie with them. Sandy followed after them, whining about having nothing better to do. That left Johnny Boy on his own. He sat outside his trailer for a while, and held the key in his hand. It pulsed quietly and he could feel it pull slightly toward the high building in the city. After a few minutes, he decided now was as good a time as any, to look for the chest and his "life."

5

There were few things in Sandy's life as sad as this. She was actually chasing after Isabelle and her foolish friends to spend time with them. There was so little to do in the caravan on the day before opening, that it was either this or Johnny Boy. She didn't know how to make use of Johnny Boy yet, if she could use him at all, so nothing would come of that. So she was stuck with the bitch Isabelle, the weakling Miranda, and the mute Jessie.

They went window shopping, (none of them could afford a damn thing) ate greasy food, and drank crappy fruit drinks since they weren't allowed to drink anything heavy until the show was over. Isabelle and Miranda had gotten around that rule since they had the time to drink the night before. They got to have their fun, and Sandy was stuck with following them around while they did NOTHING. They talked about nothing, laughed about nothing, and by the end of the day Sandy was sick of them and decided to go on her own. Anything was better than following these fools around.

No one gave any protest when she said she was taking off. They shrugged, said goodbye, and reminded her they had to be back to the caravan by nightfall.

She wandered around the city by herself for nearly an hour. She window shopped a lot herself, walking through the high end side of town, and looking at the elite dresses that she once wore while people who once bowed and scrapped at her feet, walked wide around her like she was infected with something. After a while she couldn't stand the way they avoided her eyes and she headed back toward the lower sections of the city. Back toward the artist, factory workers, and beggars that seemed to be keeping her prisoner. It was down there, in the darker sections of the city that she started seeing the fliers

Fliers pasted all over the poles and walls of the buildings. Some were tattered and worn, like they had been put up months ago, but others were fresh and had probably been put up that morning. They were all printed in

54

black ink though, and they all said the same thing:

THE TIME IS AT HAND
TAKE BACK YOUR RIGHTS
ESCAPE THE CRUELTY OF THE ROYAL
JOIN THE REVOLUTION

"Just a bunch of pissed off people desperate to get more," she thought to herself as she pulled one off a brick wall, "unorganized as shit. How're you supposed to join the fucking revolution?" She flipped the flyer over, nothing on the back.

She balled it up and threw it to the ground. She turned to walk back toward the caravan.

"You seem angry."

There was a boy leaning against one of the light posts. He was a good foot taller than her, with bright cream colored skin and a head of dirty blonde hair. His face was handsome and his eyes were a bright ray of blue that she had never seen before. His mouth pulled into a huge smile showing a set of even, but discolored, teeth. His clothing was old and hung loose on his thin body. He stepped away from the post and walked toward her.

"You look cheated," he said, "like you're ready to join in the fight to take what is rightfully yours." Sandy didn't respond, she looked into his eyes. They looked full of something, but whether it was intelligence or simply energy she couldn't say. He held out his hand to her.

"Icarus, Icarus Mayweather." Sandy reached out and took his hand.

"Sandy Delgana." She said. He was cute at least, and he was better company in the last few seconds than the girls had been in over an hour.

"Pleasure to meet you Sandy." He said with the same wide smile, "so tell me are you interested? Want me to show you what I'm talking about? Want to get what you rightfully deserve?"

He had no idea.

6

He talked as he led Sandy through the streets. He spoke of the revolution with lots of energy, but he didn't speak of anything specific. Sandy realized pretty quickly that he wasn't anyone important in the hierarchy of the revolution, just some random member who spat out all the propaganda without really knowing what he was talking about. Still, he was entertaining enough and maybe he would take her to someone useful.

He led her to a restaurant called "Haven." It was a shabby place with peeling paint on the walls and only a few old wooden tables and chairs in it. There were only three people inside it, a woman with two screaming kids at her feet. She could hear some old man in the kitchen singing some old song she didn't recognize. It smelled just like the dining trailer in the caravan; oil, bacon, and smoke.

Icarus led her to the back of the restaurant where there was a single wooden door on the wall. He tapped it twice and it creaked open just a crack. Someone was inside. She could see a head of deep brown skin and two long black dreadlocks, but everything else was in shadows.

"The world has turned its back on us." The figure in shadow said.

"So we hit it from behind." Icarus said. Sandy rolled her eyes.

The door opened and Icarus stepped in pulling Sandy along with him. Inside was a set of stairs leading down to a dimly lit room. The figure that had opened the door was already at the bottom of the steps and disappeared into the room. Sandy hesitated for the first time, not really wanting to follow someone she barely knew into a darkroom, in the lower level of a restaurant, in a city she barely knew. She reached around and touched at a small hunting knife that she had stuck in her back pocket. She pulled it out slowly and held it in her hand.

"What's wrong?" Icarus asked. He was already at the bottom of the stairs.

"Nothing." She said, and followed him down the stairs, into the room.

There were a lot more people in the room than it was probably meant for. People were lined up along the walls, some standing against it and others sitting in front of them. There were several people sitting toward the center of the room all of them sitting and staring toward the open space in the center as if something was going to rise out of the opening in front of them. There were several dark men with dreadlocks around, Sandy couldn't tell which one had opened the door.

Icarus motioned her to the corner of the rooms and they leaned against the wall. The room had the steady hum of people talking in low whispers. Sandy heard all of it but nothing interested her. They were talking about someone named Bill. *"Bill is so great. Bill is remarkable. Bill is so smart. Bill is going to lead the way to a new world."* And so on. Other than the fact that the leader's name was Bill she wasn't getting anything of interest out of these people.

She was just beginning to wonder what she could've possibly been thinking when she agreed to come here, when someone came toward the center of the room. She couldn't see what direction he had come from but everyone moved out of his path as he went by.

He was thirty-five, maybe forty, with a scraggly brown beard and short brown hair. His clothes were worn, like everyone else's, but they fit him perfectly showing a body full of muscle. He stood tall and confident looking over the people around him like a commander overlooking his troops.

"Maybe that's exactly what he is." Sandy thought. The room fell silent as he took a breath.

"My friends," he said, "are you tired?"

A low murmur of agreements from the people.

"Have you grown tired of working yourselves to death for those people in the towers?"

A slightly louder murmur of agreements.

"Building their homes," low applause, "cooking their food," the applause growing louder, "cleaning their messes, while they look down on you!" The room exploded in cheers and powerful whoops. "DON'T YOU DESERVE MORE!" The applause in the little room was defeaning, but Sandy's smile was huge. This was so wonderful, a group of people who were desperate for more, who hated the people in power right now, and above all else were easily led. The group was chanting: *BILL! BILL! BILL! BILL!*

Bill motioned with his hands for everyone to be quiet. The applause and chanting fell away. Bill smiled, his teeth were very large and very white. He took a deep breath and began again.

"Its time for the change to begin. Its time for us to move past the old world, past this system of the haves and the have nots. Its time to build a true equality. Its time for a world where the common man can have all his hearts desires!"

More applause and chanting followed this. The room was full of bright optimistic smiles. Sandy smiled too, watching the self righteous Bill preach to the converted. It was entertaining but nothing of any real use. They were talking that was all. Everyone talked about rising up and that was why everyone stayed at the bottom. No one ever actually moved for the top, and if they ever did they turned back the second they encountered a problem. These people weren't going to be any different, not with this over dramatic fool leading them.

"We must find a way," Bill had started talking again while Sandy was lost in her mind, "a way to get to Queen Abigaile." That sentence clicked in Sandy's head. She knew a way to get to the Queen. She could feel it, the feeling she had that day she killed the prince's girl, that feeling that came when an idea entered her head.

"What're you gonna do when you get her?" Sandy called out. The room fell silent and a lot of faces turned toward her, some of them angry that she would interrupt the great Bill in the middle of his speech. Sandy didn't falter though, it had clicked in her head, the idea was there buried in her mind like some strange fossil. All she had to do now was dig it up bit by bit. She would need to work this little group, and to do that she would need to work Bill.

"She will be the first of the elite to fall," Bill said with conviction, though he seemed a little thrown off by her sudden interruption, "once she falls the rest will tumble around her."

"I know how to get to her." Sandy said, she hoped the smile on her face looked genuine enough. She stepped toward Bill, moving with the same grace she had used in a better time of her life. The confidence must have been visible on her face because most people moved out of her way as she walked. One man, a very large man sitting in front of her gave her a glare and refused to move. She kept walking and threw her foot out hard and caught the man in the base of his spine. He hissed and moved out of her way.

"Sorry." She lied without looking back at him. No one else got in her way as she came into the center of the room. She walked up to Bill, stopping less than an inch from him. He was much taller than her and she stood on her tip-toes so she could look into his eyes. His confidence faded away before her, as she had suspected no one else ever tried to stand on even ground with him.

"Listen carefully." She said.

7

As Sandy told her plan to the room, the other three girls were walking along the great bridge each sipping at small bottles of punch they had bought with their little bit of spending money. Isabelle walked against the edge, liking the feeling of the cold air that seemed to rush up from the water below. Jessie walked along the opposite edge glancing at the passing travelers. Miranda walked between them sipping at her punch.

Jessie pulled her hair back from her face and reached into the breast pocket of her white blouse. She pulled out a small black pad of paper and a thin pen. Isabelle glanced over at her as she scribbled something onto the paper and then held it in front of her so that Miranda and Isabelle could both read it. It read:

Has he asked you out yet Isabelle?

"Who?" Isabelle asked. Jessie looked at her like she thought Isabelle was being stupid. She wrote something else and held the pad out again.

Who do you think? JB.

"Johnny Boy?" Isabelle asked. Jessie nodded. Miranda glanced at Isabelle curiously. "No. He hasn't and I probably wouldn't say yes if he did." She thought about the way she felt when he looked at her and wondered if she really would say no.

Jessie wrote something else.

Awfully picky aren't we? None of the other guys on the caravan do more than stare at your tits anyway. Shouldn't look a gift horse in the mouth.

Miranda laughed. Isabelle turned on her.

"What are you laughing at?" Isabelle said, trying to sound angry and not doing a good job. "I don't see you and Ramon spending any alone time."

Miranda's face was suddenly very red. Jessie scribbled something else.

Yeah. What about you and Ramon. You gonna go for it or what?

"I don't even think of him like that." Miranda said. That was clearly a lie. Isabelle was laughing and Jessie's smile had grown very wicked. She wrote again.

You're sure?

"Yes!" Miranda nearly shouted. Her skin was beginning to look like the red punch in her bottle.

Can I have him then?

Isabelle erupted in loud laughter and stopped before she fell over. Jessie was smiling brightly and Miranda could feel the smile playing on the corners of her mouth. She tried to push it away. She failed.

She laughed too.

Johnny Boy was lost.

He had known this would probably happen, was certain it would actually. He didn't know the city layout at all and it wasn't like he had anyone he could take with him. Still, he had set out to look for the chest and he had no intention of going back to the caravan until he at least knew where it was, even if he couldn't get to it yet.

He had taken off into the city, following the direction the key pointed. Taking it out of his pocket when he was sure no one was watching, turned in the direction it pointed, and then put it back in his pocket. This had seemed effective enough, whenever he got turned around it always righted him. But soon enough he had come into a section of buildings that seemed to come to one dead end after the other. He tried to backtrack and somehow got turned around again.

He had been able to keep the ocean and the bridge in sight to use as a key point, it was easier to tell if he was turned around if the ocean was suddenly on his right side. Now that he was toward the center of the buildings, the bridge and the ocean weren't in sight anymore. It was just one large brick or concrete building after the other. The key was still pointing but now he would have to either climb onto the roofs or break through walls. He couldn't break through walls of course, and he couldn't find anyplace to climb. The old fire escapes on the side of some buildings didn't look safe. Most of them hung loose with several sections of them rusted to crumbling. He could swear that he heard them creak anytime the wind blew.

"So you gonna quit little Jawnee?" A voice that Jawnee recognized as one of his dead brothers said in his ears. *"Gonna quit and just go back to being the good little kitchen helper?"* He ignored it as best he could and tried to find his way out of the maze he had gotten stuck in. He wasn't planning to give up yet but until he had the ocean in sight again it wasn't going to make much difference what direction the key pointed. Rita's voice overrode his brother's and she was much louder.

"Why not give up? You don need it anyway." Rita said. *"You already proven that. Ya ain't had it for over two months and your fine. Why bother?"*

"Because its important," Johnny Boy said not realizing he was talking out loud, "I can live without it yeah. But its important and I want it back."

He found one large road that seemed to cut straight across through several others. He could see the ocean in the distance, so he started down the road. "I want it back. It belongs to me and I'm gonna get it back."

Rita didn't respond. She seemed to fade away as she had done a dozen times over the last two months. He used to be happy when she faded but he was realizing it was only a matter of time before she started up in his head again. He could only hope she would keep teasing him and not start saying anything really viscous. Back in the Oasis she could be pretty horrible when she wanted to be. His mind started to pull up a memory of her waving a torch in his face and he beat it away before it could creep all the way to his conscious mind.

As he neared the ocean he could smell the fruits, and cooked meats of the market. He came out on the same part of the city that he had been in when he came here with Ramon before. The market had the same traffic of customers it always had and the ocean breeze shot through Johnny Boy's nose. It was a welcome feeling after the claustrophobia he had felt while lost in the city's center. He found a small wooden bench that overlooked the ocean and sat down. He wasn't eager to get lost in the center of the city again. He looked out over the ocean and his mind wandered away.

He held out the key in his hand without thinking about it and it spun around pointing back to the center of the city. He didn't look at it. He stared out over the ocean and enjoyed the sound of the waves and the feeling of the mist that was blowing into his face. He could see the farm land on the other side of the bridge to his left and the open ocean on his right. The sun was high in the sky over the water, he still had plenty of time before he had to head back to the caravan. Plenty of time to find where his key was pointing.

He got up and started into the city again. After another hour or so he found himself lost and wandering back into the market. Every time he got turned around, Rita would pop into his head and mock him again. He would curse at her and she would fade. Unfortunately, people around him weren't eager to talk to him or give him directions after watching him talk to himself. He got lost two more times and ended up back at the market each time. Eventually he sat on a bench and let his mind wander again.

It wasn't until the setting sun caught his eyes that he realized he had completely spaced out. It was already half into the water, casting a beautiful orange light into the sky. The orange faded to purple as it went up, then blue, and finally black. Johnny Boy stood up with a start and looked around. The market was closing, people were leaving and store owners were taking down their food, loading them into carts to take home. Johnny Boy stared at the key in his hand, the key pointed to the same point as always.

"Think ya have any chance of finding it and makin it home before dark boy?" Rita asked. *"Ya ain't that fast."*

He cursed at Rita again, making a woman and her kids walk away from him, and stuffed the key in his pocket. He walked along the coast until he finally found a road he recognized and headed back to the theater and the caravan. A day wasted walking in circles.

"Damn it."

9

Sandy returned to the caravan before anyone else did. She stuck her head up to the window of Andy's trailer as she did, and was happy to see that Andy was still having his meeting. Cook, Curtis, and all the other senior members of the caravan were still inside and still talking. She quickly patrolled the rest of the caravan and once she was certain that no one else was around, she made her way to the final trailer.

She couldn't pick the lock that held the large steel door of the trailer shut. She was able to pull open the window that sat on the side though, and she climbed through it to get inside. At first the thick brown bag she had over her shoulder got stuck and she couldn't get it free. She pulled and it finally came free and fell to the floor in the trailer before she could catch it. It hit the ground with a loud bang and she froze in terror waiting to see if anyone was going to go checking on the sound. A minute went by with no sound of footsteps and she snatched up the bag.

The room was dark with only the light from the window streaming in to show her the surroundings. The walls were lined with shelves that were full of pieces of metal and parts for the caravan that Sandy had no understanding of. In the center of the room was the large ATV that Ramon had used when he and Johnny Boy were sent ahead, and two large dune bugees sat on each side of it.

She went up to the first dune bugee and reached into her back pocket. She pulled out a thin slip of paper and unfolded it to read the directions. The man she had kicked in the back, she thought his name was Lucas but she couldn't remember, had written her a very detailed set of instructions to do what she wanted to do to the bugees. He was useful enough, maybe worth remembering. She followed the instructions to the letter and then repeated the entire process on the second bugee. When she was done she climbed back out through the window and headed toward the bathroom trailer to shower and change clothes. Nothing to do now but wait for opening night.

CHAPTER 6
OPENING NIGHT

1

The crowd flooded in quickly on opening night. People paid Sandy and Jessie two coins per adult and one coin per child at the door while Cook and Curtis stood ready to throw out anyone who caused trouble. Several of the audience members were part of the revolution and Sandy told each of them where to sit as they came in. The other customers she told to sit anywhere they wanted, but for the revolution members she was very specific.

2

Johnny Boy was set on the huge spotlight at the top of the theater. He had been taught when to narrow the light and focus on the center and when to pull it back and light up the entire stage. It was easy work and he would be able to enjoy the show.

Although he didn't know it, he would be in the perfect position to save someone's life.

3

Isabelle was standing behind the giant curtain, stretching her legs. She could hear the low murmur of voices as the crowd started filling the seats and her heart began beating faster. The nervousness that came over her before every show. It made her blood pump hotter and faster. She took a deep breath and tried to focus herself. She didn't need to be nervous. She knew the routine she had done it a thousand times over the last week. She knew the cues from Miranda's flute perfectly. The veils around her face and in her costume were all perfectly set so they wouldn't fall off or snag in her hair when she spun. She was ready. It was just another dance routine, just another crowd.

She was ready.

4

Nathan had bitched and moaned all through the day leading up to this. He whined about having to give up the number he used to do with Isabelle, since he absolutely refused to do it with a man. He whined about having to do a new routine with Ramon instead. He whined about the routine being stuck in the middle rather than being the opening or closing act. He whined about how cheated he was. He whined and whined all day.

Andy finally told him to shut the hell up and get ready. Nathan had done that and now he sat on the side of the stage, just out of view of the crowd, watching Isabelle stretch, letting his mind focus on his upcoming performance.

5

Queen Abigaile barely noticed anything her attendants said as she sat down. She gave no notice to the wine that was poured in the glass before her. She thought nothing of the occasional glances from the children in the stands who were waving at her. She could care less about the nervous tension that her Captain of the Guards said he felt.

She thought only of the chest.

Normally she would've sat in the highest balcony level and her attendants would've sat in the level below her. Now the chest was set in the highest balcony level, she sat in the level below, and her attendants were put down one level further. Which was just how she wanted it. The chest was above her, always in her thoughts, the only thing that mattered anymore.

When one of her attendants had tried to move the chest, saying they could just store it inside her carriage, she had beaten him savagely until she was pulled off him by her guards. No other attendant dared touch it and Queen Abigaile had things the way she wanted.

She was directly under the chest.

The chest was directly under the spotlight on the roof.

65

Andy stood before the back of the curtain. His blue suit shined even in the dim low lights, it would blaze under the spotlight. He looked over at Ramon and another stage hand who each stood at different ends of the curtain. They were both waiting for his signal, their hands on the ropes connected to the curtain.

After a while he saw Sandy and Jessie come around the side of the curtain, each with two enormous bags of money in their hands. They went past him dragging the heavy bags toward the caravan. Once he saw them climb inside he snapped his fingers. Ramon waved his hand toward Johnny Boy, and the spotlight clicked on. Andy nodded to Ramon and the curtains opened up. His eyes shut in the sudden light, then adjusted. The audience was silent, and he stepped out onto the stage, his arms spread wide.

Showtime.

"LADIES AND GENTLEMEN!" Stage Master Andy shouted over the crowd. "WELCOME TO A NIGHT OF WONDER AND AMAZEMENT! WELCOME TO A NIGHT WHERE YOU WILL SEE PEOPLE OF AMAZING SKILL PERFORM FEATS OF BEAUTY, WONDER, AND DEATH DEFYING STUNTS! WELCOME TO ANDY'S SPECTACULAR PERFORMERS!"

The audience erupted in applause. Andy stepped back, his arms still stretched out, and the spotlight followed.

"WE BEGIN WITH A BEAUTY FOR YOUR EYES AND EARS! THE WONDER OF TWO ANGELS FALLEN FROM HEAVEN TO GRACE YOU WITH THEIR TALENTS!"

Two girls; a thin cute one dressed in a long white gown holding a flute and a curvy one dressed in loose fitting veils and a long skirt cut up on both sides, came into the light. The girl with the flute walked to Andy's right, the girl in the veils to his left.

"THE ANGELS OF SIGHT AND SOUND! ISABELLE AND MIRANDA!"

Andy stepped backward out of the light and disappeared into the shadows. The spotlight pulled out a little, growing larger. Miranda stepped stage left and Isabelle moved to center stage.

Isabelle bent one leg up, balancing on the other. The skirt fell away from her raised leg allowing her bare thigh to glow in the spotlight. She held both of her arms high, her palms up, and her fingers pointed toward the starry sky. She raised her planted foot, and balanced on her toes. There was a low whistle from the crowd and a murmur of admiration at her balance. Her eyes closed and she seemed to drift off into another world.

Miranda held the flute to her lips, and blew out a sweet note that filled the night air. That note melted into a slow melody that swept across the crowd. It rose and fell like waves and soon Isabelle began to rise and fall with it. Her legs, arms, hips, face, and hair all seemed to move with the music in perfect harmony. The veils flapped in the air and reflected the spotlight into the curtain behind her, casting a beautiful symphony of colors on it. Some members of the crowd awed at the sight but most simply sat, allowing themselves to be pulled into the sights and sounds of the performance.

It was fortunate that no action was needed on the part of the young man running the spotlight. He, like everyone else in the theater, was completely captivated by the music and the dance. The only person not truly captivated was the Queen, whose eyes kept shifting to the roof over her head.

The boy running the spotlight never even noticed that the key in his pocket was pointing straight down and pulling on his pants. He had eyes only for the beauty that danced in the center of the stage.

The music began to fade as Isabelle started into a final, long spin. The colors of the veils spun around the back curtain into a beautiful rainbow. The color reflected off the curtain and over the crowd bathing all of them in a brilliant mixture of colors. The music ended and Isabelle fell into a bow, her left leg extended so her bare thigh glowed in the spotlight again.

For a moment there was silence, and then the applause began. It was a small sound first and then it grew into a deafening sound full of cheering, clapping, hooting, and hollering. Miranda came to center stage next to Isabelle. They held hands and took a long bow before falling back into the shadows as the spotlight narrowed down again.

Andy stepped back into the spotlight. Behind him in the shadows large poles, trapeze ropes, high dive boxes, and a large circular track were moved onto the stage.

"AND NOW LADIES AND GENTLEMEN!" Andy said. "THE GREAT STUNT PERFORMERS!" The spotlight pulled back and the entire stage lit up. Several smaller lights around the stage also lit up as twelve men flipped and twirled onto stage. They flipped and landed on each other's shoulders, until they made a twelve person pyramid in the center of the stage. The boy on the top (Nathan) flipped off and landed on the high platform. The boy directly beneath him (Ramon) leaped up toward the platform. Nathan caught his hand and pulled him up. The rest of the pyramid slowly broke apart; some flipping onto other platforms and then pulling others up while the ones at the bottom barrel rolled to the side of the stage.

The sound of loud drums erupted from behind the stage as the stuntmen performed. The beat growing quicker and stronger as they swung on trapeze and sailed through the air. As they hung suspended in the air for those brief seconds, Miranda's flute sang in high notes that seemed to dance and the performers spun in the air. The audience screamed, applauded and cheered throughout the entire performance.

The group of revolution members in the back row of seats watched the show with great interest. Some of them became so immersed that they stopped looking for their signal.

Two huge dune buggies flew onto the stage with a roar of their engines and circled around the stage as the performers flipped over, rolled away from, and landed on them. They never slowed as they sped around the stage and never skidded or tipped in turns. They hit the ramps and leaped onto the track. They spent the rest of the performance circling on the track while the rest of the performance went on. The two performers driving the bugees felt the hum of the engines under them but didn't hear the slight clicking sound that was coming from them. They couldn't. The engine was too loud and the crowd was even louder.

8

Johnny Boy watched the stunts with only half the interest that he had shown for Isabelle's dance.

Over the last few weeks his crush on Isabelle had faded slightly. He was so busy with the jobs he'd been given that he didn't obsess with her like he used to. Watching her dance though was like watching some sort of angel floating in the clouds. As she spun and her hair cascaded across her face, his crush came flooding back to him all at once. By the time she was done he couldn't think of anything but her and he went from wanting to talk to her to wanting to hold her close and let her scent completely engulf him until there was nothing left in his world but her.

Once the stunt show started he had pulled the spotlight back, lit up the stage and now he was just watching. This part ran very long and there was really nothing for him to do until it was done. After they were done he would narrow the light again to focus on particular performers as they did their own routines but for now he simply watched.

Since there was nothing to occupy his thoughts he could now feel the key pulling on his pocket.

He tried to pull it out but it kept pushing down, it was like someone else was pulling on it in the opposite direction. He finally got it out of his pocket and it immediately slipped out of his hand and fell onto the floor of the roof.

The key vibrated for a moment and then stood up on its tip; the key end pointing down while the small round handle pointed to the stars. Johnny Boy's eyes went wide. He looked at the key for a moment and then crawled toward the edge of the roof. He looked over the edge and down at the crowd.

His eyes started at the people in the front row and traveled back; over the children and parents, over the back row of people who seemed distracted by something, and then into the six levels of balconies. The lawyers and bankers in the bottom two levels, the Queen's servants in the next two levels, the Queen herself in the fifth level, and...Johnny couldn't see what was in the top level. He leaned forward a bit more, gripping the edge of the roof tightly hoping his weight didn't shift too much and send him over the edge. He looked into the top level again. He finally saw what was inside and nearly fell over.

There it was. His chest was sitting all alone in the center of the top balcony. It wasn't being guarded by anyone and there was nothing else in the balcony but the chest.

What were the odds?

Johnny Boy backed away from the edge of the roof and made his way to the ladder he had used to get up there. He snatched up the key on his way, so eager that he didn't even feel the strain it took to get the key off the ground. He still had time before they would need the spotlight to move anyway. He had time. And even if he didn't, who cared? This was important.

9

    Queen Abigaile stood up from her seat, her heart leaping into her throat. She heard something over her head. The sound of footsteps. Someone was in the upper balcony with her chest! She spun around and made for the door, when the attendant sitting outside her door tried to stop her she swung her hand and caught the man in the throat. He fell back gagging, hit the wall, and slid to the floor coughing and clutching his throat.

10

    Johnny Boy managed to crawl in through the half open window that sat near the ladder. He had to push it up a bit further which was difficult with one hand since the window seemed to be stuck, but he did it. Once inside it was easy enough to get to the chest, the doorway leading in was blocked by nothing but a simple red curtain. He pushed it aside and saw his chest standing there in the very center of the room. Beyond the chest the opening act was still going. He still had time before he needed to be back at the spotlight.

    He walked around to the front of the chest and trailed his hand across the worn battered wood. He knew it was his, he knew it. He bent down in front of it and traced his fingers around the little keyhole.

    The key in his hand pulsed again but it didn't pull anymore. It didn't need to anymore, it was where it needed to be.

    Johnny Boy placed the key into the hole and it clicked quietly as it fell into place. Something made him take a breath and beads of sweat broke out on his forehead. He twisted the key and he could hear the lock open up. The lid lifted up and a smell of grass, water, and apple juice wafted into his nose. He lifted the lid up more and looked down into the chest.

    It was almost completely empty. The simply wooden floor was as chipped and worn as the outside and small splinters were decorating it. Among the splinters were a huge red pendant on a long gold chain, and a small white ball. The ball was no bigger than a marble, but it gave off a small white glow. Johnny Boy could see through the white light to the wooden floor of the chest. He reached down and froze.

He was reaching for the ball but his hand seemed to be turning to pick up the pendant. He tried to pull it away and nothing happened. It was like his hand had suddenly gotten a mind of its own.

"Ya can't get away!" Rita was laughing in his head. Her voice was much louder now. *"ah deals ah deal an its time ta pay up."*

His hand touched on the red jewel and he could feel the world falling into gray. He could feel the strange disconnection, the feeling that his body wasn't his anymore, starting to grow out of his hand and across his entire body. Everything was going hazy and he could feel himself falling.

Then he could hear his sisters in his head. Both of them screaming. *"FIGHT IT LITTLE JAWNEE! FIGHT!"*

He pulled his hand off the pendant. It was hard, his entire arm felt like it weighed at least two hundred pounds, but it finally came free and he immediately turned it and snatched up the white ball. Rita was screaming in his head again.

"PUT THAT DOWN!"

"Shut up." He hissed quietly. She was fading again but she had been so loud before, like she was screaming right into his ear.

"Why don't you just put it back boy?" Rita said in a reasonable voice. *"Ya know. For safe keeping. Where is it safer than in that chest?"*

"Shut up and get out my head, you controlling hag." Johnny Boy said. He held the ball in his fingers looked at it for a moment and then put it in his mouth. It took a little work but he managed to force it down his throat with a long gulp. All at once he felt warm again, wonderfully warm. It was back, that feeling was back. The feeling that people got when they were doing something that truly mattered. The feeling that came when a person kissed their lover, or hugged their kids, or painted, or danced, or anything that gave them a true sense of happiness. Why had he ever willingly given this feeling up? Yeah he could live without it, but what kind of life would he have had if he had just forgotten about this?

The curtain that blocked the doorway was torn down. Johnny Boy looked up and saw an older woman glaring at him. Her dress was long and elegant, made of what looked like blue silk. Her fingernails were painted red, but the fingers were white from how tightly she was gripping the door frame. Her face was pulled into an expression of such murderous rage that Johnny Boy was certain she was going to kill him. Her hair was tied through a large piece of jewelry on her head. Johnny Boy realized what it was when he was able to turn away from her hate filled face long

71

enough to look at it. It was a crown. This was the Queen of the city.

"Holy crap," he thought, *"the Queen is going to kill me."*

The Queen growled at him like a dog. Spittle flew from the sides of her lips. She clenched the door frame tighter, her long nails being bent back against it. One snapped in two but she didn't notice.

"Mine." She growled at him.

"Okay." Johnny Boy reached out and closed the lid of the chest. The pendant was still inside. She could have that. He nearly took a step back, realized that he would fall out of the balcony if he did, and took a step to the right instead. He held his hands out toward the chest, "take it."

The Queen didn't seem to hear him. She wasn't looking at the chest. She was moving toward him. She was hunched forward, still growling, with the spittle still dropping out of the corner of her mouth.

"Give it back!" She growled.

Johnny Boy backed away from her, moving to the right as he did, hoping to get around her and not get backed into a wall. He was nearly to the door when she hissed like a cat and lunged at him.

She hit him with enough force to push him to the ground. He slammed his head hard on the floor. The world seemed to be behind a gray curtain as his head threatened to go blank. He only laid dazed on the ground for a second but it was enough time for her to actually try and shove her hand down his throat. He bit down and she pulled back, wrapping her hands around his throat instead. He pulled at her hands but she slammed her knee down between his legs and the mind numbing pain left him unable to keep his grip on her hands.

"Give it back!" She hissed as her grip tightened around his neck.

11

As Queen Abigaile's fingers closed around Johnny Boy's throat, the dune bugees engines exploded.

Sandy had been very specific in her plan when she pushed Bill out of the center of the room earlier that day and explained the situation to his followers. She had taken great care in how she placed everyone, all of them directly underneath the Queen, ready to overrun the few guards at the balcony entrance when the signal came. People had asked her what the signal would be, and she had told them simply; "You'll know it when you see it." She had then taken Bill aside and with a wonderful

72

combination of sweet talk, strategy, and seduction got him to introduce her to Lucas who gave her the detailed instructions on how to plant two small, timed fused bombs onto the dune bugees and how to make them go off half way through the show.

It worked perfectly, the dune bugees exploded and the two riders were thrown into the air. The tires and pieces of the engines, flew out into the stage slamming into the crowd and crushing a lot of innocent people.

One man dove in front of his wife as a tire flew at her. He saved her life but his left arm was so savagely damaged in the process that it would later have to be amputated. Another man five seats away had just enough time to register the engine that was flying at his face right before his world went black for good. A little girl was screaming several rows back and her mother yanked her out of her seat just as a burning tire slammed down on it. The entire front row was full of people screaming as they climbed over the seats. The panic swept back through the aisles like a wave and soon everyone was screaming and running.

Icarus saw all of this and he froze in fright as the crowd screamed in fear and people began moving toward the exits. Some people were pushed to the ground by the people behind them and then trampled. He made eye contact with one old woman just as she was disappearing down to the ground and felt certain he would throw up.

Bill however did not notice this. He leaped up from his seat and stood on top of it. His hands shot out and he screamed at the top of his lungs.

"REVOLUTION!"

Icarus didn't move but everyone else around him shouted with Bill and then climbed over their seats and into the first level of the balcony. The social elite inside it screamed in surprise. Some tried to fight them off but they had no success. The entire group was overrun by the revolution. Most of them were injured, a few of them were killed.

Bill pulled a long hunting knife out of a bootstrap on his leg and charged through the first balcony into the hall. His blood pumped through his head so loud that he couldn't hear the screaming of the people in front of him, or the battle cries of the people behind him. Everything around him was fading away. His mind had gone blank. He was here, it was finally time. He was going to take what he deserved. After all those years of watching everyone in his family suffer and starve while breaking their backs in order to feed him and his sisters. After watching his father lose his leg in the factory and have to quit working. After watching his sisters starve to death. After spending his life being treated like shit by those who lived in the towers above him. After having to watch his wife die because he couldn't afford to take her to see a doctor when she got sick. After all of that, it was time for revenge. Slow and wonderfully painful revenge.

Two royal guards, their blue armor reflecting the light and flames from the stage, were running at him. They had rifles slung around their backs and swords on their hips. In the heat of the moment they each drew their swords instead of their gun. In the narrow hallway though, they can't move well enough to attack Bill at the same time. One of them had to pull back while the other charged. Bill drove his knife into the head of the charging one. The bone crunching sound seemed to overpower the sound of the chaos around them. The blood gushed and the man fell to the ground.

Before either Bill or the second guard could make any move, the rest of the revolution flooded into the hall and charged past Bill (making sure not to trample him) and descended on the second guard. The poor guy didn't even get a chance to scream.

The flood made its way up to the higher balconies.

12

The stage was in complete anarchy. The dune bugee pieces flew in every direction. Ramon dove to the ground as one of tires flew at him. It went over his head and into one of the tall lights. The light fell over and Ramon rolled to his left to keep from being crushed by it. Glass flew everywhere and some of it went into Ramon's right side.

Curtis was struck from behind by the front end of a dune bugee. His spine shattered as he was thrown into crowd. He slammed into the seats and his rib cage was crushed as front of the dune bugee fell on top of him.

Nathan rolled out of the way as a tire flew toward him. He climbed to his feet just as one of the wires holding up the curtains was struck by another tire and snapped. The trapeze and two platforms fell to the ground crushing two stunt performers and a stage hand beneath them, and the wire flew at Nathan. Nathan dodged as best he could but the wire flew into his right leg. It didn't sever the leg but it cut very deeply, nearly to the bone, and all feeling went out of Nathan's right leg. No feeling ever really came back to it.

74

Isabelle and Miranda were lucky, they were behind the stage watching as the bugees exploded and, thanks to angle, most of the debris flew away from them. The few bits that did fly at them were easy enough to avoid. Miranda watched the chaos with her hands over her mouth and her eyes so wide they looked like they were going to fall out of her head. Isabelle looked all around trying to figure out what she should do. What she could do?

Andy flew past the stunned girls and headed into the fray. He grabbed Nathan, who was clutching his legs and biting his lips trying not to scream at the sight of the flowing blood. Andy dragged Nathan backstage and left him with Miranda and Isabelle.

"Get him back to the caravan!" Andy called as he dove back on stage to try and get someone else out of the danger zone. Miranda grabbed Nathan and dragged him back from the stage a bit more. He screamed out, not in pain but in despair. He should have felt a huge pain rip through his right leg as she dragged him, but he felt nothing.

13

Sandy watched from the other end of the stage with great satisfaction. Jessie stood next to her, her face twisted in a look of horror. Cook flew past them and went onto stage to try and help. She wasn't like Andy though, Cook was too big and wide to avoid the wreckage. A stage light came down and hit her, pinning her to the ground. Sandy was mildly annoyed to see Cook struggling to get up (the cow just wouldn't die) but at least she was hurt that was something.

One of the huge platforms to Sandy and Jessie's left started to fall over. Sandy pushed Jessie in front of it and Jessie had just enough time to look at Sandy in shock before it crushed her.

14

The explosion had distracted the Queen for maybe five seconds. Johnny Boy took the time to kick her off him. She fell back and slammed into the wooden chest. There was a loud cracking sound, and the Queen gripped her arm and howled in agony. It was like she had slammed into a block of steel instead of rotted wood.

She didn't stay down though, she climbed to her feet and growled at

Johnny Boy again. Her left arm hung limp and at a very painful looking angle but she paid it no mind.

Johnny Boy ran out of the room and headed away from the window, it would be easier to run down the stairs than climb back onto the ladder. Besides, he had felt the explosion. He needed to get back to the caravan. Voices were down in the lower levels and quickly coming up the stairs, very angry voices. Without stopping to think, Johnny Boy turned around and headed for the window. He ran past the curtain covered door just as the Queen came flying out of it, howling like a banshee. He leaped out the window, caught the ladder, and began climbing down. Near the bottom someone was slamming into the ladder hard, making the worn out screws that held it in place shake and start to come undone. He looked down. Two men, one of them a royal guard and the other an average guy in old clothes, were fighting beneath him. The guard had the edge, he was much bigger than the man and was slamming him into the ladder. He kept hitting it over and over and the ladder was starting to lean. The bottom screws had come undone, and the top ones were too worn to hold it in place. Johnny Boy wasn't going to make it low enough to survive the fall without breaking a leg. He climbed back up to the roof.

He made it onto the roof and heard the ladder clatter down a few seconds later. He leaned over and looked down to see that the ladder had landed on the two men. Neither one was moving. He turned his head toward the stage and looked in horror at the chaos before him. What the hell happened? He looked over the edge of the roof and looked down at the crowd. The seats were empty, except for a few pieces of wreckage from the bugees that had flown into the seats. And the bodies. Bodies were all over the seats and he could feel his stomach twisting.

He had to get off the roof. He looked down at the brick walls that outlined the open balconies. He climbed over the edge, got his foot and hands planted in the crevices around the bricks as best he could, and began climbing down slowly.

15

A young mother named Becky Richardson had joined the revolution in hopes of giving her daughter a chance at a better life. It was this thought that she kept firmly in her head as she charged at the Queen in the top level of the balconies. The Queen dove back into the room and clutched the old wooden chest tightly like it was her child. She growled and hissed like a cornered animal and her eyes swung over all of the people who flooded into the room. Her eyes stopped on Becky.

The Queen's mind was pretty much gone, but she was ready to sink her teeth into this young woman's throat and tear it open. As she lunged though, Johnny Boy lost his footing on the brick wall and fell. He reached out desperately and caught hold of the Queen's hair as he flew past the window. She was pulled back and slammed into the balcony railing. She stopped Johnny Boy's fall and he let go of her head as he got a holding on the brick wall again. He climbed on paying no attention to her after that.

Becky had no concept of what had just happened, and didn't realize that she had just been saved from having her throat torn out. Bill strode past her and sank his knife into the Queen's throat. The Queen gurgled, clawed at her throat, and died. The people of the revolution applauded.

16

As Queen Abigaile felt her life's blood flow out of the opening in her throat, her eyes fell on the wooden chest. She tried to turn her head so she could look at the stage, so she could see where the boy who had taken her prize was going. She couldn't move her head. Her entire body was going numb.

"Mine." She thought as the world went dark around her. *"Mine."*

17

Johnny Boy made it down to the floor, and ran to the stage. The chaos was pretty much over at this point. The entire thing had lasted only a few minutes but the damage was horrifying. Bodies were all over the seats and the aisles leading out. He stepped over several people as he made his way up to the three small stairs that led onto the stage.

The stage looked like hell from a distance, actually standing on it Johnny Boy thought he had walked into some type of war zone. Blood stained the floor in huge puddles. He could see where several people had been crushed under fallen lights, and stage props. The glass from the shattered stage lights littered the floor. Screaming could be heard from behind the stage but he couldn't tell who was screaming, or where in the back they were screaming from. Suddenly Johnny Boy couldn't seem to move. All the adrenaline that had gotten him moving when the Queen attacked him, was now completely gone in the wake of it all. He stood in the center of the stage while Andy and Ramon were running around checking on people in the wreckage. It took Johnny Boy several seconds before he realized they were calling for him to help. He staggered for a second and then ran up to help them lift the large stage light that had Cook pinned to the ground.

He glanced to his right and could see Isabelle, Miranda, and Nathan off stage. Miranda tied a bandage around Nathan's leg, which was bleeding very badly.

Johnny Boy looked to his left and saw a fallen platform. Under it he could see a large clump of hair, and a single hand sticking out while a huge amount of blood formed a puddle around it.

Jessie.

Once the stage light was lifted and Cook was pulled out from under it Johnny Boy ran away from everyone and threw up.

CHAPTER 7
STUNNED

1

The theater was very quiet after the few survivors were tended to. Andy looked over his group as they tended to each other, either bandaging wounds or comforting one another. He had started with seven stage hands, twenty two performers, and seven crew members. Now there were seven people total; Miranda, Isabelle, Johnny Boy, Nathan, Ramon, Cook, and Andy himself. Everyone else was dead. Everyone but Sandy that is. Sandy Delgana had simply disappeared.

2

The revolution hide out in the basement level of the restaurant Haven was full of high cheer. Bill was praised as the heroic leader that drove the knife into the throat of the "villainous" Queen Abigaile. Beside him, Sandy Delgana was praised as the angel who had come to them and given them their freedom on a silver platter. Their names were chanted while their wine glass and beer mugs were filled. Sandy made sure that hers was watered down.

Bill praised everyone as great heroes who would forever be known as the people who changed society. The entire crowd drank that up almost as quickly as the wine and beer.

After a few hours most of the revolution members had gone home for the night, looking forward to continuing the process of "rebuilding" society now that the main obstacle was gone. It did not occur to anyone that while the Queen had been the most powerful member of the upper class she was far from the only one that could pose a threat to their goals. They hadn't thought about that before, and they certainly weren't thinking about it now. Not while they were all drunk on victory, beer, and wine.

While most of the members went home, several others passed out drunk on the floor of the basement.

By the time the victory party was clearing out, Bill was having trouble walking in a straight line. Sandy took him by the hand and led him to the back corner of the basement, where the light was lowest. He fell onto the floor and leaned against the wall, his breath rank with the smell of beer and his eyes half closed. Sandy sat down next to him, draping one of her legs over his thighs. She rested one hand on his arm and the other on the back of his neck. He turned to her and smiled.

"You're a true hero," Sandy said, "you're going to be a great leader." His smile widened. He could still understand her at least, and that was good. "What are you gonna do now? What's the next part?"

"Wer gon overrun the resh of em." Bill said. Sandy understood him well enough, the stunt performers on the caravan had gotten drunk a few times around her, she knew what to listen for. He was almost out though.

"Will I be there to help?" She said, filling her voice with as much hopeful innocence as she could.

He looked at her and his hand wrapped around her waist pulling her close. She let herself be pulled into him and pretended to be nervous.

"Yur gon be there till the end." He said. "Right nexsht ta me." Sandy smiled wide as he passed out. It was always nice when she heard exactly what she wanted to hear.

3

While Sandy sat with the drunken leader of the Revolution, the crew of the caravan sat inside the dining trailer in total silence.

No one could think of anything to say that would make any sense of the situation. No one could really think at all. Johnny Boy had thrown up so violently at the sight of Jessie crushed underneath the platform that his stomach and throat burned. He sat next to Isabelle on the long table, hunched over and breathing hoarsely. He tried to speak once, found that he couldn't think of what to say and decided not to risk feeling the burning in his throat get any stronger. He simply sat there and occasionally glanced around the table.

Isabelle and Miranda were next to each other but both seemed lost in their own minds. Nathan was poking at his right leg, his face crestfallen. Ramon sat with his head down. The only people not at the table were

Andy and Cook who were outside talking to a large group of Royal Guards. Johnny Boy guessed that the caravan was probably being blamed for everything, including the assassination of the Queen.

That thought made Johnny Boy think back to how the Queen had pinned him down to try and strangle him to death. She had wanted his life, but he couldn't imagine why. That little white ball was only worth anything to him. If anything she should have wanted the pendant, that had more value. Someone probably had it by now, either the Guards or one of the people who had killed the Queen. Rita would be angry at the thought of her pendant being lost.

That thought made Johnny Boy smile a bit. It faded quickly though as he looked across the table at the horror stricken faces.

Andy and Cook talked to the two guards for almost an hour before finally coming back inside. They stopped at the door and looked over their remaining group with tired eyes. Johnny Boy had always thought that Andy looked fairly young despite his age but the age showed very clearly on Andy's face now. Cook seemed even more stony than usual. Neither of them said anything for a while.

Miranda opened her mouth to say something but Andy held up a hand and she closed it again. His hand was steady, and that made Johnny Boy feel a little better. If Andy was still together, shaken or not, then they could all still pull through this.

"We have a lot of work to do and it has to get done tonight," Andy said, his voice was calm and steady, "first we have to take care of everyone still on that stage." Miranda and Ramon each twitched at that. "We have to gather them together and take them out of town to bury them."

"Why out of to-" Nathan began.

"We're leaving here as soon as possible." Andy started to pace left and right, his hands were clasped behind his back and his fingers kept clenching and unclenching. "The Queen was assassinated tonight. Those guards are expecting there to be a few uprisings as a result, and their asking me to transport some of the more elite members of the Queen's Council out of the city." He stopped and turned to face everyone. Cook came around him and sat between Johnny Boy and Isabelle. Andy regarded them all for a moment and then went on.

"There are not going to be uprisings. There is going to be a full scale war. Just like the one in the King's Towers on the other end of the lands.

This city is going to be ripped apart over the next few weeks and I don't want us anywhere near this place when that starts to happen. We're loading everything up now, gathering up the bodies, burying them and then heading East as fast as we can."

He paused and seemed to stop breathing for a moment. Johnny Boy wondered what this man was like when he was truly angry, when this perfect level of control snapped.

"So," Andy said, "Miranda, Johnny Boy, and Isabelle are going to empty out the far back trailer. Move everything into the empty passenger cars. Nathan, Ramon, Cook, and me are going to start gathering up the bodies. Once the back trailer is empty we'll load them in their and then move out."

Nobody moved.

"Get to work."

Cook stood up, Ramon followed her, and soon everyone was up and moving.

4

They unloaded all of the boxes in the back trailer in total silence. Miranda grabbed up the little boxes of screws, nuts, and bolts. Isabelle and Johnny Boy worked together to unload the large boxes full of engine parts for the vehicles and the caravan itself. They stood staring at the huge ATV for a moment and then decided to set it in neutral and roll it out rather than starting it up. Johnny Boy glanced at Isabelle a few times and she would look back at him, but her face was blank and she never held his gaze long enough for him to get any concept of what she was thinking. Miranda kept her head down the entire time.

After they had finished taking everything out they began the process of loading the things into the empty trailers. Johnny Boy's trailer was the closest one of these and he loaded a lot of things into it. He had no intention of sleeping this close to the bodies. He would just move into one of the empty trailers further up.

When they finished they opened the large back door of the trailer and stood aside as the bodies were loaded into the back trailer. Andy and the others had wrapped them up as well as they could in the cut pieces of the two huge curtains. There were a lot and by the time everything was loaded and the caravan began to move away from the city, the first hints of light were creeping into the streets.

5

They buried the bodies in a valley nearly a days travel from the nearest farm. There were a lot of silent tears as Andy said a brief prayer over the bodies.

As the sun began to set, the caravan continued east toward the rising moon.

6

About an hour later the caravan was heading away from the edges of the farm lands into the valley area around it, driving far enough out so that they would be out of sight of the city and the farm lands by the next morning.

Johnny Boy walked across the small platforms that connected the trailers together and made his way to the dinning trailer. He walked slowly, hoping that the feeling of the wind cutting across his face would help him keep his head together. He had tried to sleep but he kept seeing that small clump of hair and the single arm sticking out from under the platform. Each time he woke up and feel asleep again it would be there waiting for him. He had a feeling that it would be a while before he got a good night's sleep.

He was certain that the dinning car would be empty, it seemed that no one wanted to really be around anyone else right then. Even Miranda and Isabelle each seemed to want time to themselves for a while. So it was a bit surprising to Johnny Boy when he found Cook sitting inside a wooden chair in the corner of the room.

She wasn't drunk, at least Johnny Boy didn't think she was. But he saw the large black bottle at her feet and he could tell by the smell coming out of it that it wasn't full of water. Her head was turned down when he came in but she looked up when she heard his footsteps. Her eyes were red and puffy, her cheeks were glowing in the light coming in from the windows, and her nose was running a little. She turned her head back down and her face was hidden from him again, but he could see tears running down her fat cheeks. She picked up the bottle from the floor and took three huge swallows before sitting it back down.

"That lil bitch did it." she muttered. She said it so low that Johnny Boy wasn't sure if she was talking to him or herself. "That bitch Sandy killed her. I just know it. I feel it in my bones. She always hated her, I never knew why."

She looked up at Johnny Boy and the pain in her eyes was horrifying to see on a woman who had seemed untouchable for the last two months.

"Jessie was a good girl," she said and her voice finally began to break, "she was a good girl and she loved Sandy. She loved her, and that bitch killed her. Jessie was a good girl!"

Johnny Boy went to one of the small tables. He grabbed a chair and pulled it to her. He sat down in front of her and reached out, laying his hands on hers. He never thought about it, he just did it. She clutched his hands tightly.

"Jessie was a good girl." Cook cried.

7

Isabelle slept uneasily. She kept having images of the explosion; of the bodies, and the falling platforms. She kept hearing the screaming from the crowd and from Miranda as she had stood next to her backstage. It kept her from sleeping for more than a few minutes at a stretch.

In the bed next to her Isabelle could hear Miranda's soft cries and moans as she tossed and turned in her bed. Miranda's nightmares seemed pretty bad too but she never woke up, she was riding them out.

"Or is she trapped by them?" Isabelle had thought.

Isabelle would get up, pace around the room, and try to sleep again. Each time she woke up a few minutes later, touching her face expecting that blood had splattered on it. There was plenty of sweat but no blood.

Eventually she got tired of trying to sleep and she walked to the dinning car so she would have more room to pace around.

Johnny Boy was in there, and Cook was asleep in the corner, a black bottle of what smelled to Isabelle like bourbon was clutched in her arms. Her wet cheeks told Isabelle she had been crying. Johnny Boy was watching her, sipping at a small cup of tea with a hot pot sitting next to him. Isabelle could see the steam rising out of it's spout. He looked over at her as she walked into the room.

"You can't sleep either huh?" He asked. She nodded and sat across from him. He tried to smile at her but he couldn't seem to do it. The corner of his lips twitched but that was all. "You want some tea?"

She wanted something much stronger than tea, whatever was in Cook's bottle would have worked, but she nodded to him. He got up and went into the kitchen. He came back with a small cup, filled it with tea, and handed it to her. She drank it slowly, letting it warm her body, it was actually pretty good.

"Do you," Johnny Boy began. She looked up at him and found that she didn't feel that strange drowsy feeling when she looked into his eyes, "do you have any idea how it all happened?"

Isabelle shook her head. She didn't know, and she didn't want to think about it. She wanted to talk about something else, anything else. She looked at his face, haggard and tired, and asked him a question that sat in the back of her head.

"Johnny Boy?" She asked. "How old are you?" He looked at her with a bit of confusion.

"Seventeen." He said.

One year younger than me?" She thought. He was still looking at her, wondering where the questions had come from. She decided to keep going.

"Where are you from Johnny Boy?" She had meant to ask him that a long time ago but it had simply faded away as interest in him had died.

He blinked, not expecting that question, and then answered.

"I'm from the Oasis," he said, "far away from here." He tilted his cup a little left, then right, then forward, then back. His eyes never left hers but they seemed so dazed and far away. A very different expression from the lovesick look he had been giving her before.

"The Oasis?" she asked. "What's it like?"

"It's a beautiful place. Lots of grassland and valleys. A huge lake is in the center of my part of it." He sipped as his tea. "I lived there with my big sister."

"Where is your sister now?" Isabelle said and then wished she hadn't. If his sister was dead then she wasn't going to get them off the subject for very long.

"She's still in the oasis as far as I know." Isabelle tried not to let her relief show on her face. Johnny Boy's eyebrow raised a bit as he looked at her. "You were afraid she was dead weren't you?" He did smile this time, his lips pulling back into a teasing but kind smile. Isabelle found herself returning it. She didn't know that in the back of his mind Johnny Boy was thinking about the sister and brothers that were dead.

"Yeah I did. I thought I might have just made the mood even worse."

"I don't think that's possible."

"What were you doing out in the middle of nowhere when we found you Johnny Boy?"

"I really don't remember."

Cook coughed lightly and they both turned to her. She snorted, moved around on her chair a bit, but didn't wake up.

"I was making a delivery," Johnny Boy continued and turned his attention back to Isabelle, "Some cheap little red pendant to some old woman in a town a few miles out of the Oasis. I don't know what happened I blacked out while traveling and woke up in the caravan."

"And you lost your delivery?"

He didn't respond for a minute.

"Yeah."

Something in his tone told Isabelle that he wanted to change the subject. She was trying to think of something she could say when he did it for her.

"Your dance was wonderful." He said. "I've never seen anything that beautiful in my life." Some of the daze was starting to fade from his eyes and Isabelle thought she could feel the familiar feeling that always swept over her when she looked at him.

"Thanks. It was Miranda's dance though, she put it together. The music too."

He didn't say anything to that, just kept looking at her. The daze was completely gone and his eyes shown again as the two black pools they had always been when he looked at her. That feeling was getting stronger, she was getting sleepy. She didn't turn away this time, or try to fight it, she wanted to sleep. She wanted to sleep without nightmares and something told her she would. She set her cup aside without realizing it and laid her head on the table. She was asleep almost immediately. The last thing she heard was Johnny Boy's voice distant and far away in her mind.

"I'm glad you're okay Isabelle." He said.

She slept until long after the sun rose. She had no nightmares.

CHAPTER 8
WATCHING

1

The Oasis that Johnny Boy called home was usually very quiet at this late hour of the night. The few frogs that sat in the small crevices of the huge lake gave out soft croaks while crickets chirped in the tall grass just outside of the village. The small ranches and farm houses were mostly dark with only the occasional light or candle glowing in the windows. Most of the people were usually asleep. On this night however, no one was sleeping peacefully, and no animals were making their soft sounds. The furious howling of Rita Hatchworth kept everyone and everything awake.

Rita's home, the only all wood shack in the village, sat just inside the tall grass that surrounded the town. Its one small window next to the door gave off a bright flash of red light every time she screamed. She would howl, curse at the tops of her lungs, and then howl again.

Rita was a woman of nearly one hundred years, a nearly bald head with only a few wisps of gray hair in it. Her face had the sunken look of melted wax and her fingers were long and thin. Her lips were a dry gray and her body trembled at all times. Her eyes though were always alive, awake, and cruel. They glowed white in the dark and seemed to catch the moonlight coming through her window and absorb it before shooting out into the room around her.

The inside of the room was nothing but a bed, a stove, and two doors; one leading outside, the other to the bathroom. Against the wall sat three enormous metal chests and hanging above them were four pendants, each different colors, and one empty peg. Every time Rita's eyes fell upon the empty peg she would howl again and the light that seemed to glow out of her eyes would turn red.

"What da he think he is!" She screamed, "We had ah deal!" She picked up a wooden stool near the chest and flung it. It hit the window at great speed and flew threw it. The window shattered in a glorious explosion of glass and the stool flew nearly twenty feet before falling into the lake. Rita barely gave any notice.

"He cain't do this ta me! Little boy dun forgot who da hell he's playing with! I'll find ya, ya bastard!"

She stopped stomping around her home for a moment and closed her eyes tightly, her few remaining teeth were bared and her flared nostrils puffed in great pools of air.

"Where are ya boy?" She said.

Through her closed eyes, the world was black and empty. Then suddenly the world went red and she could see through the jewel of her lost red pendant. She cursed to herself.

"Where's the boy? Ah don't want the stupid pendant!" But the pendant was all she seemed to be able to see. The boy was gone from her minds eye. He had been gone ever since he found his soul and took back what he promised her. He would pay for that. One way or another.

The pendant was being held by someone, she could see the tips of fingers on the edge of the small red circle she was seeing. The room she was seeing looked old and worn, made of wood and full of people who were asleep on the floor.

"Where did you find this?" Some young female voice asked. Rita recognized that language though she couldn't remember how many years it had been since she'd heard it.

"It was in the chest that the Queen was protecting when we killed her." A man said. His voice was timid and submissive, whoever the young woman was she was clearly in charge.

"You shown it to Bill yet?" The young woman's voice asked.

"No Sandy." The young man said, "I...I wanted you to have it."

The pendant rose up, it had been tossed in the air and suddenly the fingers that had been holding it, clenched around it in a fist. Rita could almost feel the young woman's pulse through the pendant.

"Thank you Icarus." Sandy said. "Why don't you make sure that Bill gets home safe. We can't lose our leader now right?"

Icarus gave out a babble of agreement and Rita saw some shadow pass through the cracks of Sandy's fingers. The pendant moved again and now the jewel pointed directly at the face of the young girl who must have been Sandy.

"Gawdy looking thing." Sandy said into the jewel. Rita wanted to smack her, these pendants were easy enough to make but they were nothing to simply brush away as cheap jewelry. "Queen had no taste at all."

Sandy looked at the jewel in disgust for a moment, and then the look faded. Her eyes widened and she leaned in bringing the jewel closer to her face. Rita's breath held in her lungs. Sandy blinked and then she pulled it away from her face again.

"Who the hell?" Sandy said and then she looked into the jewel again. "Who the hell are you ya old hag?"

Rita's eyes shot open and she stumbled back, nearly falling over. Her breath came out in a shocked gasp and she clutched at her chest, sure that her tired old heart was going to stop beating from shock. It didn't, and after a moment she calmed down stood in the center of her little home. She closed her eyes.

The jewel was no longer in the girl called Sandy's hands. It was completely black. A brief flash of light came in and she could see the small hints of lint and fabric surrounding her small field of vision. Sandy must have put the jewel in her pocket. There was the sound of voices all around her, all of them saying goodnight to Sandy or screaming things like *"Victory"* or *"Revolution."* Rita listened until the voices had all faded and their were only two voices.

"You sure you don't mind me staying down here?" Sandy was asking. She spoke with a slight hint of fear in her voice that Rita knew was fake.

She liked this girl.

"Are you kidding," a deep masculine voice said, "the Angel of the Revolution is always welcome to use my restaurant however she wants. Stay for as long as you want."

"Thank you so much." Sandy said in a bright, cheery tone. There was the sound of someone walking up stairs, a door closing, and then there was nothing but silence. After a moment, there was laughing. It was quiet at first, and then it grew until it was nearly manic. It had to be Sandy and even through the muffle of the pocket it was perfectly clear. Sandy laughed hard and loud for nearly five minutes before she finally stopped. Rita could hear her sniffle for a minute and then give off a few more hiccups of laughter.

"Fell in my lap." Sandy said, still laughing a little. "Good things do happen to good people."

"Good people." Rita chuckled. Suddenly Sandy went silent and her small laugh died.

"Who said that?" Sandy said.

Rita's heart nearly stopped, she hadn't meant to project that. She was certain she hadn't projected it. This time she was going to project. She wanted some answers.

"I said you ain't no good person." Rita thought and she could see Sandy's hand reach into the pocket and pull her out. Sandy's face appeared, looking scared. "You just a manipulative little thing ain't ya girl?"

"Who the hell are you?" Sandy asked. Her grip was tight around the pendant and Rita could see her finger tips pressing into it.

"I got question first." Rita said, the girl had thrown her for a minute but she wasn't going to let some random little shrew take control of any conversation with her. "Where am I? And what happened to my chest?"

"Who are you?" Sandy said, and the fear seemed to be fading from her face.

"Rita." Rita replied. "Now where am I?"

"Frisco" Sandy paused, "My city."

"I can tell you're lying girl."

"It won't be a lie for very long." Sandy's shock had melted into something more like sadistic glee. "I've got everything I need now to make it happen."

"Do ya?" Rita said. "Well then tell me where mah chest is and where mah boy is and I'll leave ya to it."

"Boy?"

"That fat good for nothing that was suppose to be delivering this for me."

Sandy's face contorted in thought for a moment, and then a sudden thought must have occurred to her because her face lit up.

"Are you talking about Johnny Boy?"

"Yes that's him! Jawnee! Now where is he!"

"Oh he's gone by now." Sandy said. She sounded like she couldn't have cared less. "He headed east with the rest of those useless little peasants."

Rita could already feel the anger building up in her again. She suppressed it as best she could, she didn't want to start screaming and throwing things around again. She took a breath and Sandy's face drew in close to the jewel.

"You still there?" Sandy asked.

"I need you to go get him for me." Rita said. "He has something that belongs to me and I want it back."

"Hmmm," Sandy seemed to consider for a moment and then gave Rita that sadistic smile again, "nope."

"I can make it worth your time." Rita said.

"How?"

"Point me at one of those chairs?"

For a moment Sandy just stared at the jewel and then Rita's vision moved around the room until a simple wooden chair was directly ahead of her, sitting against the wall. Rita looked at it for a moment, and then scrunched her face in concentration. The chair exploded in a blast of wood and dust that seemed like it should have been deafening to Sandy in the small quarters but Rita knew Sandy would only hear the sound of splintering wood. Rita's vision spun around and she was once again looking at Sandy. Her lips were straight and unmoving but her eyes were wide.

"Do me this favor and I'll let you call on me to do this whenever you have need of it."

Sandy said nothing but her eyes were no longer wide. She shrugged. "I have a whole army of people," she said, "you're not that useful." Sandy studied the jewel quietly, turning it around in her fingers, and ignoring everything Rita said to try and convince her.

"But maybe," Sandy finally said after several minutes of quiet study, "I'll do it for something else. You got any other little tricks?"

Rita could feel the anger building in her again. She wanted to focus on this girl and watch her explode like the chair. But she needed her, at least for now, if she wanted to find the boy. Her hatred for him was much stronger than her anger at this insolent little brat. If she had to make a deal, she would make a deal. It was just a matter of deciding what to offer her. She could cast almost any spell through her pendant but she wasn't going to tell this girl that. The girl was a little too in control of the situation as it was. But there was one trick that she could do that she was sure Sandy would like. She focused on Sandy's face.

Sandy's eyes widened in shock and she pulled back. If Rita was doing this right, and she knew she was, then Sandy was looking at a huge red dog that was hovering over her and baring enormous teeth. The low growl and then barking that Rita heard confirmed that the illusion was playing just right. Rita relaxed her focus and Sandy's face quickly went back to normal, though her breathing remained fast and ragged.

"Is that interesting enough for you?" Rita said. She was sure that her irritation showed in her voice but she didn't really care.

"Okay." Sandy said. "I can find use for that. You want Johnny Boy then, I'll find him. But once I do, where am I suppose to take him?"

"Just find him." Rita said. "I'll take care of things beyond that."

"Fine." Sandy said and then Rita's vision went blank as the pendant was stuffed back into the pocket. Rita called to her but got no response. After a while she stopped trying and let the image of the pendant fade away from her mind. She opened her eyes and stared out into her empty little home. She had been so close to having the perfect little pet in that boy and now she was making deals with bratty little girls that she would've slapped senseless under normal circumstances.

She deserved better than this.

2

She couldn't find him. Her little brother, little Jawnee Sond, was completely gone from her limited sight. She had him clearly in her minds eye for a long time but she had to compete with Rita for his attention and often Rita won. She was just so much better at this and for the first time Suroa regretted not letting the old hag teach her when she was younger. Now she had use for the skills and she understood why little Jawnee had wanted to learn even though Rita scared him. Regretting didn't change the facts though, she had only been able to get passing words to Jawnee and he hadn't always listened. Thankfully he hadn't always listened to Rita either.

Why the hell had she let him go in the first place? She beat herself over the head with that question. She had two younger brothers and one older sister before little Jawnee was even born. When her mother died in childbirth everyone took to Jawnee as the last remaining remnant of her essence. Everyone but their father. He never really had the chance to tend to his youngest son, he died about four months after Jawnee's birth while on a trip to the land beyond the Oasis. Suroa could still remember the day that his body was returned to the Oasis as she and all her siblings watched; Jawnee in the arms of Becca, the oldest girl. After that it had been one tragedy after the other. Slowly everyone was gone but Suroa and Jawnee.

He was all she had, why the hell had she let him leave on a delivery for that witch? Hell, why had she even let him near that little witch? Hadn't Becca always told her that Rita was a calculating, manipulative shrew? She had tried so hard to protect Jawnee, but he didn't want to be protected. He always did things on his own, and in the end she had simply used her sight to watch him.

But now he was gone. He had faded from her line of sight when he swallowed that marble. She had wanted him to do it too, screaming at the top of her lungs for him to hurry and swallow it, to take back his life, even though she knew he probably couldn't hear her. She had known that if he replaced that missing thing Rita would lose her sight. She just hadn't thought she would lose hers too.

She could still feel his presence, which meant he was still alive *(thank the powers that be)* but she couldn't actually see him in her mind anymore and she couldn't hear him. Rita probably couldn't either *(thank the powers again)* but if Suroa could feel Jawnee's presence then Rita could too. Rita would find some way to get to him, if she hadn't already.

Suroa hadn't slept in a long time but she felt no fatigue. Her little brother, little Jawnee, nothing else mattered at that moment. She closed her eyes and thought of Jawnee, she thought of him as hard a she could.

"Please Jawnee," she thought, *"answer me please."*

Nothing. She kept trying though, pushing out with what little sight she had. Pushing out to her little Jawnee, the only one of her brothers and sisters still alive. The only thing that still mattered.

CHAPTER 9
LADY SANDY

1

Sandy didn't waste anytime getting Bill to work. It proved surprisingly easy, apparently Bill saw her as a angelic guide just like the other members of the revolution did. He looked at her with a mixture of awe and longing whenever she spoke.   He did exactly what she told him without question or hesitation.

Over the next week, as Andy's caravan rode on, Sandy began a massive purging of the social elite from the city of Frisco. It began with an assault on the palace, where the royal guards and the late Queen Abigaile's advisors were attempting to restore some type of order. The group of revolution members had nearly doubled since the assassination of the Queen and they stormed the palace at midnight the night after Rita and Sandy made there deal.

The guards fought hard, the sound of the battle cries and rifle fire rang out throughout the city. However they were outnumbered. Twenty revolution members to every guard. The attack took only twenty minutes and the palace was taken. Not a single guard was spared, per Sandy's orders. and their weapons were given to the revolution members. Sandy moved into the palace along with Bill and managed to talk him into allowing her the Queen's personal room as her own private quarters. She was certain that Bill would come to her room sooner or later and try to take her. She may well let him if it gave her even more control, but she wasn't in any hurry to let that happen.

The next day the new "Free City of Frisco" began to exterminate anyone who would not immediately turn over all their worldly possessions to the people in the lower levels. By that night, most of the towers were full of dead bodies. The citizens in the lower level were attempting to move into them. When several of the new guard tried to stem the tide of people, just wanting more time to remove the bodies from the towers, they were accused of rebuilding the oppression and overrun by the citizens. Several other guards panicked, fired on the citizens, and soon the city was in a full scale riot.

Sandy spent all of her time during this riot inside the Queen's Tower. She slept in the huge bed while the explosion and gunfire and screams outside rang across the night air. Her sleep was mostly dreamless and she remembered none of her few dreams when she woke up in the morning to find many of her followers, but even more citizens, were dead.

Bill fell under a lot of criticism after the riots. His leadership was questioned as was his ability to handle the new powers that had been given to him. Neither Bill nor anyone else seemed to be aware that the decisions were really coming from Sandy. All she had to do was whisper them in Bill's ear, or give a stirring little speech to a few of her troops and her plans always came into fruition. Part of her just wanted to sleep in her bed and watch while the world fell to hell around her. Once it did she could start to rebuild it. Let the people lose their faith in Bill while their faith in her builds up. Their children could be raised seeing her as a goddess. Why not? They already thought of her as something grander than just a little girl with a decent idea. It wasn't so unlikely that they would eventually start to view her as something more than human. It would take time, and it was going to be a lot of fun to watch.

Still, she had made a deal with Rita. Besides, part of her still wanted to see the caravan burn. She wanted to see Cook, Andy, and everyone else who had made her life a disgrace on that giant hunk of metal dead. She wanted to finish what she started on that stage. It wasn't important anymore, but she was going to have to send someone after the caravan anyway. Why not take care of unfinished business while she was at it? It was important for a future goddess to be thorough after all.

She decided to send a little group to go after the caravan. It would have to be people that she could count on and there was only one person in the revolution other than Bill that she really knew.

2

Sandy called Icarus into her room on the fourth night after the riots had started. When he came in she was dressed in the longest white dress she was able to find. The entire time she spoke she kept her face in an expression of sorrow and stayed in front of the huge window so the light from the fires engulfing the city framed her figure.

"Icarus," she said, "I need to ask you something." She loaded her voice with fear and uncertainty. "Do you trust me?"

"Of course I do." He said at once his voice so high it was almost funny. She thought of how confident and cool minded he had been when they met. She was seeing the real Icarus now. Timid, weak, and (above all else) eager to please.

"Its just," she said. She made sure to pause for effect, "I need someone I can trust and Bill is-"

"Bill is what?" Icarus asked. Sandy shook her head and let her eyes tear up.

"Its nothing."

"Plant the seed for later." She thought to herself.

"The people in the caravan I used to be part of. I think one of them could be dangerous. Dangerous to our cause." She let the tears fall and then turned away from Icarus, burying her face in her hands. Through the cracks in her fingers she could see Icarus' reflection in the window. He looked like he wanted to comfort her but was scared to touch her.

She smiled.

"There gone Sandy." Icarus said in a reassuring tone. "They left the day after you led Bill in killing the Queen."

She had *led* Bill. Sandy bent her head lower and pressed her hands tight over her mouth to stifle her laughter. Bill had been leading these people for over two years and she had usurped him in less than one month. It wasn't that surprising though. All Bill had done was give stirring speeches, rob a few banks, and post up fliers. Sandy had given them what they wanted, a real change. She hadn't even been trying to do it either. It was just a moment where the right opportunity presented itself and she knew how to take advantage of it. They were taking to her so fast because she was a true leader. She had all of this because she had earned it. She deserved it.

"I've had a dream." she said. Wiping the tears from her eyes and turning to face Icarus. She had to keep her eyes turned down for effect, so she couldn't read his expression anymore. "I saw them coming back. They turned us away from the right path and" she turned away again. She was making it up as she went along but it didn't sound half bad she thought.

"And they killed me, and turned everything we've managed to take back from those elitist pigs to dust." She buried her face in her hands and let out loud cries of agony. This time Icarus did come up and put his hand on her shoulder. She immediately spun around and buried her face in his chest. She sobbed against him and could feel his heartbeat triple immediately. He wrapped his arms around her and held her tight. She cried into his chest for as long as she could before she felt it had been enough. She pulled back and turned away from him, she went back up to the window.

"I need you to find them." She said. "I need you to take someone with you and, and kill those people in the caravan.. I know that's horrible but I'm so scared. There's so many people who could suffer because of them." Somewhere in the streets a woman let out a blood-curdling scream as another streak of fire shot into the sky. "Take as many people as you want, but please promise you'll be safe. I don't want to lose you Icarus." Icarus's eyes widened and his cheeks went red. It was true she didn't want to lose Icarus. How many people were this blindingly loyal? She was certain she could send him to hell if she wanted and he'd go without a second thought.

He proved her right.

"If I have to do this to save everyone," Icarus said, "if I have to do this to protect you. Then I'll do it. But I'm not sure who I can bring with me. Maybe Lucas? The one who showed you how to use the bombs, you remember?"

Sandy did of course, the memory of the caravan exploding was one of her more pleasant ones. She nodded slowly, and sniffled.

"Yes. I think Lucas would be a good choice." She said. "There is one other thing though. One thing I saw in the dream."

A deal was a deal after all.

"There is a boy. He's a little fat with dark brown skin. He's not like the other ones. I think he could help us, he could be really useful in ensuring our safety here in the city. Bring him back alright? Bring him back alive please? He answers to Johnny Boy I think."

Icarus nodded, and turned away from her. He left without another word. Sandy waited for as long as she could. Then she laughed.

CHAPTER 10
ON THE LAKE

1

The lake town of Tablay is a small town of about two hundred people. The homes are brick and wood cottages, each has two bedrooms and one bathroom. Most of the town sits on the roads a few miles away from the enormous lake that sits directly on the borderline of the continent. Three houses sit on the lake side and look out on the lake and the large spruce trees that surround it. The sounds of birds and crickets completed the scenic feeling that earned the town the reputation nickname "Town of Escape." It was a town for the elite who desperately wanted to get away from the hectic life of the kingdoms and get back to the "simple life."

Tourism was very low during this time of year though, and the caravan of Andy Che Pen now sat along the lake. In another month or so the summer travelers would begin coming into town but for now the members of the caravan had the lake to themselves.

The group was very quiet for the first few nights along the lake, but Andy knew that would change. Eventually they would be able to move on. They would never forget of course, but they would be able to get past it and keep moving. Some of them already were; Ramon, Isabelle, Cook, and Johnny Boy all seemed to be doing much better now that they were in a more scenic place. Isabelle had taken to swimming in the lake, Ramon was going on long walks along the forest trails, and Johnny Boy seemed to be helping wherever he could and however he could.

There was something different about Johnny Boy, but Andy couldn't quite put his finger on what it was. He hadn't changed in any note worthy way, except for the weight he was beginning to lose, but there was something different about him. He seemed more together and happier than he was before. It was like the boy had finally managed to get some of his crap together. Andy spent a few days when they first got to the lake, showing Johnny Boy how to do basic maintenance and steering on the caravan. He had wanted to learn and Andy was glad to teach him. Johnny Boy learned fast, asking all the right questions and taking his time with each little task Andy sent him on; changing the oil, changing the tires, repairing the brake pads, etc. With so many of the people gone, he needed all the help he could get and Nathan wasn't proving to be any help at all.

Nathan's right leg was all but useless now. He could still walk on it but slowly. If he used a cane it would be easier on him but he absolutely refused to. When Miranda brought him the cane he had acted like he was going to hit her with it and then hurled it into the lake instead. He spent all of his time feeling sorry for himself, sulking in his room. He refused to work and snapped at Andy when he asked him to.

"I LOST MY FUCKING LEG BECAUSE OF YOUR DAMN SHOW!" Nathan roared at him. "I'M NOT DOING A DAMN THING FOR YOU!"

Normally that would've gotten Nathan beaten and thrown out, but Andy's own guilt kept that from happening. He had recruited Nathan years ago under the promise of adventure and excitement but he had also made a silent promise to himself that nothing would ever happen to Nathan or any other member of his show. He had failed at that and there was nothing to do now but try and repair the damage as best he could. He hoped Nathan would come around again, but in the back of his mind he doubted it. The boy had always been pretty arrogant about his speed and agility and those two things were pretty much gone. Nathan was going to be little more than a grumpy old man in a young man's body.

Miranda wasn't doing very well either. She helped out with the cleaning and cooking. She tried to smile whenever someone's eyes met hers. She sang little songs under her breath. However, she walked around the kitchen in a daze, the smile was hollow on her face, and the songs were dull and flat in her throat. At night everyone could hear her moan or scream in her sleep. Whenever she was away from the group and sure no one was watching, Andy would see her sitting under a tree with her legs pulled up and trembling.

There was so much to do, so much damage to repair, and Andy was sure that there was nothing he could do about it. Nothing except pray.

2

Miranda couldn't get any real sleep at all. She would keep dozing off and finding herself on the side of the stage, watching everything fall apart around her. Sometimes she would find herself center stage, watching the bugees explode and kill everyone around her. She woke up screaming every time. Isabelle would try to talk to her and Miranda would refuse every time until she gave up and went back to sleep. Miranda didn't want to talk about it, she couldn't find the words for it. She knew that Isabelle was only trying to help, and she loved her for it but there wasn't anything she could do anyway. Talking about this wouldn't help. How could anything help this?

One morning after another horrible nightmare, Miranda woke up to find herself in a large bed inside a wooden cottage room instead of her small bed on the caravan. After a moment of panic she realized that she was sitting inside the bedroom of one of the lake houses that Andy had rented. Isabelle had made her move into it last night, maybe thinking things would be better if she slept somewhere else. It hadn't helped, the bed was more comfortable but it didn't do anything for the nightmares.

She got up, nearly tripped over her legs since her knees felt like jelly, got dressed, and went out to the lake. She stood on the porch for a while and let the cold air blow through her hair. She could see Isabelle swimming in the lake, her head rising out of the water as she took a deep breath and then disappeared beneath again. Miranda watched her for nearly ten minutes, and for a moment her mind slipped away from the replay of the stage. She simply watched Isabelle move around in the lake, her figure turning into a faded silhouette as she swam deeper into the water. Miranda was so taken in this simple train of thought that she didn't notice Ramon coming up to the porch until he was standing at the bottom of the steps.

"Miranda." Ramon said. She didn't respond at first and he moved up one step toward her. "Miranda?"

She looked down at him and her mind was pulled back into the present. She gave him a smile that she hoped would look genuine, though the look in his eyes said it wasn't. She turned away from him and looked back at the lake.

"Hi Ramon." She said.

"You okay?" He asked then shook his head realizing what a stupid question that was. "Is there anything I can do to help? I mean can I maybe...can we talk or..." He trailed off.

"I just want to be left alone Ramon," she said. Johnny Boy was walking along the edge of the lake watching Isabelle swimming. He sat in the dirt along the shoreline and laid back staring up at the sky. He seemed to be doing better in the last few days. She wondered how he bounced back so fast. Given everything that happened.

Miranda sat down on the stairs and laid her head in her hands. The memory of the stage was creeping back into her thoughts again and she could feel her skin crawling. Ramon took another step up and he was now standing next to her. He sat down next to her, held his arm out to put it around her, then changed his mind and pulled his arm away from her.

"I had a crush on Jessie." He said.

Miranda turned to look at him, her eyes wide in surprise.

"I was planning on asking her if she wanted to see the town with me the day before opening night, but she had already left with you. So I went with Nathan and the guys. I figured I could ask her out on a date or something after the show. I wasn't sure if she would say yes but I figured what did I have to lose ya' know?" He stopped and stared out over the lake. The gentle kindness that had been on his face was giving way to pain. Miranda suddenly realized that the look on his face was probably the same look that had been on her face for the last several days. He turned away from her and tried to settle his face. When he turned back to Miranda his face looked like he had aged nearly thirty years in two seconds.

"I don't really know what to do." He said. "I'm trying to keep myself busy but its driving me crazy cause I can't...I can't...I can't stop seeing it ya' know."

Miranda was crying now, she could feel the tears streaming down her cheeks but she didn't bother trying to wipe them away. She tried to speak, coughed, and cleared her throat.

"Its worse when you're asleep isn't it?" She said.

Ramon looked at her and nodded. Without thinking she reached out and wiped away the tears on his cheeks. He was shocked by this but didn't pull back. She smiled at him and although the smile was exhausted it was a real smile this time.

"I don't know what we're suppose to do." Ramon said. Now he wiped the tears off her cheeks.

"I guess we just have to work pass it." That had been what Isabelle had said to her. She had wanted to smack Isabelle when she said that but now it was the only thing that came to mind. There wasn't anything to do but get up and keep moving. Nothing to do but accept the horror of it and then try to keep going.

Ramon and Miranda sat and watched Isabelle until she got tired of swimming and headed back toward the caravan. She waved to them and they waved back. Once she was out of sight they just watched the lake until Cook called Johnny Boy to help get dinner ready.

They headed toward the caravan together and passed Johnny Boy. He was still lying on the lake shore but his eyes were closed and he was snoring lightly. A butterfly landed on his nose and Miranda giggled for the first time in weeks. Cook came stomping out of the caravan and screamed at Johnny boy to wake up. He leaped up and Miranda's giggle turned into laughter. She laughed so hard that the tears started in her eyes again. Ramon laughed along with her and they hurried after Johnny Boy into the caravan.

3

An hour later, Johnny Boy laid out the food on the table; a batch of fried chicken, a large bowl of mashed potatoes, a large bowl of gravy, salad, fruits, and two huge jugs of fruit juice. Cook finished cleaning the stove and came out of the kitchen to join everyone at the large round table. Johnny Boy, Ramon, and Andy had removed all of the other tables and benches out of the room and sold them. The plan had been to make the room seem less haunted. Now the room just seemed empty. When Johnny Boy laid down a plate the light *chinking* sound seemed to echo around him. It was a very unsettling feeling.

Everyone sat down and began to fill up their plates. Johnny Boy sat down next to Isabelle who smiled at him and then proceeded to fill her plate with salad and potatoes. Miranda and Ramon talked quietly on his other side. Both still looked tired but they didn't seem far off anymore. Andy and Cook were talking quietly too but their faces still looked haggard.

Nathan was nowhere in sight.

"So," Johnny Boy began, Isabelle turned to face him with a fork full of mashed potatoes inches from her face, "how was your swim?"

"Fine." She said and stuffed the fork into her mouth. "This is really good. Did you make this or Cook?"

Johnny Boy could feel his heart lift up.

"I did." He said proudly. "I made almost all of it. Cook just supervised." He paused. "She supervised very loudly."

Isabelle began to laugh and held her hand to her mouth to keep her food from spilling out. She hunched over for a minute and everyone turned to look at her. The laughter died slowly and then she sat up again.

"What's so funny?" Ramon asked.

"Nothing." Isabelle said still chuckling, "Nothing."

The door opened with a bang and everyone turned to see Nathan limping into the trailer. Johnny Boy had the impression that Nathan was being overly dramatic about his walk, he had seen Nathan move around with more ease than he was now. Johnny Boy couldn't understand why Nathan wouldn't just use a damn cane.

"Hey Nathan." Ramon said, "How are you? Ya hungry?"

Nathan didn't respond. He glared at the faces around the table and limped over to it, falling into the seat next to Ramon with a defeated slump in his shoulders. He grabbed a plate and started filling it up with chicken and mashed potatoes. Everyone watched him in silence for a moment, waiting for a snide remark or angry outburst. He kept his head down and stuffed food into his mouth.

Johnny Boy decided to at least try and get back that smile that had been on Isabelle's face before Nathan came in. He leaned toward her and when she realized what he was doing she leaned in to meet him. He tried to think of something else to say that would make her laugh, realized it wasn't something he could do when he was actually trying, and decided instead to ask her what he had been wanting to ask her for the last few days.

"Listen," he said, "I was wondering if after dinner. You maybe wanted to take a walk or something?" She smiled, it wasn't the large toothy grin that had been on her face when she laughed but it was a warm smile. She raised a fork full of salad to her mouth.

"Sure." She said and stuffed the food into her mouth.

4

After dinner Miranda sat inside one of the old wicker chairs inside the cottage. She was watching the sun set over the trees and twirling her wooden flute around in her fingers. She wanted to play, but she didn't think she could. She was sure she would bring it to her lips and suddenly not be able to draw enough breath to make any sound at all, much less any music.

"Then you can't play," She thought to herself. *"Its not the end of the world, its not like you can't survive without music. You don't need to."* But she did need to. She wanted to. She had to.

After a while she brought the flute to her lips and began playing. It was a slow ballad with a lot of long drawn out notes that echoed throughout the cottage. The echo made the notes overlap giving the impression that there were actually several flutes playing together in a beautiful symphony. Although she didn't realize it, the sound was traveling out of the cottage and across the lake, relaxing everyone who heard it; from Ramon sitting on her porch, to Johnny Boy and Isabelle who were about to begin walking along the forest trail.

She played until her lips were dry and her finger tips felt sore. Then she laid back in the chair and drifted off to sleep. She didn't have any nightmares.

5

The forest has a small dirt road that runs through it. There were a few small little lantern post standing about twenty feet apart from each other on the road, giving off a gentle glow of yellow light so that travelers could make out the road in the night and still see the stars overhead. An owl was hooting somewhere in the trees and crickets were chirping.

Johnny Boy and Isabelle were walking along the trail with a fair amount of distance between them. She was leading the way by a few feet glancing back at Johnny Boy out of the corner of her eye, while he stared up at the stars. Miranda's music faded away on the wind as she finished playing and Isabelle let her attention return to Johnny Boy. He hadn't said a word since they started down the path and now he wasn't even looking at her. It was bit a annoying to Isabelle. She hadn't been expecting a big romantic moment. She knew he wasn't going to say or do anything that made her want to rush into his arms. But she had been expecting a little attention from him. Hell, if he wasn't going to talk to her then why ask her out here?

"Johnny Boy?" she asked.

He stopped looking up at the stars and finally turned his attention to her. His eyes locked with hers again and she felt that familiar calming warmth sweep over her. She surprised herself when she realized (not for the first time) that she was actually starting to miss that feeling whenever she went too long without it. It was almost like the feeling she got when dancing, the sense that everything else was fading away and there was only the feeling.

"Are you going to talk to me at all?" Isabelle asked. Johnny Boy smiled and stepped up toward her.

"Sorry." He said. "Couldn't come up with anything interesting to say."

"Then why did you ask me out here?"

"I like spending time with you that's all." He looked around the forest and his smile grew a little wider. "Its nice out here and I figured maybe you would like it out here too." He met her eyes again. "Why do you look at me like that?"

"Like what?" She asked.

"Whenever you look at me, you look like you're sleepy." His head tilted a little to the left. "I'm not that boring am I?"

Isabelle laughed. She had heard a lot of words to describe Johnny Boy since he had arrived, she had used a lot herself, but 'boring' had never been one of them. That wasn't the only reason she laughed though. She had been worried that maybe he was making her feel this way intentionally. Maybe he was a witch after all and he was hypnotizing her. That apparently wasn't the case, and that made her happier than anything else he had done for her over the last few days. He had done a lot for her over the last few days too. Mostly just talking to her, listening to her, and doing whatever he could to make her smile. Having him around had made looking out for Miranda a lot easier, since she had less to deal with on her own.

All of these thoughts mingled in her mind and made her laugh even harder, it just felt too good for her not to laugh. Johnny Boy simply watched her, his smile a little uncertain now. She wiped at the tears at her eyes and looked at him. They had kept walking all this time. He had moved to her left side and she moved a little closer to him so that their shoulders were nearly touching.

"You're not boring," she said, "I don't know why that happens when I look at you. I guess-"

Something large crushed several sticks in the trees to her right. She stepped back and Johnny Boy came around her, standing between her and the trees before she realized he had moved. Whatever it was took another huge step and more branches were crushed underneath its step. Another sound followed it, something being dragged through the dirt. It was hard to tell if the thing was moving toward them or away from them. The sound didn't sound any louder or softer than it had the first time. Isabelle could feel the hairs on the back of her neck standing out. Her mind was screaming, the same thought over and over.

Dangerous. It's dangerous and it wants to hurt you! Get away from it!

Isabelle reached out and gripped Johnny Boy's arm. She could feel it trembling in her grip. His face was solid but he was scared too, he could feel whatever it was looking at them and he knew it was dangerous. He stepped away from the trees and turned to face her.

"Let's go." They said at the same time. Normally that probably would've made them smile, maybe even laugh again, but not this time. They took off back toward the caravan at an uneven but very quick stride.

6

Lucas gave Icarus a glaring look as he picked up the long rifle barrel off the forest floor. He looked back up toward the couple, watching them as they half walked-half ran back down the path toward the lake. They had been close enough for Lucas to deal with both of them, but Icarus had first stepped too hard on a thick clump of branches and then dropped his rifle. The sound was enough to get those two moving.

Icarus clutched his rifle tight in arms. He gave Lucas an apologetic smile. Lucas turned away from him and adjusted the shoulder strap of his shotgun. The rope tied to his belt was pulling his pants down a bit and he pulled them back up. The rope had to be thick enough to tie the boy up if they were going to drag him back to Frisco without him breaking free and running. It was going to be a royal pain in the ass dragging him back to the truck they had hidden in the forest, but it was either that or take him on foot, which would take a few weeks. The truck would only take about three days at high speeds.

Lucas was certain that he could easily handle the boy and the girl, but he wasn't sure he could deal with everyone at once. He remembered the guy who ran the caravan from when he was on stage. Lucas' main thought when looking at the guy was *"That guy would kick my ass in a straight fight."* That thought had earned Andy a lot of respect in Lucas' mind since there were very few people who could kick his ass. He wasn't going to try and charge the caravan.

They could've dealt with these two so easily; knock the girl out, tie the boy up, and get moving before anyone noticed. Now he would have to come up with a different strategy.

"Let's get back to the truck," he whispered to Icarus, "we're gonna have to think of another way to do this." Icarus didn't argue. They turned and made their way back to the truck hidden about a mile deeper into the woods. The best plan Lucas could think of, was to kidnap the boy and destroy the caravan. How he was going to destroy something that big when he didn't have any explosives to do it, that was where the real strategy was going to take place. He would have to come up with a special type of bomb since he had so little supplies.

7

Johnny Boy and Isabelle spent a long time standing outside the caravan once they were out of the woods. Neither one had that feeling of danger anymore, and both were almost sure that it had just been their imaginations. That they had just been nervous so deep in the woods at night.

That was what they told themselves anyway.

After a while Isabelle was back to the relaxed feeling she had been in before that fear had swept over her. This was mainly thanks to Johnny Boy and that warm feeling that came from his eyes. She wanted to ask him about that, to see if maybe it was some type of hypnosis after all, but she couldn't find the words. *"Why do I feel funny when you look at me?"* It felt like something a little girl going through her first crush might say.

As the two of them sat outside Johnny Boy's trailer she decided to ask the question she had asked him all those months ago, in what felt like another life.

"Johnny Boy?" He turned his eyes away from the stars and looked into hers. That sleepy warmth flew through her. "Are you a witch?"

He didn't say anything for a long time. He turned back up to the stars for several minutes, and Isabelle had a sense that he was trying to form the right sentence in his head. His language was nearly perfect now, but maybe it wasn't completely perfect yet. He finally turned back to her.

"I don't think so." He said. "At least, not the way that everyone seems to describe a witch. I don't raise the dead."

"But I do hear them." Johnny Boy thought.

"I don't know how to talk to animals or anything. And I can't hypnotize anyone."

"I wonder about that." Isabelle thought.

"But I do think that I'm different." He continued, "I can't say how exactly but I don't think there's anything magical about me. Not the way you guys have described it."

Johnny Boy stood up and walked toward the lake. He scooped up a rock and flung it. It bounced across the water and faded from Isabelle's sight before she could see it stop. She got up, followed him to the water, picked up a rock, and flung it at the lake. It sank straight to the bottom. Johnny Boy chuckled and gave her a playful grin. She smiled back.

"Don't look so damn pleased with yourself." She said. His little grin widened.

"He can be so cute sometimes." She thought.

"Isabelle, do you plan to stay with the caravan forever?"

Her smile disappeared into a look of confusion. "What do you mean?" She asked.

"I mean, is there somewhere you wanted to go? Something you wanted to do?"

She shrugged.

"I just want to dance really." She shuffled on her feet. She remembered her father. When she had left to get on the caravan he had told her plainly that if she did she would never be welcome in his home again. No daughter of his was going to waste her life away spinning around. You worked on the farms or you worked in the city, those were the options in that home. Whenever someone brought up the subject of her future she could hear her dad in her ears. Johnny Boy was probably going to start asking her why she would want to waste all of her time dancing when she was smart enough to make real money. It was what everyone had asked her at some point, even Miranda.

"You're a great dancer." Johnny Boy said. "I wish I could do anything as amazing as what you do. When you dance you seem to light up everything around you." He shrugged. "Guess that's an overly dramatic way of saying it though. But you definitely had that effect on me."

He took a step toward her, and she could feel the warmth in her body getting stronger as his eyes came closer to hers. She immediately thought of pulling back, but she didn't do it. She stood still and let him come up to her.

"I don't really know what I want to do." He continued and she could smell the barest hint of something on him. A pleasant little smell of forest flower. He had put some type of cologne on after dinner, before they went on the walk.

"So cute sometimes." She thought again.

"I never really put much stock in things like that. Everyone around me was always ready to tell me what I should do that I just followed their directions. The only time I did something that no one thought was a good idea, I ended up bloody and bruised with two broken arms. But I don't regret doing it, cause if I hadn't I wouldn't have met any of you. I wouldn't have learned everything I've learned out here. And I wouldn't have gotten to watch you dance. Whatever I do, I'm hoping I always get to watch you dance."

He leaned down close and kissed her lightly on her lips. It was barely a peck, a light feeling on her lips. It was so faint that she was almost sure she had imagined it, but that warm feeling flew over her body stronger than ever and she leaned into the kiss without realizing it. It took her several seconds to realize what she had done and pull away from him. His eyes were wide in surprise and his mouth was hanging open a little. That face made her laugh and she tried to keep it in. It came out as a small giggle. Johnny Boy let out a small laugh in response.

For a minute they tried to hold it in, but soon enough their giggling turned into laughter again.

Isabelle had kissed plenty of guys in her life, and this was the first time she could recall laughing afterwards. This was something that she was sure would've hurt Johnny Boy's feelings but he was laughing just as hard as her. It just felt right to do it. Later on that night she would realize that it wasn't the kiss, it was the release of it. She had been laughing a lot lately because it was the only way to let out all the strain she was feeling other than screaming. She wasn't a woman prone to crying. In those late moments of the night, she had been letting it out in small giggles and burst of laughter but it hadn't been nearly enough. Now it was all flooding out and Johnny Boy joined in. They laughed until there were tears in their eyes and they couldn't breath. Once it subsided they felt better, the stress lifted from their shoulders.

When the stress faded, the momentary heat faded with it. Isabelle was sharing the cabin with Miranda so Johnny Boy walked her to the door. At the door Isabelle said goodnight, gave Johnny Boy a quick peck on the lips, and went inside. Miranda was fast asleep in the large wooden chair, her flute in her arms, and Isabelle threw a blanket over her before going to the bedroom.

As Isabelle layed in her bed, she looked out the window at the stars and thought of what Johnny Boy had said.

"Whatever I do, I hope I always get to watch you dance."

If there was a cornier thing he could've said, she couldn't think of it. But he had meant it and as Isabelle drifted off to sleep she thought that it wouldn't be so bad to have Johnny Boy around to watch her dance. Dancing was her main thing after all, it didn't give her life purpose, but it made her happy.

8

Nathan had watched Johnny Boy and Isabelle kiss by the lake. When they left toward the cabin, he had to hobble over to his door and crack it open to see them. Once he was sure that Johnny Boy wasn't following her in, he closed the door and went back to his bed. His right leg gave a dull throb around his cut but he could barely feel it. He barely felt anything in his right leg anymore. His right leg, his life as a hunter and performer were all as good as dead and it was all Johnny Boy's fault.

When that realization fully hit him Nathan had exploded into a temper tantrum. He smashed his weapons rack and watched as the swords and knifes flew all across the room. He ripped apart his pillows and sheets. He pulled at the mattress, lost the footing on his good leg and tumbled back pulling the mattress half way off. All the time his teeth were gritted in a viscous snarl and his mind replayed on that thought. *It's his fault! It's his fault! It's his fault!*

It had to be Johnny Boy's fault. That tingling feeling, the uncertainty that had been creeping into Nathan's body since the day they found that boy was a warning. He could see that now, his body had been trying to warn him of how dangerous Johnny Boy was and he hadn't been able to see it. Now he was suffering because of it, because he had allowed Johnny Boy to stay here. Because he hadn't killed Johnny Boy when he had the chance. He let that old fool Andy keep him around and now he was watching Isabelle (a woman who was supposed to belong to him) fall into some type of hypnosis. That was the only explanation for her steadily growing affection. It was impossible for anyone to take to that boy through anything other than hypnosis.

"He's evil. He's a witch." Those thoughts kept running through Nathan's mind for the rest of the night. *Its Johnny Boy's fault. Its his fault that I'm like this. He's evil. He's a witch. He has to pay."*

Isabelle too. Isabelle may be under Johnny Boy's spells now but that hadn't always been the case. She had acted like she was too good for him even before he'd found that fat shit laying in that circle of blood. So grand and glorious, the sensual Isabelle who couldn't ever settle for one of the lowly stunt performers. Who couldn't even stand being touched by one. Little miss perfect and her little stick figure of a roommate. To hell with her! To hell with all of them! He would be better off without them. He should have left the caravan when Sandy did. Anything would've been better than this. Anything would've been better than looking at all of them sitting at that damn table. Looking at Isabelle give that warm little smile to the goddamn witch. Anything would've been better than this.

"He has to die." He thought. *"That witch has to die."*

9

Lucas ran his plan by Icarus for about an hour before falling asleep in the open back of the truck. Icarus stayed awake and stared up at the stars.

He could still feel Sandy pressed against his chest. The swell of her breast, the smoothness of her skin, and the scent of her hair. She trusted him, she trusted him more than Bill. That feeling gave him the strength that he was going to need to kill the people in the caravan. Maybe Lucas lacked the will power needed but Icarus didn't. If these people were going to harm Sandy, then he was going to kill them. Anything for Sandy.

Lucas' method was a different type of bomb. It worked perfectly, if savagely, last time. It would work this time to, and this wasn't like the

111

people who unfortunately got caught in the crossfire at the show. These people were evil, Sandy said so. He would just have to figure out how to get that Johnny Boy guy away from the caravan first.

He could use that Isabelle woman maybe. Lure her away first and use her as bait. Then once Johnny Boy came running after her, he could kill her and grab him. If Lucas agreed to that, then fine. If he didn't then maybe Icarus would be bringing Johnny Boy back by himself.

First things first though, they had bombs to make. Once those were done he would have to find places to place them. And also, he needed to take a closer look at the Caravan.

CHAPTER 11
BEING WATCHED

1

The next morning, as the sun began rising over the trees, Isabelle went for her usual morning swim in the lake. After a half hour she came back to the shore and found Johnny Boy sitting on the beach holding a large mechanical part in his hands. He wasn't looking at her but studying the part from every angle. His eyes had a far off look, the same look she saw on Miranda when she played her flute.

"What's that?" she asked. He looked up, and she could see his eyes trail across her body in her swimsuit for a brief instant. When he met her eyes he smiled and she returned the smile.

"One of the parts of the caravan's spare engine." He said as he stood up. "Andy gave it to me to look at. He said that he wants to switch the engines out before we head out next month."

"We're here for a month?" That took her by surprise. "I figured we were leaving in another day or something."

Johnny Boy shrugged.

"I'm not in any hurry to leave." He said. "Its nice here, and its always fun to be in a nice place with good company."

"Hey Johnny Boy!"

Johnny Boy turned to see Ramon standing in front of the head of the caravan. "Andy wants you in here, and bring the engine piece with ya!" Ramon disappeared into the front trailer.

"Work, work, work." Johnny Boy said, still smiling. He picked up the small little engine piece, and turned toward the caravan. "See ya later?"

Isabelle nodded. She watched him walk away for a moment and then headed back toward her cabin. Her thoughts went back to the kiss they had shared on the lake shore only a few hours before. From there her mind went much further back to the time when her father told her about his first meeting with her mother.

When Isabelle was five her Dad had taken her on his knee one day and told him the story of how he met her mother. Back then her relationship with her father had been much better, at five it had been perfectly fine for her to want to spend all her time dancing. She had been able to perform for him and he would laugh and applaud while she would dance around to the music her mother would play on a wooden guitar.

Her father told her that when he first met her mother she had been traveling through the small town on a small horse drawn carriage that had broken down in front of his farm. While her parents and his parents tried to repair the wheels that had broken off the carriage, they had spent all their time talking. Actually, she had spent all their time together talking. He simply listened. He told Isabelle that her mother had been the exact opposite of all the other girls he had met before then. The other girls in the farms around the way had been quiet and docile creatures looking for someone who would tell them what to do. Her mother had been so aggressive and confident that by the time she had left with her family, he hadn't been able to think of anything but her for days. Isabelle had always hoped to eventually meet someone like that, who completely blew her mind and wouldn't leave her thoughts no matter how much time they spent away from her.

Isabelle had many crushes over the years, several times she fell in love, but the feeling never stayed. It would fade and very quickly. Eventually she would lose the lovesick feeling and start to see them for who they were. Once she did that, she always saw things she didn't like and couldn't live with. She had never found the perfect one who blew her mind in that first meeting, and kept that feeling alive long after that. It had never happened and it wasn't happening with Johnny Boy. With Johnny Boy there hadn't been any sudden feeling of love that washed over her (that feeling she got from looking in his eyes was nice, but not the same) and it hadn't happened when he kissed her. Johnny Boy wasn't mind blowing or awe inspiring. Johnny Boy was pleasant. He made her smile and that was enough. She wasn't in love with him though, she knew that much. He was cute, but she wasn't in love with him.

Not yet anyway.

Miranda wasn't the one to see Icarus spying on the caravan over the course of the day. Nathan caught sight of him early in the morning but he kept all knowledge of Icarus's presence to himself. Miranda did find signs of him in the middle of the day. She found several footprints in the grass directly behind her bedroom window.

She had been watching Isabelle and Johnny Boy at the lake bed that morning and wondering about the way they were acting to each other. The difference in their body language from how it had been before they arrived in Frisco was impossible not to notice. Johnny Boy's newfound confidence (where the hell had that come from?) and Isabelle's newfound comfort around Johnny Boy was strange. When had she'd gone from being uncomfortable around him to enjoying his company? But then, Miranda had to admit, she had gotten much more comfortable around Ramon lately hadn't she?

When she had finished playing her flute last night Ramon had been outside on her porch. She saw him through the window but fell asleep before she could even think to go talk to him. While watching Isabelle and Johnny Boy at the lake she wondered about where he must be. She saw him come out of the caravan and call Johnny Boy. When Johnny Boy headed toward the caravan, Ramon disappeared, and Isabelle headed back to the cabin.

"You and Johnny Boy are sure getting along." Miranda said. Her voice still felt a little dead to her but Isabelle didn't seem to notice. She sat in the old wicker chair by the door and looked over her shoulder at Isabelle. Her bare feet stuck out from under the long blue dress she was wearing. "When did that happen?"

Isabelle smiled and shrugged. "I don't know," she said, "he's kinda cute when ya get to know him." She gave Miranda a playful smirk as she went toward her bedroom, she didn't close her door but simply disappeared out of sight.

"What about you and Ramon?" Isabelle called out, "You two seem to be spending more time together."

"I don't know." Miranda said and tucked her feet under herself in the old chair. "It helps having him to talk to that's all."

Isabelle came back out in a pair of black jeans and a simple white shirt that just covered her stomach. As she stretched it rose up to reveal her belly button. Miranda looked at her simple blue dress and felt that familiar pang of envy. As usual, Isabelle didn't see it. Why should she? Isabelle didn't have a problem with fading into the background like Miranda did. Wherever Isabelle went she was noticed, Miranda was so easy to overlook. That was why she was always off to the side when she played her music after all.

Miranda came out of her thoughts and saw Isabelle staring at her. Miranda's jealousy must have shown on her face.

"What is it?" Isabelle asked, "You look like you're angry at me."

"I'm not angry. Just, just wish I looked like that in jeans."

Isabelle couldn't think of anything to say to that. She knew that there were women who didn't like her because of her looks. She had just always figured Miranda was above that. In her eyes Miranda looked fine, innocent and sweet, the look that suited her.

"You look good to me." Isabelle said. Miranda shrugged and picked her flute up from the small table next to her chair. She twirled it idly in her fingers. "Are you going to stay in here today?"

Miranda stared at her flute and shook her head. "No." She said. "I'm gonna walk around for a bit. See what else there is around the lake."

"Can I come with?" Isabelle asked. She tried not to show the worry that had crept into her. Isabelle was thinking about that feeling she had gotten when on the trail with Johnny Boy. That feeling of something dangerous being nearby, something in the woods that wanted to hurt them. The feeling had gone away fast enough, and she kept telling herself she had just imagined it. Still-

"Sure." Miranda said.

They wandered through the forest for most of the morning, talking a little at first, then giggling, and finally laughing full and loud as they reclaimed that relationship that had faded after the show. It was while they were making their way back to the caravan that Miranda asked Isabelle about Johnny Boy.

"What do you think it was that changed him?" Miranda asked. "I mean you think he's gotten confident overnight or maybe it's a spell?"

"I think he's just comfortable around us now is all." Isabelle said. "And I don't think he's a witch. I think he's just different." Isabelle smirked.

"I guess." Miranda didn't sound convinced.

"What is it?" Isabelle asked.

"I just wonder. So much has happened since he showed up."

Isabelle blinked. Miranda couldn't be thinking what Isabelle thought she was.

"You don't think Johnny Boy caused all of this?" She asked.

Miranda shook her head.

"No I just- I just wonder if maybe its because he's around. Like a- a curse or something."

"No." Isabelle said, then she paused, "No! No I don't think so. It's just been a- a really horrible season that's all. And its over now. We-" Miranda had turned away from her. "Miranda?"

The two of them had walked around the back of the cabin they were sharing and Miranda was staring at something near the window. Isabelle walked up behind her and looked down. The dirt around the window was soft and dark. In it were two deep footprints.

They looked like the type of work boots that farmers wore. There were a few more footprints in the grass but they were fading, the ground wasn't as soft. Only the two by the window that looked into the living area (and the chair Miranda had been sleeping in) were clearly visible. Miranda's face went pale.

"Those are two small to be Johnny Boy's," Isabelle said, "or Ramon's, Nathan's or Andy's." She placed a hand on Miranda's shoulder. "Let's go get Andy."

Miranda nodded.

3

Andy studied and followed the prints from the window into the woods for a few feet before he caught sight of the tire tracks. He looked at them the trail disappearing into the woods. Following them was like following that trail of blood. It felt like he was hunting for Johnny Boy again.

Johnny Boy had wanted to come along, so had Ramon, but Andy wouldn't let them. Nathan was no help and he wanted there to be someone other than Cook watching the area while he was gone. Even so it wasn't a good idea for him to go too deep by himself, he knew that. But someone was watching them, someone had been watching Miranda sleeping and he wasn't taking chances. He wasn't losing anyone else. He took a breath, readied the rifle that had been slung around his shoulder, and headed off into the woods after the tracks.

He had done this on his own before. He had been separated from his unit once when he was still a soldier and still under fifty (it seemed like an eternity ago) and he'd survived wandering through the woods for nearly three weeks with only the few supplies in his backpack. He'd come out battered, tired, and alive. He'd become known as the "Wood Man" after that. It wasn't the best nickname he'd ever heard, but it fit. After that he always seemed to be sent on solo missions.

By the time he left the platoon, he had gained an excellent sense of direction and a wonderful appreciation for the time he spent alone. Now as he traveled he could remember that feeling very clearly in his mind. That feeling that you get when you're in a place where you can do or say whatever feels right to you. That feeling of true freedom you rarely get in society. Combine that with the knowledge that you know you can survive anything that comes your way, and these moments of solitude become very important to a man with such a large family in his caravan. But that wasn't what mattered right now. What mattered was that there may well be someone planning to harm Miranda or Isabelle or someone else in the caravan.

He followed the tracks for nearly an hour before he found it. A small truck parked in a clearing deep in the woods. It had a large open back and its blue paint was fading. Andy studied the clearing, looking for any sign of someone nearby before he finally moved toward the truck. There were footprints all around the truck but they weren't recent. Whoever had been watching Miranda hadn't been anywhere near the truck for a while, but he hadn't come across any tracks going the other way as he moved in this direction. He hadn't heard the sounds of someone (judging from the footprints two someones) passing by in the woods around him. They weren't heading back to the caravan, he was sure of that. So where were they?

Andy opened the passenger side door and stared into the truck for a moment. It smelled of beer and there were a few discarded sandwich bags and beer cans on the floor but other than that there wasn't anything of use. He closed the door, took note of the long thick rope in the truck bed, and then went back to studying the footprints around the truck. He found what appeared to be the most recent set of footprints and followed them toward a different section of the woods. He followed them through the trees until he came out on an expanse of barren land. The trees were dead and knocked over. The grass was slowly turning into swamp land and the footprints had disappeared entirely.

"Shit." Andy thought. All this tracking and he hadn't found them yet. He turned around and headed back toward the truck.

He would camp out. He would find a good hiding spot near the truck and wait for them. When they came back he would wait for his opening and then-

But what if they went back to the caravan. He had seen two distinct sets of footprints but that didn't mean there were only two. There could be more people. There could be more trucks. He didn't know why there would be a group of people.

"But why would Sandy have killed so many people in my family? In HER family?" He thought. Take no chances. As he reached the truck again, and once more searched for signs of someone watching, he decided against camping out. If they did come back to the caravan, he wanted to be there waiting for them.

He went up to the truck and did another cursory inspection of it. Nothing had changed since his last inspection. He looked at the footprints again but none of them led into a new path, they just circled around the truck. It looked like one of them had been pacing back and forth in the clearing for some time.

Who were they? Some random travelers who were just looking around? That was possible but he knew it wasn't the case. He just knew it. No these two (he was sure it was two) were here for the caravan. Why? He didn't mull it over in his head too long before he came to a decision on what it must be.

Johnny Boy.

As much as Johnny Boy had grown over the last few months. As much as Andy had come to think of him as just another member of the caravan. As much as Cook liked him. As much as Isabelle was taking to him. Andy couldn't let himself forget how he found Johnny Boy. The trail of blood that had disappeared. It seemed like one of those bizarre things that a traveler could come across but it hadn't been a random event. No, Johnny Boy was a change in things. Even after the initial interest in him had faded everything felt different once Johnny Boy was around. The chaos at the show wasn't Johnny Boy's fault, Andy didn't think so anyway, but Johnny Boy's presence had played a part in it. He was different, witch or not, and he had a way of changing things around him whether he knew it or not.

Those two were there for Johnny Boy but, they wouldn't get him. Johnny Boy hadn't been part of the caravan for very long, but he was still part of the caravan. He was part of the family, and Andy was going to protect the few remaining people in his family.

The sound of a twig snapping pulled Andy out of his thoughts. He dropped to the ground and readied his rifle. The sound of footsteps through the trees was growing louder, they were coming this way. Andy looked around and hid in the trees just out of the clearing. He took his rifle in his arms but he didn't take aim, not yet. The sound of cracking twigs was getting louder still. The person coming was doing a piss poor job of hiding his presence. Andy listened but he couldn't hear anything that sounded like another person. Either he was a much softer walker or the first person's steps were just drowning him out. Whatever the case, Andy watched and listened.

A tall, skinny boy came stomping out of the woods. He was dragging a large plastic bag in both hands and it hung nearly to the ground. Once he was out of the wood and in the clearing Andy listened for footsteps but he heard nothing. When the larger, muscular boy came walking out later without making any noise at all Andy was already certain who was the most dangerous of the two. He was also sure that the skinny one was the one who had been looking in through the window.

"What's in this thing Lucas?" The skinny one asked as he started to lean back. He was losing his battle against the weight of whatever was in the bag and it was intent on pulling him down to the ground.

"Stuff for that caravan." The big one said. He had a large bag slung over his shoulder too but he was having no trouble holding it. "If we're really gonna do this the way that Sandy wants-"

"Lady Sandy!" The skinny one shouted. Andy felt his mind go blank and his blood boil. He readied his rifle. He could take care of them both without any trouble but not yet. He wanted to hear as much as he could, and after that he wanted to ask some questions.

"Since when are we callin her Lady Sandy?" Lucas asked. He tossed his bag into the truck bed and the truck lurched for a moment under the new weight. The skinny boy couldn't raise his bag high enough to drop it in and eventually had to just swing it into the truck. It hit the bed with a sharp bang that told Andy the bag was full of something large and blunt. It sounded like metal but he couldn't be certain.

"She is our savior Lucas!" The skinny one said. He was practically screaming it. "If not for her we would've just listened to Bill talk about all the ways we *could* change the world instead of actually *doing* it." He rubbed his shoulder. "Without her nothing would have changed."

Lucas gave of a grunt that didn't sound very enthused to Andy. Sandy was their savior? At least to the skinny one she was. Andy couldn't be sure but he suspected he had been right about the chaos that was going to engulf the city after they left. With the Queen dead there would be a power struggle. Sandy must've been in the right place at the right time. Or put herself in the right place at the right time. Either way though, this didn't explain what these two wanted with the caravan, and until he knew that he didn't see the use in killing them. If he did that now, for all he knew, Sandy would send out another (more dangerous) group of people.

"Find out what they're planning," Andy thought, *"and why they were planning it."*

"We have a lot of work to do Icarus." Lucas said. "We have to go back to the swamp."

"You said that you had all the stuff you needed." Icarus said. "How much of that stinkin swamp water do you need?"

"You want a big boom." Lucas said, "Then we need more swamp water. Stop being a cryin little girl and go get it." Icarus poked out his lower lip and stomped off toward the swamps. Lucas watched him for a while and then leaned into the truck bed.

If Andy had given the truck bed more than a cursory glance he may have noticed the compartment built into it. But he hadn't, just as he hadn't noticed that Lucas saw him (just barely) in the trees when they first came to the clearing. So when Lucas came back out of the truck bed with the rifle in hand and took aim, Andy hesitated.

4

Two gun shots rang out through the woods at almost the exact same time. The sounds broke through the nervous silence of the caravan. Everyone in the dinning trailer leaped up, Isabelle and Ramon ran for the door while Cook went into the kitchen. Miranda, who had been sipping on a cup of tea, screamed and clamped her hand down on Johnny Boy's. It wasn't intentional but Johnny Boy's hand had been in the right position and once her hand closed on it she didn't want to let it go. He talked calmly to her as he pulled her hand off and then ran to the door. He squeezed past Isabelle and Ramon and stepped out onto the lake.

They didn't have to say it. They all knew what those sounds meant. Cook came lumbering out of the kitchen with a huge shotgun slung over her shoulder and a rifle in each hand. She tossed the rifles to Johnny Boy and Ramon.

"Go get Nathan," Cook said to Isabelle, "tell him time to stop feeling sorry for himself and get his ass out here."

"But his leg-" Isabelle began.

"Move!" Cook hollered back. Isabelle stopped talking and ran toward Nathan's trailer. Cook turned to Johnny Boy. "You're gonna stay here, when Nathan gets here you follow after us." She looked at Ramon. "We go now."

Ramon nodded and the two headed off after the gunshots. Johnny Boy watched them and could feel tightening in his throat. He looked over his shoulder at Miranda who was still sitting in her chair. Her skin was white and her hands were trembling. She looked the way Johnny Boy felt.

He considered going up to her, comforting her, but something held him back. His eyes turned in the direction of Nathan's trailer and that made his stomach tighten along with his throat. When was the last time he had seen Nathan?

"What does that have to do with anything?" He thought. *"It was at dinner last night wasn't it. Its not important."* But it was important he just couldn't remember why. He thought back as well as he could. Back to the dinner table, to the smile Isabelle had given him when he asked if she wanted to take a walk. His mind stayed on that smile but there was something else in the corner of his eyesight. Something important. It was a blurred image, someone across from Isabelle. It had to be Nathan from that angle, but what about it?

"It's the way he was looking at her."

It was so obvious. That moment when Isabelle was laughing and smiling at him, the look of loathing that had always been saved for Johnny Boy had shifted to her.

"Oh shit."

"Johnny Boy?" Miranda was looking at him, studying him, and her face had gotten several shades whiter. Johnny Boy's face went back in the direction of the trailer.

"Stay here." He said, and before she could ask him anything he went running toward Nathan's trailer. Something was pulling in his head.

122

Isabelle wasn't defenseless he knew that, but Nathan was dangerous.

5

Isabelle pounded on Nathan's trailer and the door swung open. He hadn't been bothering to lock it apparently. The room inside was dark, the curtain drawn over the tiny windows and Nathan's collection of weapons were knocked off their shelves and scattered all over the floor. A small mirror that Sandy had left in the trailer was on the ground in pieces with shards of glass sticking out and reflecting the light from the doorway back at her.

There was no sign of Nathan though.

"Nathan?" she said as she pushed the door a little further open so the light would fill the tiny space. Nathan definitely wasn't in here. She took another sweep of the room with her eyes, looking for signs of blood in case something had happened to Nathan. Maybe the person who had been looking at Miranda sleeping, and watching her and Johnny Boy in the woods, had done something to Nathan. There was no blood but the room was a mess. The pillows had been ripped apart, the sheets had been pulled off the mattress, and the mattress hung half on the bed frame and half on the floor. The weapons hadn't fallen off their wooden stands after all, the wooden stands had been smashed and hung in long shards.

Isabelle took a step into the small room, carefully stepping around the broken glass. She wasn't sure what she was looking for but she wanted to look around more for something, some sign of what happened to Nathan.

As she stepped into the room she heard what sounded like shuffling feet behind her. Before she could turn around though, there was a dull *thunk* sound, a sharp pain in the back of her head, and then everything went dark.

6

Nathan came out from behind his doorway and looked down at Isabelle unconscious on the floor. He was afraid for a moment that she might have fallen on the glass. That his little tantrum earlier had resulted in scarring her body, the only good thing about her, but she fell well away from the broken glass. A small trickle of blood was creeping out of her hair. He looked at the cane in his hand and could see a small spot of blood on the tip.

"At least this thing is good for something." He thought. He threw it aside and then scooped Isabelle into his arms. It was a little difficult having to balance on one leg, but he managed. He carried her over to his bed and threw her on it. He looked at her laying there for a minute. She couldn't say "no" to him now. This wasn't the time though.

He turned and headed back toward the door. He could already hear someone running toward him. He hid back behind the door and picked up his cane. He hoped that this time it would be Johnny Boy.

7

Johnny Boy caught sight of Isabelle lying face down on the mattress before he was even near the trailer. He went from a light jog into a full run. He flew into the room without taking notice of anything around him. He reached Isabelle and picked her up in his arms. She groaned and he breathe a sigh of relief. He ran his hand over her face and through her hair. When he pulled his hand back there was blood on his fingers.

"What the hell happened?" He said, Isabelle groaned in repsonse and her eyelids fluttered. Johnny Boy took a quick look around the room and caught sight of Nathan just as he flew across the room. The cane flew through the air in an arc and caught Johnny Boy across the cheek. He fell to the ground and Isabelle dropped back to the mattress. He hit the ground hard and his hand fell on the broken shards of glass. The blood flowed from his palm and he could feel blood in the corner of his mouth as well. The world seemed to have blurred.

Then two feet came into his line of sight. He looked up in time to see Nathan bring the cane across again, hitting him in his other cheek. A scream of pain shot through Johnny Boy's mouth as he clutched his hands to his mouth. A tooth came loose and he could feel the blood flowing even quicker. He tried to get up and Nathan brought the cane into his side sending him back to the ground, this time on his knees. The cane came down on his back, then the back of his head. The blurring grew and now everything was getting dark as well as blurry. He barely felt the next blow to his head and the darkness got even thicker. He expected another blow but it didn't come. Through his muffled hearing there was the sound of the cane hitting the ground, and then something that sounded like screaming.

A pair of feet came into his blurred vision one dragging slightly while the other bounced around trying to keep balance. Two more feet seemed to be flying around in the air. They went out of sight again and a dulled crashing sound tore through the haze in his ears. Johnny Boy tried to move his legs but he couldn't seem to get any messages from his brain to his body. The sound of angry voices came through again and this time they were followed by a loud smacking sound.

"Get up!" he screamed in his head, "You have to get up. Isabelle's laying on the bed, she's out cold, you have to move." His legs didn't budge, everything was still hazy and blurry. He was helpless. Completely and totally helpless.

8

Miranda watched Johnny Boy leave after Isabelle, then looked into the woods where Cook and Ramon disappeared. She felt rooted to the chair.

"Its happening now," she thought, "its going to be finished out here. You saw so many people die in front of you and now you're going to watch the last members of your family go. Andy is going to die. Cook and Ramon are going to die, and Isabelle-" But Isabelle was fine, she was going to get Nathan right now and they would help Cook and Ramon. Then they would find Andy and everything would be alright. Just wait here and everything will be alright. Just wait for the others.

She sat in silence for a full minute and could feel every single second tick away in front of her. She got up and started to pace around but she didn't even finish one time across the room before she stared back out through the open door of the trailer. The trees were quiet and the birds weren't chirping. The entire forest was still dead even though several minutes had passed since the gunshots. Everything was so silent. She was hugging herself, swaying from right to left. Her eyes turned down to the floor.

It was driving her crazy. It was quiet, so darn quiet.

"Why isn't there any noise! What's taking Isabelle and Johnny Boy so long? It should only have taken a few seconds. Nathan should be running into the forest right now!"

Where was Nathan? Now that she was thinking about it, when was the last time she had seen Nathan? He hadn't left his trailer since- since when? Dinner. She hadn't seen Nathan since dinner the night before.

Suddenly a jolt of fear ran through her. What if something had happened to Nathan? What if that person who had been watching her sleep had done something to Nathan? What if Isabelle and Johnny Boy had gone into the trailer and found him lying dead?

She shook her head, swinging it back and forth as hard as she could. She wanted the thoughts gone, she couldn't handle anymore of it, she had finally gotten those nightmares to fade away and now she was going to have nightmares of the last few members of her family dead.

"No!" She screamed, not realizing she screamed out loud. She ran for the door, completely forgetting about the night that Nathan had hung over her, menacing her and trying to bully her out of doing the show with Isabelle. All she thought about was the feeling of losing another member of the family she'd traveled with all these years.

Miranda ran out of the dinning trailer and ran toward Nathan's her eyes wide and tears already forming in her eyes. She knew what she would find, she would find Nathan dead. Isabelle and Johnny Boy would be standing over him with looks of horror on there faces. Then that person who had been watching her last night would come up behind her and then everything would fade into darkness forever. It was going to happen, that was all there was to it, all that she loved would be carried away.

She reached the trailer and saw the door hanging open. There were shards of glass on the floor and three figures inside, one of them on floor.

"Nathan." She thought. But it wasn't him, Nathan was standing up and he was swinging something (his cane) over and over on somebody. *"Johnny Boy."* She realized. Nathan was beating Johnny Boy to death! Miranda ran toward the open door and now she could see Isabelle slung over the mattress. She was unconscious and Nathan was beating Johnny boy to death.

"Nathan stop!" She screamed. Nathan didn't respond, the cane came up again and flew down again. Johnny Boy fell off his knees and hit the floor hard. Nathan was walking around to the front of Johnny Boy. The cane rose up.

"He's going to bring it down on his head! He's going to kill him!"

Miranda moved without thinking. She flew across the room and jumped at Nathan. She gripped the hand with the cane in it and sunk her short nails into the skin. Nathan screamed and began swinging his body back and forth. She wrapped her free hand around Nathan's neck and pulled back as hard as she could. Nathan stepped back, trying desperately to try and keep his balance on his one good leg. His foot caught on a broken sword and the two of them fell backwards. Miranda felt Nathan's full weight land on her chest and all the air flew out of her. Nathan rolled off her.

"BITCH!" He screamed and brought his hand across her face with enough force to make the room spin. His hands gripped around her throat and the world started to grow hazy in her eyes.

"YOUR FAULT!" He was screaming but it was already fading in the haze. "YOU AND YOUR GODDAMN ROUTINE!"

Her hands reached out, fingers flexing in desperation. Her fingers closed around a large shard of glass and she gripped it tight in her hands. The palm of her hand cut open and blood started to flow around the shard. Without thinking she swung out and the glass cut high across Nathan's face.

Nathan screamed. Blood flew from his left eye and he let go of her throat. He threw his hands over his eye and blood flowed through his fingers. His other eye glared at her with savage rage. She clutched at the glass in her hand and held it out in front of her like a knife. He lunged at her and she screamed, throwing her arms out. The glass went into Nathan's side with a sickening *squish* sound. Blood flowed across Nathan's shirt and he fell on his side. Blood started dripping to the ground in a small but steady stream. Miranda looked at it and then the bloody shard of glass in her hands.

She looked at the glass and then back to the blood.

The glass. Back to the blood.

The glass. Back to the blood.

Her mind seemed to have gone blank in fear and horror. Nathan was still glaring at her but he couldn't move anymore. The combination of his useless leg and deep stab wound made moving impossible and breathing painful. He tried to crawl toward her and the blood flowed faster.

"Bitch!" He hissed through gritted teeth. Miranda dropped the blade and backed away from him, her eyes full of fear and her mind still blank.

Behind Nathan, Isabelle had begun to stir and in the woods a second gunshot rang out.

Andy hunched over, feeling the gunshot wound in his side. He could still breath evenly and there was no blood in the coughs he was occasionally giving out. Nothing vital had been hit, he would live through this. Lucas hadn't been as lucky. He was laying on his back a good several feet from where he had dropped his rifle. Andy's shot had caught him in the head and thrown him back. The sound of running footsteps was coming from the swamp, Icarus was running back to the clearing. Andy struggled with the rifle in his hands, the pain in his side flared up but he managed to ready the rifle.

Icarus came flying out of the woods with a huge bucket of swamp water in his hands. He saw Lucas's body in the clearing and dropped the bucket, staining his new shoes. Then he simply stood there, his eyes wide. Andy took aim and fired.

Icarus's right leg flew out from under him and he spun in the air a moment before falling face first in the clearing. A quick howl of pain flew out of his mouth followed by a groan and deep hissing sound as he rolled around in the dirt. His eye finally came to rest on the rifle and he began crawling toward it. Andy was already on the move though and there was no chance of Icarus beating him to it. Andy kicked the rifle aside. He swung his rifle wide and caught Icarus in the mouth, shattering two of his teeth. Icarus reeled back and covered his mouth with his hands, a scream came muffled through them. Andy grabbed Icarus by his hair and pulled him up. The boy was light and rose up easily.

Footsteps were tearing through the trees behind them. Andy dropped Icarus and took aim with his rifle, forgetting about the pain that was ripping through his body.

Cook and Ramon came tearing into the clearing, guns at the ready, and Andy lowered his rifle. They both saw him and lowered their guns as well. Icarus had begun trying to crawl away and Andy grabbed him by the hair again, throwing him into the side of the truck. Icarus let out another scream of pain as his weight fell on his injured leg.

"Who is this?" Ramon asked. He ran toward Andy and stepped over Lucas body, he gave it only a quick glance and came to stand over Icarus. Cook came more slowly, breathing heavy from running through the woods. She took a longer look at Lucas, studying his face.

"This is Icarus," Andy said, gesturing with his rifle, "that was Lucas.

They were planning to blow up our caravan."

Ramon's face went first to shock and then to anger. He glared down at Icarus who looked almost hysterical with fear.

"Who are you?" Ramon screamed. He thought back to the footprints outside Miranda's window. How this guy (and he was sure it was this guy) had been watching her sleep. Had he been planning to blow her up too? Plant bombs around the caravan and the cabins? Was that his plan? Icarus wasn't answering, he was biting down on his lips and shaking his head side to side.

"I know I've seen him before." Cook said. She'd been staring at Lucas but now she turned her focused look on Icarus. "I've seen both of them. I think they were in the audience."

Ramon's fear came shooting back up, completely overpowering the anger. The nightmares that had been fading from his dreams came rushing back with enough force that he thought he was actually back on the stage. He could smell the blood again and hear the screaming. Feel the heat from the explosions.

"-ent you here?"

Ramon came out of his nightmare vision. Andy and Cook were both leaning over Icarus who was still shaking his head.

"He asked you a question child." Cook said. "Who sent you here?" Icarus didn't answer, his head still shaking like he was trying to knock the memory out of his mind. Cook took her huge right foot and kicked Icarus's bullet wound, he stopped shaking his head and started screaming again. Andy stepped away from them and turned his attention to the bullet wound in his side. He would have to deal with that soon. He also wanted to deal with Icarus in a more thorough method than this. He wanted as much as he could get out of this boy before they decided what to do with him.

More than anything else, he wanted to get back to the caravan. He didn't like the idea of all the fully capable people being away from Miranda, Isabelle, and Johnny Boy. Nathan was there but that didn't fill Andy with the comfort it once had.

Andy went to the truck bed and grabbed the rope that was sitting inside it.

CHAPTER 12
LOSING EVERYTHING

1

Icarus was handcuffed in the far back trailer. Johnny Boy found it strange (and in some ways creepy) that it was the same trailer he had been put in when they first found him. Nathan was in the next trailer up from Icarus and that made Johnny Boy much more nervous. He didn't like the idea of those two so close to each other. He didn't like either of them on the caravan at all. Especially Nathan. Nathan wasn't going to give up on killing anyone just because Isabelle and Miranda had stopped him.

Isabelle had woken up just after Miranda had stabbed Nathan and she wasted no time in beating him into unconsciousness with his own cane. When Andy, Cook, and Ramon returned with Icarus, Nathan was handcuffed to one of the large wheels of the caravan. When Andy heard what Nathan had done he struck Nathan across the face four times. If not for the bullet wound he had in his own side Andy probably would've beaten Nathan within an inch of his life. Instead he had him thrown into an empty trailer and tied him up.

Miranda was trembling like a leaf in a strong breeze for the rest of the day and wouldn't even go to the caravan for dinner that night. Isabelle had only left her alone long enough to get two large plates of food from the dinning trailer and then she headed back to the cabin with only a quick (very small) smile at Johnny Boy. He didn't really feel like smiling either. He wanted to go into the trailers and beat both Nathan and the other guy until they were covered in their own blood. Things had been going so well. Everyone was moving past their nightmares, the caravan was in the middle of a much needed overhaul and after this they would've moved on. They would've moved on to new places, new things, and he could've seen it all. He could've-

kept running

He didn't want to admit to that but he was running. He had left the

Oasis because he hadn't wanted to marry, but that wasn't why he was still gone. Even after he'd gotten his "life" back he'd stopped practicing his tricks. It wasn't like he didn't have the time to do it, none of his responsibilities were so time consuming that he couldn't practice. So why had he stopped?

"*Because of Rita.*" He admitted to himself, *"because Rita might be waiting for me. She might be looking for me."* That was why he had stopped, why whenever he had free time he just wandered around or slept. He finally had his life back but he hadn't done anything with it. Hell, he was worse off now than if he hadn't taken it back. There was no excuse for it now.

"Time to stop running." He thought. Once he had finished all of his chores for the day he went to his trailer and locked the door. He drew the curtains over his little windows and then sat on the floor with his eyes closed. The world was dark and silent. Exactly as Rita had always told him to make it before he practiced.

When he was ten and Rita had first taught him this trick he had to spend nearly three hours trying before he could fall into the right mind set. Now he could do it almost immediately. No sooner had he closed his eyes than he could feel the floor fall away beneath him. The sound of rustling grass filled his ears and soon the image of the Oasis began to come into his mind's eye, then the Oasis was gone and a mass of colored ropes flew around him.

No red. Please, no red.

There were blue ropes, green ropes, purples ropes, but no red. No red that he could see anyway and that was good. Rita wasn't here. She might be looking for him, but she hadn't found him yet. He reached out and pulled on a green rope. The smell of flowers filled his nostrils. His mind's eye filled with the vision of a valley of flowers. It was definitely a man made garden, flowers of every color from all over the world seemed to stretch beyond his sight. The smell was a beautiful mixture that made Johnny Boy smile.

Miranda would love this place.

He let go of the green rope. He knew the place he'd just seen, but not from the Oasis. It was somewhere between here and the Oasis, somewhere he'd been when he first left home. He was amazed at how little of that time between the Oasis and the caravan he remembered. If he had seen something like this vision of flower he should have remembered it.

I should remember a lot of things. Like how I ended up in this caravan to begin with.

A blue rope this time. The smell of ocean water was everywhere and the sound of crashing waves. A stone house on the beach, a beautiful home with a wonderful view of the ocean.

Isabelle.

Johnny Boy was smiling again. He let go of the rope. He had never been to that place, he was sure of it.

What was it Rita had said before? Time has little purpose for you. Whatever that was supposed to mean.

He let go of the blue rope. He reached for the purple but they were all gone. There was a single yellow rope flying through the darkness but it was too far away for him to reach. He tried to reach it, stretching out with his mind, but it wouldn't come any closer. He had never seen a yellow rope before, not that he could remember, but it wasn't red and that meant it wasn't Rita. Red hadn't always been dangerous but since Rita got into his head, red ropes were always bad news. This yellow one though was different. It came closer and he could only just brush against it before it pulled away again but there was an image.

Eyes. A pair of beautiful silver eyes staring at him. There was a smell of roses in his nose and the feeling of silk underneath him. He couldn't see anything but the eyes for a moment and then everything went dark again. The yellow rope pulled away from him and then began to fade away into darkness again. Johnny Boy looked after it hoping it would come back into his range. For a moment it looked like all the ropes were gone and then something came into vision. Johnny Boy's throat tightened.

Red ropes were creeping in. The blue ropes were pulling away and red ropes were wrapping around him. The green ropes were gone and now the red ropes were wrapping around his neck and pulling him down.

"FOUND YA BOY! FOUND YA AND YA AIN'T GETTIN AWAY THIS TIME!"

Johnny Boy pulled out of his vision with a scream and fell backwards, hitting his head hard on the floor of his trailer. The room was still pitch dark and silent but he was back in the caravan. He was home again.

His heart was beating hard in his chest but there was no sound of anyone coming toward the door. No sounds of worried concern from him screaming. Either he hadn't screamed out loud or no one heard him.

Rita had found him. He hadn't realized until now that she hadn't been in his head since he got his "life" back. He'd gotten away, he'd finally gotten away from Rita for good. He'd escaped and now she had found him and she was going to drag him back. He had to run. He wasn't sure where or how but he was going to have to run. He couldn't go back, if Rita got hold of him again there was no telling what she might do to him. This time she would do more than remove his "life" from him, she would probably destroy it or take it into herself.

He shook his head. That wouldn't happen. He would find a way to escape from her. He ran this far after all.

"Don't think about it." He thought. *"Think about something else. Anything else."*

He thought about the silver eyes. Did he know someone with silver eyes? No. He could remember where he would've smelt roses however. He'd seen a few roses when he was maybe five.

He had been on a walk with his oldest sister Becca, about two years before she died, and they'd come across a rose bush that was freshly blooming about two miles out of the Oasis. He'd only been five then and he'd never heard of or seen roses before. He had reached out to grab the red flower before Becca could stop him. When the thorns poked into his palm, Johnny Boy let out an ear piercing scream. He'd run back to Becca with tears streaming down his cheeks and Becca had scooped him up in her arms and rocked him back and forth until he'd calmed down. Then she bandaged his hand and kissed his wound.

"You gotta be careful little Jawnee." She told him as she carried him away from the bush, which he had suddenly gotten very afraid of, "Sometimes pretty things bite. And when they do they always bite hard."

"You're pretty," he'd asked, "do you bite?" She'd laughed.

"All pretty women bite hard honey. You gotta be tough so they don't hurt ya."

That was the only time Johnny Boy had ever been near roses but Becca had green eyes.

"Pretty things bite." He'd forgotten about that little saying of hers. In fact he hadn't thought of Becca, or any of his dead family members, in a long time. Becca had been the best of them. She was pretty, strong, and always so sweet to him. Suruo was trying so hard to be like her but she wasn't the same. Of all the family members he'd lost, he missed Becca most of all. She'd been the closest thing he could remember to a mother.

He could remember the day she died. He'd come inside from playing and his remaining brother and Suruo had been crying. He knew immediately that someone had "left." That was how it was explained to him, he had never been around when any of them died so it was simply that they'd "left" and never came back. He had begun crying right away wondering who it was, and when he realized that Becca was the only one not in the room his crying had turned into screaming.

"Pretty things bite." Those silver eyes were pretty but he was sure he had never seen them before.

Time has little purpose for you.

What did that even mean?

Johnny Boy shook his head and crawled into bed.

2

Sandy would forgive him, Icarus was sure of it, but that didn't make him feel any better about his failure. He'd failed to bring her that Johnny Boy guy and he'd failed to kill the other people in the caravan. How could he face her now? How could he look at Sandy and tell her he'd failed? That the people who were going to kill her were still alive and well. That he had lost Lucas, a brilliant man who could've helped Sandy in a dozen other tasks. How could he ever face her again?

Icarus looked down at the thick handcuffs on his wrist that held him to the heavy metal bed frame. He'd pulled on it as hard as he could but it barely moved. Now he lay on the floor of the trailer, his arm bent at an uncomfortable angle, and cried silent tears of self-loathing.

"What am I going to do?" He said to himself, "What am I going to do?" He rolled away from the bed, felt his arm snag as the handcuff caught, and rolled the other way.

He had to get out of this, he had to get away and come up with a new plan. He couldn't go back a failure. He *wouldn't* go back a failure. No! He was going to do what he came here to do. He would bring that Johnny Boy guy back to Sandy and he would kill these people before they had a chance to hurt her. He would do it!

He yanked on the handcuff again, he pulled until the cuff started to cut into his wrist. The bed didn't move at all, and the chain on the handcuff remained strong. Icarus looked down at his wrist in furious agitation. He had a wild moment where he actually considered chewing his own arm off but dismissed that idea almost immediately. That was insane.

Icarus rolled away from the bed and looked at the trailer around him, hoping there would be something (anything) he could use. He'd already done this a dozen times since being put in here and there was nothing. Other than the bed and its one pillow, the room was completely empty. There wasn't even a curtain on the tiny window, the large woman (he was pretty sure they called her Cook) had ripped the curtain off after handcuffing him to the bed. Icarus couldn't think of anyway it might have been useful but apparently she had.

There was nothing to work with; just himself, the handcuffs, and the bed. He pulled on the cuffs again. No movement. Again the thought of actually chewing off his arm passed through his mind.

This time he dismissed it a little more slowly.

3

Nearly four days after they tied him up, Andy decided that it was nearly time to let Icarus have some food. Johnny Boy volunteered to bring the food to Icarus. Ramon had wanted to do it but Johnny Boy convinced him to take care of Nathan instead. Ramon hadn't really wanted to deal with Nathan anymore than Johnny Boy had but he agreed. Andy told Johnny Boy to wait though. He didn't want Icarus to eat until after he had answered some questions. Johnny Boy sat outside the trailer with a tin cup of water and a plate of food while Andy questioned Icarus.

4

The first thing Andy saw when he stepped into the trailer was that there were several deep bite marks around Icarus's wrist. Andy felt a sudden jolt of uncertainty at that. Anyone who would actually try to gnaw there own arm off was either suicidal or insane. Either way Andy suddenly doubted that starving Icarus was going to make him anymore cooperative. Still, he had answers if Andy could figure out a way to get them. If starving didn't work he would come up with something else. He had done it before.

The second thing Andy saw was the fake courage on Icarus's face. He was trying to look completely calm and was failing horribly. His lips trembled slightly and his eyes were too bright. He was scared and that was good. But, the bite marks said he wasn't right in the head and that was bad.

Andy stomped across the room, his face set and a dark, cold, feeling falling over him. He grabbed Icarus by the hair and flung him against the wall. Icarus groaned as his handcuffed arm was pulled at a bad angle. Andy grabbed him by his throat and glared into his eyes.

"Why are you doing this?" Andy asked. His voice was deep and dark. If there was one thing Andy had learned as a solider it was command presence. No matter what the situation you never lost your control, you never let yourself come undone or show anyone around you that you were scared or uncertain. You always gave off a sense of absolute power and total control that would calm your allies and terrify your enemies. Andy focused all of this command presence onto Icarus.

"I'm doing my part." Icarus said. His voice trembled but it was focused. The voice of a man who was doing everything he could to cling to something. "I'm doing my part in making Frisco a better place for everyone in it."

"What does Frisco have to do with anything out here?" Andy stood up and glared down at Icarus, who shrunk back against the wall. "We left that city behind. You can do whatever the hell you want in there its no concern of mine."

"Liar!" Icarus shouted. His face filled with anger and then immediately fell back into fear. "You're planning to kill Sandy. You're going to take away everything she's built for us."

"Sandy? Sandy Delgana?"

"She came to us to lead us into a better place and you're going to kill her. She foresaw it! You won't do it! I'll find a way! I'll protect her from you and bring her back Johnny Boy!"

"Johnny Boy? What does she want with Johnny Boy?"

Icarus began to speak and then stopped. His face went from fear to uncertainty. He didn't know. He was a fanatic following orders. Andy glared down at the boy who was still trying to look defiant. He didn't know anything else that was useful. Still what he'd known was enough. Sandy Delgana.

The little brat he'd been dealing with for years, was running things in Frisco now. She'd been the one responsible for the explosion that destroyed his show. Cook had always said it was her but Andy hadn't wanted to believe it. That didn't explain what she wanted with Johnny

Boy though. There was nothing of use from Johnny Boy, nothing he could do for her and if he'd known anything about Sandy it was that she only went out of her way for things that were of use to her.

"Where are the bombs you were making?" Andy asked. Icarus's eyes went wide and he looked like he'd just had a great idea. That look made Andy feel another pang of uncertainty. "Where are they?"

"I don't remember." Icarus said. He was a very bad liar. Andy bent down and smacked Icarus across the face.

"Where are they?"

"I don't remember."

Andy stared into Icarus's eyes for a moment and Icarus kept shifting his eyes around, unable to lock eyes with Andy for more than a few moments. Andy stepped away from him and went back to the trailer door. He cracked it open and Johnny Boy stood up with the tray in hand.

"Give it here." Andy said. Johnny Boy gave no protest and handed the tray over. Andy pulled it in and closed the door. Icarus caught sight of the plate and his face immediately went from false calm to desperation. There was only a small biscuit and a few pieces of bacon on the plate but Andy was certain that Icarus wouldn't be very picky about his meal right now. Andy sat against the wall opposite of Icarus and laid the plate in his lap. He knew his caravan well enough to know that he was just out of reach of Icarus no matter how far he stretched.

"Where are they hidden?" Andy asked again. Icarus didn't answer and Andy ate one of the pieces of bacon. Icarus's face fell and a groan crept through his lips.

Andy had once gone nearly four days without food. He had barely made it through that and he was a much stronger man than this child. He ate another piece of bacon and gave out a small moan of pleasure. He overdid it a bit for effect but the bacon was very good. Icarus looked like he wanted to leap at the plate but instead he pressed himself against the wall even harder. Even if he had leaped at the plate he wouldn't have reached it. Andy ate another piece of bacon.

"Where are they hidden?"

Piece by piece Andy went through the entire plate of bacon and drank down the tin cup of water. Now there was nothing left but the single biscuit. Andy ripped it in half and began idly nibbling at it. Icarus's eyes focused on the half of biscuit remaining.

"Where are they hidden?"

Icarus let out a long defeated groan.

"They're under a rock in the swamp." Icarus said. There was skidding sound as Andy pushed the tin plate and its half of biscuit across the room. Icarus snatched it up with his free hand and nearly swallowed it whole.

5

When Andy came back out he led Johnny Boy and Ramon to the swamp. Johnny Boy brought up the rear as they marched through the woods. It amazed him how they never seemed to make any noise as they moved. His footsteps seemed to fill the air with a loud crunch as he stepped on leaves and twigs. Neither Andy nor Ramon seemed to step on anything that made noise. Once they reached the swamp it was more of the same. The two of them always seemed to plant their feet on just the right spot in the murky water and Johnny Boy seemed to constantly fall into it nearly to his waist. He was freezing cold and his clothing weighed him down as he turned over the larger stones, looking for anything that might have been a bomb. The three of them turned stones over until the sun began to set.

Johnny Boy sat on top of a dead tree trunk that floated around in the muck. Sweat had covered his face and soaked through his shirt, staining the only part of his clothing that hadn't been covered in swamp water. Ramon rested on a large rock that they had overturned earlier only to find a very angry snake beneath before immediately replacing the stone. Andy was replacing another overturned rock with a dark look creeping into his face. Icarus was as good as dead if they didn't come across something soon. Johnny Boy was a little horrified to find that he was perfectly okay with the idea of Icarus being killed.

Johnny Boy got off the log and sank back into the water up to his hips. He turned toward Ramon, meaning to talk to him about what he thought Andy would do to Icarus when his foot struck something in the water. He howled and winced, grabbing at his foot. He looked down through the water and could just make out the shape of something beneath him. For a moment he considered ignoring it, just leaving it alone and leaving Icarus to whatever he got. Then an image of his sisters disapproving faces crept into his mind. He sighed, bent down and pulled up the large rock from under the water. A large black bag lifted slowly off the ground but didn't float all the way to the top. Johnny Boy pulled it up and opened it.

Inside there were four small cans with thin layers of film wrapped on top of them. He could hear the swamp water slushing inside of the cans. He couldn't see how these were bombs but-

"I think I've found them." Johnny Boy said although his uncertainty was clear in his voice. Andy and Ramon both turned to him and walked up to examine the bag. Andy took the bag from his hands and pulled one of the cans out. He sniffed at the can, pulled the film of it, and dumped the swamp water out. Then he dumped the rest of the cans out.

"Let's get going." Andy said.

6

Once Andy had left, Icarus looked down at the bite marks on his arm and reconsidered his plan.

Andy had given him one shining glimmer of hope without knowing it. The little homemade bombs were his last chance. If he could get to them he could place a few of them around the caravan and still take care of everyone. It wouldn't be as thorough as Lucas had been planning but it would work. The bombs in the swamp were only the most recent ones, the greater bulk of them were just a few feet into the woods between the swamp and caravan, carefully hidden. If he could get out. If he could get to them.

Icarus looked down at his arm again. The idea to bite into his arm until he bleed and then using the blood to slick his hand and slip out of the cuffs, had lost a bit of its intensity now that he was no longer starving. That little piece of biscuit hadn't been near enough to slate his hunger but it had calmed it a bit. Now that rationality was creeping back into his mind, he was becoming a little slower to move. Besides now he had an idea.

He would need to be able to move quickly once he was out. He would have to get the bombs, move them into position under the caravan and then place the few droplets of acid onto the film. Once he did that he would have to grab Johnny Boy and get away from the caravan before the acid ate through the film and ignited the swamp water and chemicals inside the can. Then he would have to make it back to the truck with Johnny Boy in tow and then drive all the way back to Frisco. Could he really do that if he was bleeding severely from one of his wrist? Not very likely. No, he would need to find another way out and pray that Andy guy didn't think to ask if there were anymore of those bombs around.

He gripped the side of the bed frame and lifted as hard as he could. The bed shifted a little, but not nearly enough and he stopped when his arms started flaring up in strain. He let go of the bed and howled in frustration.

7

Nathan winced whenever he tried to shift his position. Like Icarus he had been handcuffed to the bed in his room, but unlike Icarus he was making no attempt to escape. Not yet. The pain in his side from where Miranda had stabbed him *(little bitch)* was still flaring up underneath the bandages Andy had slapped onto him. Added to that was the headache from the beating Isabelle had given him *(little slut)* and he was barely able to sit upright much less try to escape. He needed his body to calm down, for the burning and throbbing to go away. Once that happened he could figure a way out of the handcuffs.

Andy's treatment of him was the absolute worse part of it. The old man had promised him true freedom. A chance to see the world and experience things that no one else could shown him. He had promised that no harm would come to Nathan. Instead he had dragged him across the barren fields of the world, made him perform like a monkey in crappy towns, had allowed him to lose the use of his right leg, and now he kept him tied up like a criminal. And why? Because he had tried to take care of a serious problem? Because he had tried to remove the very thing that had caused all of this trouble? If Johnny Boy was dead everything would've been better. Things had been boring before but none of this had happened. Isabelle would have tried to stop him from doing what had to be done so he knocked her out, he hadn't killed her and she wasn't that badly hurt. If Miranda had stayed out of his way he wouldn't have had to hurt her either, but she had gotten in the way so he had to take care of her. Both of the girls were under whatever hypnosis Johnny Boy was doing and now it was clear that Andy, Cook, and Ramon all were too.

He was the only one still free of Johnny Boy's power. He was alone. Fine. If they wanted to get in his way that was fine. He wasn't going to stay on the caravan after this but he had no intention of simply limping away and letting Johnny Boy get away with everything he'd done. No real man would just walk away from something like this.

The pain in his side was beginning to dull. He crawled slowly, very slowly to the edge of the bed frame until his head was right next to the handcuff that held his wrist. He'd learned this trick a long time ago from one of Andy's more pleasant passengers and it was time to put it into practice.

The passenger had been an old man of about eighty, that had traveled with the caravan from the King's Towers to the beaches at the southern point. He had been in very good shape, able to move around with as much ease as Nathan and showed no sign of ever being tired. He'd also had quite a mouth and more than once he had fought with Andy over it. Mostly the fights had been over the way he had talked to the women in the caravan. Everyone had gotten into it with the old man at least once. Everyone hated him. Everyone except Nathan.

"Can't take nothin from people like them." The old man had said to Nathan once. "They don't know what it means to be a real man. You do kid. Don't take nothin from them." Nathan had listened to that advice for a while, but once the old man was gone he slowly slipped back into being the obedient little boy he had been before. Still the old man had also taught him a lot of tricks. Ways to fight, how to steal a few extra things from the kitchen without being noticed, and even how to slip out of a pair of handcuffs. How to twist his wrist at just the right angle and use a small little needle to pop the lock.

Now Nathan pulled the small steel needle he kept in his hair and leaned in close to the handcuffs. It only took a few minutes before the lock gave off a small click and the handcuffs came undone.

Slowly Nathan got up and left the trailer. The door was locked but while the lock was too strong to kick in it was very easy to pick. Once he was out he closed the door behind him to make sure no one would notice it. He needed all the time he could get. After a quick look around to make sure no one was watching, Nathan crept back toward his own trailer. He had to move slowly, the stab wound still howled with each step, and he kept to the deep shadows created by the moonlight. Cook came out with a small tray of food and Nathan dove underneath the dinning trailer as she passed by. She made her way to the two back trailers and Nathan prayed silently. After a moment she went into the trailer that housed the other guy. Nathan sighed and crept underneath the trailers, his wound howling even louder now, until he reached his trailer.

Quietly he climbed inside, the door wasn't even locked, and searched through the wreckage of his room. His weapons were still scattered everywhere, some of the blood from his fight had dried on the once perfectly polished blades of his swords. He could feel another pang of anger at that, it was just another sign of how much his life had been ruined since Johnny Boy arrived. He pushed it aside, letting the cold emotion that he used to feel when he went hunting fall over him. He had to be quick, once Cook had given the other guy his food she would go back to the dinning trailer and get his. Had to pick one fast. Which one?

After a moment of careful thought Nathan picked up the short sword that was still in its jeweled sheath. He pulled it out and studied the polished blade as it glimmered in the moonlight that was creeping in from the doorway. It felt so good in his hand, he swung it left and then right. He stumbled a bit in the right swing as his weight shifted onto his bad leg and he immediately shifted his weight back to his left leg. He looked down at his right leg and groaned. With a look of defeat on his face, Nathan reached onto the floor and picked up the cane.

He stuck his head outside and could see Cook leaving the dinning trailer with another tray of food, heading to his trailer this time. Wasting no time, he moved toward the woods, the walking stick gave up a soft *thump* sound as he moved but his feet didn't give any sound at all. He disappeared into the woods just as Cook came flying out of his trailer.

He moved as quickly as he could while Cook's voice exploded into the air calling for Isabelle and Miranda. She thought he had gone after them, if he had more time maybe he would've but he couldn't deal with them now. Now that he was out he needed to find Johnny Boy and once that was done he could move on. Maybe he would move into the town a few miles away from the lake, or just keep going through the woods until he was over the border.

The sounds of footsteps brought Nathan back from inside his mind and he crouched low in the shadows. There was only one noticeable set of footsteps but he knew there were three people. Johnny Boy couldn't move quietly if his life depended on it.

"It did tonight," Nathan thought with a smile, *"too bad for you witch."* He waited and listened as the footsteps grew closer. Then he saw what he wanted to see; the silhouette of three men walking through the forest. They weren't crouched low or even attempting to hide themselves. Why should they? The only two real threats were safely locked up right?

Nathan grinned again.

The third silhouette was lagging behind a bit from the other two. Everyone of it's footsteps crunched the leaves and twigs underneath it.

Nathan unsheathed the short sword. A little closer, just a little. *Crunch, crunch, crunch.* He could make out the two black balls of Johnny Boy's eyes and hear his breathing. *Crunch. Crunch.*

Now.

Nathan didn't make a single sound as he leaped out. There was slight rustling as his bad leg dragged against the leaves for a moment and then he was in the air. Andy and Ramon had spun around at the sound of rustling and Johnny Boy was looking up. The moon caught the blade and reflected it into Johnny Boy's widening eyes.

8

Time seemed to slow to a crawl for Johnny Boy as the moon light flashed off the blade and into his eyes. In mere seconds his mind seemed to fly through thoughts.

Nathan's loose! What about Isabelle! What about Miranda! How did he get lose! Why is he doing this!

Time began to speed up and the blade began moving toward Johnny Boy again. All of his thoughts were pushed away by a new one.

NO!

Johnny Boy held his hands out in front of him and tried to force Nathan away. There was a sound like a sharp boom and Nathan flew into the tree behind him.

9

Andy couldn't quite wrap his head around what happened next. There was a sound almost like an explosion all around them and Nathan flew back in the air as if something had snagged him and pulled him back. He hit the tree with enough force to cause a crack in the trunk and then he was flattened against it. His face turned right and his skin began stretching like it was being flattened against the tree. The force grew stronger, the booming sounded again, and the entire forest seemed to move. Large clumps of grass began uprooting and flying back. A loud snap came from Nathan as something in him broke. He opened his mouth to scream and his jaw popped loose in the force.

There were another three loud snaps, and Nathan's body went limp.

The strange force disappeared as Johnny Boy lowered his hands and Nathan fell to the ground, laying like a rag doll. Johnny Boy looked at the body with wide eyes and turned to look at Andy and Ramon. Both of them took a step back without realizing it.

"What happened?" Johnny Boy asked. "What did I do?"

Before either of them could say anything, if either of them could've thought of anything to say, Miranda's voice came roaring into the woods.

"ANDY! NATHAN'S LOOSE! HE'S LOOSE!"

Johnny Boy looked down at the body in the dirt again. He looked up at Andy and Ramon again.

"What did I do?" He asked.

10

It had finally moved! After pulling and straining, and pulling, and straining, Icarus had finally gotten the bed to move. His arms were screaming from the effort but he had lifted the bed frame enough to maneuver the cuff off it. He was finally free. The door was locked but he was thin enough. He opened the tiny window, and slid out that way. The cook was screaming for the two girls, something about Nathan (*must be the other guy*) getting loose. It made no difference to Icarus, he moved toward the woods behind the cottage to get the bombs and fuses he'd hidden away from the swamp.

As he passed the cottage the two girls came running out. They ran toward the cook who was standing by the lake. They never even noticed Icarus. He ran through the woods as fast as he could and found the right rock without effort. Even in the dark he found it.

"Sandy's guiding me." He thought to himself. *"She's helping me perform my duty."* He pulled out the five cans with the thin film covering them. Inside was a small vile with the acid in it. He ran back to the caravan with the bombs in hand.

Everyone was gone, the three women had disappeared. Icarus ran to the caravan and dove underneath the main trailer. He had to move quickly. He prayed that Sandy was still doing her part, still guiding him. He prayed everyone was inside as he placed the bombs underneath the large main trailer and placed the acid on each can's film. The hissing sound began immediately and Icarus crawled out from under the trailer as fast as he could. It would take several minutes, as many as ten Lucas had said, before the acid ate through. He ran back toward the woods.

Icarus was on his way back to the woods when his stomach gave out a huge growl. He stopped and looked back at the caravan. He hadn't eaten anything but that half of biscuit. How long would the trip back be? He would need his strength if he was going to bring that Johnny Boy guy back. Icarus turned and ran toward the dinning trailer. He needed food, and he had just enough time to grab something and run. He was taking a risk but his stomach had decided for him already.

He was so focused on his hunger that he didn't realize that Cook had glanced back at the caravan and could see him. He also didn't notice her running toward him until she was grabbing him by the back of his head and throwing him into the air. He hit the ground with a loud thud and she brought her foot down on top of his stomach. The wind was knocked out of him and little spots of color flew across his vision. Then he was gripped by the back of the neck and lifted up.

"Back in the room with you." Cook was saying. She dragged Icarus back toward the trailer. He screamed kicking out with his feet and punching Cook in the face. She kept moving, not even feeling the weak little punches his skinny arms were landing on her face.

"No!" He was screaming. "No!" His time was running out. He had to get loose and get hold of Johnny Boy. He had to do it without warning any one.

He swung his foot out and kicked her in the back of her knee. Her leg buckled and her grip loosened. Icarus broke free and ran toward the woods as fast as his legs could carry him. Cook tried to chase but she never had a chance of catching him.

11

Isabelle and Miranda were both horrified and relieved to find Nathan dead. It was a sick feeling in both of there stomachs to be happy at the death of someone they had known for so long, but the memory of his attack was still very clear. Johnny Boy's face was very pale and he was stumbling as he walked. Isabelle helped him for a little while until he calmed down and seemed to get his footing.

Ramon and Andy both dragged Nathan's body back to the caravan. Miranda had suggested a simple burial in the woods but Andy wouldn't hear of it.

"He was a part of the caravan," Andy said in a far off tone, "whatever else he may have been we're gonna give him a full burial." Andy's face was equally pale and Miranda noticed as they walked back that he kept throwing glances at the back of Johnny Boy's head. When they reached the caravan, Cook was running toward them panting for breath. She was limping a little. When she bent over to pant, her hand clutched her right knee.

"The other one got loose too." She said through breaths. "Ah don't know how. But he got loose and he's somewhere in the woods."

Andy's face went cold. Everything was falling apart again. He looked at the woods around him, waiting for Icarus to come leaping at them with a knife. He would probably kill Miranda, that would be the grand finale wouldn't it? If he lost the member of the caravan who was like a daughter. Johnny Boy couldn't do his little trick then, Andy was sure of that. No, if Miranda was attacked she was dead. Just like everyone else in his crew who had been in contact with Johnny Boy over the last two months. Just like Curtis, Jessie, all his performers, and now Nathan.

"Come on everyone," Andy said, "back to the main trailer. We need to talk." It would take them about six minutes before they got to the caravan. By the time they got outside the main trailer there would only be one minute before the bombs went off.

12

The silence during the walk back was horrible. Johnny Boy could feel the eyes on him, the nervous tension building in the air. His anger at Nathan came back even thicker now.

He had been doing so well. Everyone had accepted him, no one had started turning an angry eye on him after the night in Frisco, but he hadn't done anything there. This time he'd cheated death *(in a way he wasn't sure of)* and there was no doubt of what it was. He understood enough to know that that had been what everyone called magic. He'd talked to enough people over the last several months to know that magic was a widely feared thing.

"I didn't do anything wrong." He thought. *"I didn't want to die. Anyone of you would've done the same damn thing!"* He turned around and looked at Isabelle.

She turned away from him and he felt the bottom fall out from under him. He wasn't sure what, but something had just died between them before it had even had a chance to grow. Johnny Boy wished he could bring Nathan back to life just to kill him again.

They reached the main trailer and something pinged at Johnny Boy's head.

Pull back Jawnee!

He stopped about four feet from the caravan and the rest of the group stopped too, keeping their distance. Johnny Boy turned to Andy who didn't flinch but stared back with the same cold resolve he had shown when Johnny Boy had first talked to him all those months ago.

"Something's wrong." Johnny Boy said. "Something's different."

Pull back Jawnee! Please little Jawnee!

This time he recognized the voice and that made him listen even more closely. His sister. Suruo was calling out to him to warn him about something. Something in the caravan.

Hurry Jawnee! Pull back!

But Nathan was dead. And the other guy was gone, Cook had said so. They'd already dismantled his bombs, those few little things-

Those *few* little things. There had only been a few of them. They were so easily made it looked like. A person should have been able to make a lot more than just-

Johnny Boy's face fell and without thinking he dove on top of Isabelle.

The bombs went off at almost the exact same time, one setting off the other four. Isabelle and Johnny Boy were already down but everyone else was thrown back with tooth shattering force. Miranda and Ramon were both thrown into the lake while Andy and Cook skidded across the dirt. The main trailer was thrown into the air by the force of all five of the small bombs underneath it. Then the fuel canisters underneath it ignited and the trailer exploded. The fire tore through the few passenger trailers behind it and then the gas stoves in the dining trailer ignited. There was another deafening boom as the dining trailer went and took the remaining trailers with it. Then the large spare containers of fuel in the final trailer ignited in another boom. In only a few seconds the entire caravan was gone. The fire flew across the log cabins and soon those caught fire too. The burning debris flew into the trees and soon the woods were also burning.

Miranda and Ramon swam out of the lake and Miranda looked at the fire around her; the burning cottages to her left and right, the woods to her back, and the caravan in front of her. Her home. The fire and smoke were everywhere burning her eyes and filling her lungs. She bent low and started coughing, choking out sobs between each cough. She could feel Ramon wrap his arm around her shoulders.

Andy was crawling to his feet as Johnny Boy did the same. Johnny Boy limped away from Isabelle, who was sitting up and looking at the burned caravan with tears in her eyes. Johnny Boy hadn't looked back at the caravan but he was still hunched over, his eyes scrunched close and his teeth gritted. His back was an enormous black spot and a piece of burning debris was sticking out of it. He didn't seem to notice that Isabelle was crawling away from him or that Miranda and Ramon were turning their horrified looks on him. Cook got back to her feet slowly, having trouble adjusting her weight after having her balance thrown with such violent force.

13

The fire didn't travel too far into the woods. The weather wasn't hot enough and the trees were too well watered from the rains a few months earlier to catch fire. The trees that did catch burned and died. The cabin had nothing close enough to it to keep the fire going and simply burnt to the ground. The caravan though burnt for a very long time, powered by the fuel. Eventually people from the town came to investigate the explosion and were able to put it out. The former caravan members were led back down to town.

Johnny Boy trailed behind the others. None of them would meet his eyes.

14

Isabelle was happy to stay in the small bed and breakfast in the town. She was even happier to find out that Johnny Boy wouldn't be staying in it with her. She had tried but she couldn't look at him anymore. Ramon had told her what happened with Nathan, had told her and Miranda, and now that feeling she got when she looked at him was terrifying rather than comforting. All the pleasant feelings she'd gotten from him were gone. It would be her, Miranda, Cook, Ramon, and Andy in the bed and breakfast.

Johnny Boy wasn't staying, he had decided to stay in the motel on the other end of the town. Sad as she felt to have played a part in driving him away, she was glad he was gone. Maybe now things could go back to the way they had been.

Miranda had taken to spending a lot more time with Ramon, even more than they had spent on the lake. They acted like they were joined at the hip, never apart for longer than a few hours and those were usually when they were asleep. Isabelle could feel a little pang of jealousy every time she saw them together. They weren't being romantic, not exactly, but at least they had each other to lean on through all of this. The only person she could think of to go to was someone that had brought all of this chaos on them.

"Had he really done that?" She wondered about that at night when she looked out her window, which unfortunately had a perfect view of the small motel on the other end of town where Johnny Boy was. *"Had it really been his fault? Or am I just blaming him because he's the new face? Because I can blame him without feeling too guilty?"* She didn't want to think about herself that way. She didn't want to think she was torturing someone who didn't deserve it.

Someone who dove on top of you and acted like a shield.

Before they had separated from him, Isabelle had gotten a glance at Johnny Boy as he changed his shirt. His back was burned (badly) and she was sure he was going to have a large burn scar on his back for the rest of his life.

That could've been my face if he hadn't dove on top of me.

Isabelle had a lot of nightmares now, but they weren't about the show. Those nightmares had faded and were long gone, lost in the back of her mind where the truly horrible things seemed to go for all people eventually. Now they were dreams of dark, empty rooms with empty beds. Everything was empty and dead around her. No hallways, just floating rooms all around. She would float into one, float out, and then float into another. The walls had torn wallpaper on them. Each room looked like someone had come in and started ripping apart every sign that someone had lived there, but hadn't finished. The rooms still held the feeling of a person in them. The more rooms she went into the more familiar the feeling of people became and the more scared she would get. There was going to be a room, sooner or later, that would belong to her or Miranda and she would see why the rooms were empty. She would meet the person who had ripped these rooms apart. These dreams didn't wake her up screaming but they did wake her up, and each time she would find herself out of her bed and standing by the window, staring at the motel down the way.

About four days after they moved into the bed and breakfast, Isabelle walked through the town. It was a quiet place, and everyone in town seemed to be in their fifties. They were all pleasant enough though, each of them making polite conversation. It was a little boring but she appreciated that right then. Things had been way too exciting over the last few months. There was a small little diner a few blocks away from the Bed and Breakfast and she went in to have some lunch. She had sat down and ordered a sandwich before she noticed Johnny Boy sitting two tables away from her. He glanced at her and that drowsy feeling swept over her again. She turned away and ran out of the diner. He didn't follow after her. She had run all the way back to the Bed and Breakfast and had to sit on the porch steps to catch her breath.

That night she had another dream about the many empty rooms and woke up standing by the window again. She caught sight of something walking away from the motel. After a moment she realized what she was seeing.

Johnny Boy was walking out of the town.

15

"What am I gonna do now?" Johnny Boy asked himself, *"where am I gonna go?"* He had been wondering about that for the last four days. Arguing with himself about whether he should try to repair the damage done or just leave. When Isabelle ran out of the diner though, he'd decided. Now it was just a matter of deciding where to go. Frisco was to the west, so maybe he could head east toward the King's Towers. He'd never been there (*he didn't think so anyway*) and maybe things would be better there.

"That's what you were sayin when you left the Oasis. Wasn't it Johnny Boy?"

Things would be better though. If he kept moving, eventually things would be better. When things got real bad, just keep moving and things would get better sooner or later.

He went back to the tiny little bedroom in the motel and tossed the few bits of clothing he'd gained over the last few months into a small brown bag. He glanced out the window at the Bed and Breakfast. He felt like he could still feel Isabelle's taste on his lips but that was just a past memory now. Dreams about what could've been. He slept lightly and a little bit before sunrise he got ready to walk out of town and head east.

As he was getting dressed he got a good look at his back in the small bathroom window. There was a huge oval shape on his back that was about three shades darker than his skin. Every move he made caused his back to flex a bit and shoot pain through his body. It was going to be a very long and very painful trip, but he had to go. He couldn't stay here. They didn't want him here.

Before leaving he stopped at a small little surplus store and used his little bit of money to buy a large bottle of water and a few sandwiches. He took sips out of the bottle as he walked and the sun was well into the sky when he stopped under a tree to eat his first sandwich. It wasn't very good, the bread was a little hard and there was too much mayonnaise on it. It made him yearn to be back in Cook's kitchen.

"Maybe I could get a quick job somewhere. Use it to buy some cooking stuff." He said to himself. "Pot, bowl, cup, stuff like that." He took another bite out of his sandwich, not feeling the few tears that had started to stream down his cheeks.

Wasn't it bad enough he'd had to watch all of his family die around him? Wasn't it bad enough that all of those people in Frisco had died in front of him? How much more of this crap did he have to go through? It wasn't fair. It wasn't fair. It wasn't fair! He didn't deserve this. He hadn't done anything to anybody. He just tried to find a place he could be happy. Find a place where he wasn't always wishing he was someplace else, and he had found that! He had found that place! He could've spent the rest of his life on the caravan and he would've been happy.

He traveled along the old concrete roads, stopping every now and then to take a quick nap or sit in the shade while he sipped from his water. He ate his second sandwich as the sun was beginning to set over the horizon. He was once again sitting under a tree, and he knew that he was going to have to decide where to sleep soon. He could keep walking if he wanted but he was tired. Not just from the walking either, he was tired of everything. If there really was a higher, greater being in all this, as both of his sisters had sworn there was, then clearly it just wanted to torture him. What other reason could there be for this? Some people must just be made to suffer. The tears began rolling down his cheeks again as he ate his food.

He had always preferred his sisters to his brothers but his brothers had taught him a few things he was pretty sure he would need now. Now that he was alone again. If he didn't want to be found by another nice group of people, if he didn't want to ruin another set of lives, he would have to make sure that nothing could hurt him again. He would have to remember things a lot further back than just the last few months. He would have to think back to what his brothers had taught him. About the types of foods he could eat, a few simple medicinal tricks (he would need to do something about the burn on his back, it hurt like hell), and what they had taught him about camping. They hadn't taught him much, but what they had taught him would be important. **Had** been important, maybe he wouldn't have ended up bloody, in the middle of nowhere, with several months of his life knocked out of his head if he'd thought about them sooner.

His older brothers had been bullies. They taught him how to fish and how to fix things around the house, what little things he could fix at that age, but they were still bullies. They locked him in closets, would ambush him in scary mask at night when he was walking to the bathroom, and basically made his life a living hell. When he cried, something he did very often as a child, they would call him a cry baby and beat him up. Which, of course, only made him cry more. The first time he could remember when they had truly done right by him was when he was six years old.

The Oasis was usually peaceful but every so often something would happen that stirred up trouble. That time, a wolf had snuck into the farm lands and was killing the sheep and chickens. Johnny Boy's brothers had been asked to deal with it as they were the young men of the village. He had been left with his sisters and Becca had refused to let him go out after them. A few hours after his brothers had left, he snuck out of the house and chased after them. He found them crouched deep in the woods waiting for something, he wasn't sure what then. They had apparently laid out some bait and were waiting for the wolf to take it. The wolf however was nowhere to be seen but Johnny Boy had caught sight of it, sneaking up behind his brothers. He'd flung a rock at it, hitting it right between its eyes. That made the wolf turn its attention on him but his brothers spun around and shot it dead before it could get within five feet of him.

Becca had been furious with him for sneaking out but his brothers defended him. After that the teasing was much more light and playful than it had once been. They were more prone to bringing him random things they found when they went hunting, and most importantly they started taking him on simple nature walks and camping trips.

Becca hadn't really wanted them doing it, didn't want little Jawnee out in the woods. His brothers had insisted though and taught him what was safe to eat, what wasn't, how to pitch a tent, how to make a camp fire, things like that. He had only been six but he would remember a lot of these things he thought. After all, it was one of the only times his brothers had done right by him, he wasn't likely to have completely forgotten that. After the third of those trips his eldest brother had died, killed by a wolf (something in Johnny Boy had always wondered if it was somehow the spirit of the one they'd killed), and the nature walks stopped. Soon thereafter everyone in his family had died around him and it was just him and Suruo, the only person who didn't seem to be affected by whatever it was that killed the people around him.

Tears were running down his cheeks again as he sat under the tree and ate his lunch. It *was* his fault. He could tell himself it wasn't all he wanted but that didn't change the truth. All of it *was* his fault. Soon he was crying hard and stuffing the last bit of his sandwich into his mouth between sobs. He let the small piece of paper the sandwich had been wrapped in fly away in the breeze. A truck was coming up the road but he didn't pay it any mind, he was off the road and out of the way. He didn't pay any mind when the truck stopped a few feet away from him either. It wasn't until the driver of the truck got out and he heard running footsteps that he looked up.

He looked up just in time to see Icarus flying at him with a maddened look on his face. He had a rock in one hand and before Johnny Boy could react the rock came down on his head. The world went black.

16

Andy was going after him. He didn't want to, everything in his mind was telling him to let the boy go, but he was going after him. He had been planning on talking to him about moving into the Bed and Breakfast that morning. He wasn't sure about whether or not Johnny Boy was safe but he was part of the caravan. Try as he had, Andy couldn't let go of the one reality. The one thing that overpowered every single bit of logic his mind could come up with. There were so few of them left. They weren't just passengers anymore, these few people were family. Johnny Boy was part of the family.

That morning he had gone down to the small kitchen to join the rest of his surviving family members at breakfast. The proprietor, a middle aged couple who always seemed to wear matching outfits, had laid out a very nice breakfast of pancakes, eggs, and bacon before them. Cook was a little bitter at not being allowed to cook the food herself but she still ate with gusto. Miranda and Ramon were both talking quietly and throwing glances at Andy. Isabelle was simply sitting and eating, her face looking out the window that looked over the road that ran out of town.

"Is she thinking of leaving?" Andy had thought. *"Are the others thinking of leaving too?*

"Andy?"

Andy turned his attention to Miranda who was staring at him with the same big eyes he had seen that day in the storage trailer all those years ago.

"What is it Miranda?"

"Are you planning on asking him back?"

Cook stopped eating and looked at Andy. He couldn't read her face but Ramon's looked both guilty and scared. Isabelle didn't respond, she just kept staring out of the window at the long concrete road that ran on and on until it faded out of sight. Her face was cold, and dead. Her beautiful features seemed sunken, like she was made of melting wax. Andy hadn't taken to Isabelle like he had Miranda, but she was part of the family. Looking at her face like that, her expression melting, something in her having died along with all the people she had seen die over the last few weeks, it was heartbreaking. Simple as that. It was heartbreaking to see the damage of all of this.

"Andy?"

"Yes." Andy said. "I'm thinking about it." No one said anything but he could see something in their faces. It was doubt. For someone who had gotten used to seeing these four faces obediently follow his orders for years now, a look of doubt was very unsettling.

"I'm scared of him." Miranda said. "I know he's a nice guy and all but- but I'm scared of him." Ramon placed his hand over hers and she gripped it tightly. "But he's part of the caravan isn't he?"

"He's a good kid." Cook said. "Like Jessie was. He's a good kid."

"I'll go," Ramon said, "I'll go if you want."

"Why would I want that Ramon?" Andy asked. Ramon nodded and gave Andy an apologetic look. "He's part of the caravan, and I run the caravan. I'll be talking to him about coming to the Bed and Breakfast tonight."

Isabelle didn't respond, she just kept looking out the window.

"If any of you have a problem with this," Andy continued, he was looking at Isabelle as he spoke, "say so now. Once I bring him back we're gonna have to figure out how to get moving again."

"He can't come back." Isabelle said, her voice sounded as dead as Miranda's had after Frisco. "He's gone. He left town on foot this morning.

There was a moment of thunderstruck silence. Isabelle finally turned to face Andy and her face looked so old and sunken it was scary. She was guilty, that was what he realized now that he was looking straight into her eyes. What she felt guilty about exactly, he thought he knew but he wasn't sure. He suspected that it was the same guilt they were all feeling right now.

"Which way did he go?" Ramon asked. Isabelle raised an arm and gestured weakly at the window she'd been staring out of. Ramon got up and Andy waved him back down. He turned to Cook.

"Let's talk outside for a bit." Andy said. Cook sighed, lumbered out of her chair and followed him into the lobby. The wallpaper was green with pink flowers all over it. Something about it made Andy queasy.

"I'll go get him." Andy said. "I want you to try and find us something to travel in. Something big enough to fit all of us, if only for a little while."

"No problem." Cook said. "I'm sure this little town is full of large caravans for families of five or more. I'll figure somethin out."

Andy nodded and left.

If Johnny Boy had left that morning, then he probably hadn't gotten too far yet. For all the weight he'd lost, Johnny Boy wasn't very physically fit and he would have to stop pretty regularly. Andy could catch up to him on foot within a few hours. He wasn't sure what he would say to him, but he could figure that out as he walked. He got onto the main road and pointed himself east. It wouldn't be a very long walk for him, so he decided to forego water. If all went well he would be back by nightfall. With Johnny Boy in tow.

He was just reaching the edge of the town when he saw Icarus's truck fly by with a large lump under a blanket in the truck bed. There was absolutely no doubt in his mind that it was Johnny Boy under that lump. Icarus never looked twice at him just flew through town, nearly hitting two people, and disappeared to the west.

17

Johnny Boy was in his trance state again. Granted this wasn't by choice, but he was back in it again. He could pull himself out of this if he wanted. He was sure of that. Something in him didn't like that idea though. Something in him wanted to stay in this trance for a while. There was something in here, something to see and he had better do it now while he still had the time. Something important.

The ropes were weaving in through the darkness again and once again he could see the different places as he reached out. The field of flowers, the house on the beach, and most of all the silver eyes. He could smell roses again, the smell was all around him, but all he could see were those two beautiful silver eyes. This time he tried to pull back, to see more of the face that those eyes were in, and the world fell into darkness as he did. Soon it was just a pair of eyes floating in black. Then the eyes closed, and everything was gone. The ropes started slipping in again and this time a silver one flew toward him, mixed in with the blues, greens, and purples. He had never seen a silver rope in one of his trances before and he lunged out to grab it. He latched on to it just as it was about to disappear from his mind's eye. The world was filled in with dark black smoke. He could feel heat all around him, burning heat like when the caravan exploded.

"Another explosion." He thought with his heart sinking. *"Another explosion. Why? Why? Fucking Why!"*

Then the smoke began to clear away. He could see something through the fire. He was in an empty room. The room was all white with a large expensive bed and a huge window that overlooked a city. *Frisco.* The room was on fire and something was sitting on the floor in the center of the room. Rita's red pendant. It was melting, and he could hear Rita screaming. She was cursing him, damning him, swearing she would find him and kill him. Then the fire engulfed the jewel, it cracked, and Rita's voice stopped. The world was falling into darkness again but there was something else in the background. Another voice, a younger woman's voice, screaming at him with the same viscous rage that he had heard in Rita's voice. But before he could see who that voice was coming from, the world went dark again.

The ropes were pulling back but he reached out for another one, not caring about the color. He was reaching out for a blue one when he realized he'd already caught hold of one. He hadn't seen one, but then he realized why. He had grabbed hold of a black rope.

Waves were crashing outside and a breeze was blowing in through an open window. The world was coming into light again and Johnny Boy could see the beach outside with the moon and stars reflecting in the ocean water. He was inside the beach house. He was inside the beautiful house he had seen before. The one that made him think of Isabelle. There was no sense of peace this time though, and something was overpowering the smell of the ocean water.

He could feel something warm trickling out the corner of his mouth. He couldn't move his body, but he could taste it now. He was bleeding. Blood was trickling steadily out of his mouth and he could feel it trailing from a gash in his head too.

"Give me a break." He moaned. *"Let me have one pleasant **thought** if nothing else."* Without another thought, he let go of the rope and let the world fall to darkness again. He'd loved thinking about that beach house too. Fate just wouldn't give him a break.

CHAPTER 13
THE RED PENDANT

1

Sandy had to admit that Bill had been a halfway decent lover. He had been very eager for it too. Hell, she had barely had to try when she wanted him. She had managed to turn him into a very useful little tool for quite some time. She was still using his name when she gave orders, but that was fine. The higher ranking members of the revolution knew who was the real mastermind anyway. The higher ranking members knew who was the most powerful too. In the end the revolution would listen to her before they would have listened to Bill. It was because of her that everything in Frisco had begun to settle again. It was a pity she couldn't have kept Bill around a little longer.

The riots were still going on, but they were nothing like the literal hellfire they were not long ago. Now they were mostly just angry fights that would break out in bars and develop into large battle royales in the streets. Her newly appointed guards were more than able to handle those though. It wasn't even really a challenge keeping the people in line anymore.

The only thing working her nerves now was Rita.

The same damn thing over and over with that woman. *What's taking so long? Where is the boy?* On and on and on. Hell didn't that woman have any type of life beyond chasing after chunky little Johnny Boy? Still a deal was a deal and she was certain she would have use for that red pendant. With a steadily growing group of people that thought of her as some sort of spiritual figure, a skill that would look like magic was the perfect thing. Not that she needed it. She had found out that her power was pretty much absolute when she had Bill executed.

2

Once she had sent Icarus and Lucas on their way she pretty much forgot about the old caravan (at least until Rita had started bitching) and turned her attention to the more arduous task of regaining control of Frisco. Bill had been fairly useful for that. After their second time in bed she had begun with the subtle whispering in his ear. As he had laid on his back she had rested her head on his chest and raked her fingernails lightly across his belly.

"Bill?" She had said.

"Hmmm." He had moaned, he had been starting to drift off.

"Do you think things will get better now that the riots have stopped?" She had already known they would. She had plenty of people who gave her information well before they gave it to Bill.

"Hopefully." He had said. His hand cupped her bare butt and pulled her closer. "Things are going to be tough for a while but eventually everyone is going to see things differently and things will improve."

"Think we'll be able to give up this power?" She had to fight a laugh when she said that.

"Later on. When things are calm and then we can start dividing everything up; the money, the jewelry, the property, maybe even that trailer thing in the garage."

"Trailer thing?"

"In the garage. I guess it was going to be some type of carriage for when the Queen went on long trips. It looks kinda like a smaller version of that big metal car you rode into town on."

Sandy had felt a strange sense of fear at that. The caravan was still there, still under her. Still haunting her. First chance she had when things were settled she was going to set that damn thing on fire.

"Yeah," she had said, "it'll be wonderful when we can finally break things down. Level the playing field a bit." She couldn't believe that people bought all this crap that she was spitting out lately.

Bill had drifted off to sleep after that and she had slipped out of bed. She got dressed and left her large room with a quick glance at her city view. There were two guards outside, whose names she had never bothered to remember, and they straightened up as she opened the door and began down the hall.

"Lady Sandy." They said in perfect unison. She gave them her sweetest smile, a gentle bow, and began down the hall way. She wasn't sure where she was going at first but once she was in the big golden elevator she knew. She was going down to the garage, down to see it for herself. She wanted to see if it truly looked like the caravan.

"All that work to get rid of it," she had said with a laugh, "and I end up with a stupid miniature of it. At least I can order to have this one destroyed." It was a long way down from the top floor even though the elevator went from floor to floor wonderfully fast. She thought back to how it had felt to see the chaos that erupted around her when the bombs went off on that stage. It was so wonderful to see, and the feeling she had gotten when she pushed Jessie underneath that falling platform was better than anything she had ever felt. Those thoughts warmed her up and she had a smile on her face all the way down. When she reached the bottom though, her smile faded and the fear returned.

The lights in the garage were very low. The light bloomed bright in small sections and then quickly faded creating large pockets of pitch black shadow. She stepped out and felt a shock of cold concrete rise up from the balls of her feet. She realized then that she had forgotten to put on her shoes.

She had forgotten the red pendant in the room too. She wondered what Bill would think of that thing if he came across it. She wondered if Rita might talk to him.

"That would be an interesting conversation." She said quietly. The sound echoed through the empty garage and she cringed. She should have brought one of the guards from her bedroom with her. But what if he had asked her a question about why she was down here. Why she HAD to see the carriage.

She went through the garage at a very steady stride, staying inside the pockets of light as best she could. When she had to go through shadows she ran through them, her bare feet smacking loudly in the darkness. She stopped running after a while and could feel her heart pounding in her chest. She was scared, she didn't know why but she was scared. She couldn't stop thinking about Jessie for some reason, that last look of heartbreak that Jessie had given her right before the platform fell. That last look was so clear in her eyes. It was like she was watching her, following her. Soon she was running again and this time she could swear something was behind her, something. Someone. She stopped running when she was in a pocket of light and spun around.

Jessie was standing right behind her, her eyes wide and her mouth open in a mute scream. Her arms shot out and grabbed Sandy around her throat. Sandy screamed and pulled back. She slipped on her own feet and fell hard on the concrete. She screamed again and crawled away going back into the shadows, her hair hung wildly over her head. She brushed it away and looked at the shadows.

Jessie was gone. She had never been there. Sandy didn't get up, she just kept backing away until she slammed into something hard and metal. She spun around and looked at the carriage she had been searching for.

Parts of it were hidden in shadow but the front and back were laying inside some of the light pockets. It was the caravan, a smaller caravan. The main trailer that pulled everything was only about half the size of Andy's but it was the same basic shape. It pulled another large trailer behind it, that she was willing to bet worked as a kitchen. Six more small trailers behind that one and then the small caravan ended. It was rounded on the edges instead of solid box shapes, and it was painted baby blue instead of steel gray. Still, it was the caravan. It was the same caravan that she had been trapped on for years. It was following her.

She started laughing, first a small giggle in her throat and then a loud manic blast of laughter that echoed throughout the entire garage. Any guard within ear shot must have thought she was going insane. She laughed until she couldn't breath and then she coughed and gasped for air. The small shadow of the caravan being cast from the pockets of light fell over her. She was chuckling again, a soft trembling sound that was almost sobbing.

The next morning she had talked to Bill about getting rid of the carriage as soon as possible. Rita had been whining about Johnny Boy again and Sandy had stuffed the pendant inside a drawer so Bill wouldn't hear Rita's bitching.

"I think we should find some way to get rid of the carriage now." She had said. Bill wasn't paying much attention to her but she had no intention of just letting that thing sit down there if she could help it. "Bill!"

"Why now?" He had asked. "There are more important things to be worried about aren't there?"

"I think that thing is dangerous for morale." She had been making it up as she went along but later on she thought it had sounded pretty good. "it's a symbol of the abuse of power the Queen exerted, and if we get rid of it now it'll be a sign of how much things are gonna change. Of how different the city will be."

"I suppose." he had said. He hadn't seemed interested in her idea, which was a first, and it turned her attention away from that large lump of metal in the underground garage for the first time that day.

"What's up? You seem distracted."

"I've been thinking of removing the guards completely. Now that most of the riots are done."

All at once Sandy had something much more important to worry about than the ghost that seemed to be lying in wait for her outside of the tower. If she had no guards, what was she going to do when she began to build things up more to her liking? Who would handle the people in the streets (and in the rebellion) that would object. Even with Rita's help she would need the support of loyal soldiers. They were a necessity.

"We can't do that!" She said. He gave her a curious look and she realized her rage must have shown on her face. She pulled it back as fast as she could but the damage had already been done. Bill didn't come to her bed that night and the next day he hadn't asked her to show up with him at the morning meeting with the other key members of the rebellion. He had seen more than rage in her face and it had set off some type of alarm in his mind.

3

The members of the morning meeting were a fairly diverse group of people who rarely spoke to Sandy when Bill was around. When she was alone though each of them came to find her at some point or another since the revolution. Each time they had come telling her of something Bill had done in private and wanting to know what she thought of their actions. They trusted her more than Bill, anytime she forgot that one of them would show up asking for advice. It had allowed her to place a few seeds in their minds.

One of the many things she had done after first talking to Icarus was lay a small bruise on her side. It was tiny and on the small of her back but it was noticeable; dark and purple. It had been a pain in the ass putting it on such a discreet part of her body, but it had to look like it had been done in a spot that wouldn't normally show.

Then she had gotten into a fight with Bill; she could no longer remember what it had been about. She made sure it was full of screaming and shouting, she even threw a glass against the wall for good dramatic measure. She had also made sure that she wore the same virginal white gown she had worn when she sent Icarus and Lucas away. Once he had stormed out she had started to cry. She left the door to her room open so that the guards out front could see her crying. Later that day when the members of the council had shown up one by one to inquire what had happened, she simply told them that she and Bill had disagreed. She pretended to try hiding her tears from them, and turned. Through her white gown the bruise on her back had been perfectly visible.

Now that she had been left out of the morning meetings by Bill she would have to take advantage of the seeds that had been planted. She pulled the drawer open and pulled out the pendant.

"Rita!" Sandy screamed into the pendant. No answer. Rita had fallen silent when she was actually needed. Typical. It was how people worked; when you had no use for them they wouldn't leave you alone and the second they were useful they were nowhere to be found. "Useless."

She had really not wanted to have to do this herself. It was an unpleasant experience beating yourself. She had hoped maybe Rita could do a smaller version of her little spell. Or maybe make her look bruised without actually bruising her.

The bathroom that was connected to Sandy's bedroom was almost as big with an enormous whirlpool tub on the far wall and a porcelain toilet next to it. A long sink ran against the wall with a huge mirror over it. Sandy opened up one of the drawers under the sink and found what she wanted. Earlier that month she had sent out for three large rocks that she now kept in that drawer. She scooped them out and then went back into the bedroom. She pulled a sock out of the drawer next to the bed and stuck the rocks in it. Sandy took her shirt off and then started swinging the sock over her head.

The sock gave up a slight *woosh* sound over her head and she brought it down fast. The sock wrapped around her side and slammed the rocks hard into her stomach. Sandy doubled over and gave out a small choke of breath. The skin was already starting to darken and she could feel pain when she pressed her finger to her stomach. It worked though and she spun the sock over her head again. It came down with *whomp* into her ribs this time. The next one was her back, then her other side, and then her stomach again (which was accidental and hurt worst of all). Sandy stopped and groaned at the pain that was running through her torso. She could feel her grip on the sock slacking, she didn't want to do what came next but it was what she had to do. She gripped the sock, pulled back, and brought the sock up in a long arc that brought the rocks directly into her face.

4

Sandy creaked the door into the banquet hall very slowly and poked her bruised face into the room. The long table was sitting in the center of a large chandelier lit room and she could see the other senior members of the revolution sitting at the table, Bill with his back to her. One of the members, an old woman with a balding head of gray hair, glanced at her. At first her face was full of light as she saw Sandy's face and then her face fell into shock and concern as she really saw Sandy's face. The old woman gasped, which drew the attention of the other senior members and soon they were all running toward her. Bill spun around and looked at her too, first with concern then with doubt. He had caught on real quick once he caught sight of her face that time, Sandy had to give him that.

The old woman reached out and placed a hand on Sandy's back. Sandy winced and pulled away (if there was one benefit at doing things this way it was that she didn't need to pretend to be hurt, her entire body and face hurt like hell). The woman cooed soothingly to her and Sandy began another steady stream of tears. The other senior members surrounded her, none of them touching her for fear of hurting her.

"We can't bruise the goddess." Sandy thought and had to suppress a laugh. *"Who would do this to our sweet little Sandy? Who would do this to our goddess?"*

Bill stepped forward, wanting to get a better look at her, and Sandy stepped away from him. Cringing into an old man who wrapped a protecting arm around her. She gave Bill her best terrified look and the rest of the senior members turned their gaze on him. For the second time in less than two days, Sandy watched a look of understanding sweep over Bill's face. This time though it wasn't calm at all, this time there was definite fear mixed in with the realization of where the real power stood in this room. When everyone was glaring at Bill, and Bill was staring at her, Sandy smiled.

164

5

Bill was executed without anything even remotely resembling a trial. She was there to watch as he was shot by a firing squad. She had been allowed to watch and had managed to suggest (through one of the more influential senior members) that he be shot on the very stage that Andy Che Pen's Stunt Performers had been on. Once he was gone she had sat down in his chair at the meeting table for the first time. There was no pretense about who was in control anymore. "Lady Sandy" was the ruler of the "United People of Frisco." She had to work hard to keep from laughing. By the time Icarus came back with Johnny Boy, she had completely forgotten about the caravan that sat in the garage underneath the tower.

6

Icarus drove the old truck through the streets of Frisco trying not to stare at the destruction. The riots had stopped while he was away but so many buildings were just large black lumps now. Blood was staining the streets and he could hear gunshots from a few blocks away.

"Things were bad before," he whispered to himself, "but they were never like this."

He'd been talking to himself for days now. Slowly going from just saying things out loud to damn near holding conversations with himself. He didn't have anyone else to talk to, the boy in the back was still asleep and had been for a few days now Even if he was awake, what would Icarus do? Ask him to sit up front? *So tell me your life story man. We still got some time, lots of uphill ta travel.*

"Well," Icarus said in a deeper voice (although he had no idea what the boy sounded like) *"I'm just your mysterious chubby boy who wanders around with a group of savage killers."*

"Are they really savage killers?"

"Of course they are!" Icarus shouted to the silent truck, abandoning the fantasy conversation he was having with the boy. He came to a stop sign at an intersection and slowed down. There was a burning pile of garbage bags on the corner and it gave off a horrible stench. Something that looked like a very small hand was sticking out from under the bags. Icarus turned away from it and sped through the stop sign.

The thing he hated most about talking to himself was that it made him feel like he was splitting in two. His conversations had slipped into doubts about Sandy more than once over the drive back. Something in his mind was full of distrust for her. The conversations had gone both ways so far. Half the time he'd actually started thinking of just stopping the truck and dumping the boy out. Then Icarus could just drive off and try to start his life anew. The other half he had ended up driving toward the city with his foot literally crushing the gas pedal, determined to get back to Sandy as soon as possible. Now another argument was building in his mind and the destruction around him was going to add a lot of fuel to the Anti-Sandy Side's fire.

"Are they really killers? Wouldn't they have killed me on sight?" Icarus said to himself.

"They killed Lucas! They shot him!" Icarus screamed out immediately.

"They weren't doin anything before then though were they?"

"Sandy said they were evil."

"Sandy said a lot of stuff though. What da ya think she'd been telling people while you were gone."

"Sandy's an angel."

"You and Lucas had been cool once. You weren't friends but you were cool."

"And they killed him!"

"If they hadn't, you would've."

"That's not true!"

"Is too. You were thinkin about doing it if Lucas didn't prove himself devoted enough."

"I never woulda done it."

"Really?"

"Yes!"

The truck gave a lurch as his foot first lifted off the gas and then stomped back down on it. He jumped and gripped the steering wheel hard enough to turn his knuckles white. He pulled to the side of the street and stopped the truck. His breathing had grown hoarse from all the screaming and now he was panting, his throat stinging with each little gasp for breath. He giggled a bit and then threw his head back in a howl of near manic laughter.

"I'm goin insane." He said, still laughing. "I'm losin my mind." He laughed loud and hard for nearly five minutes. After a while his laughter died and he glanced into his rear view mirror. He fell silent as he stared at the road behind him. He had been staring out that window for a long time since he blew up the caravan.

"Last chance." He said.

Then he blinked. Why had he said that? Last chance for what? His eyes flickered to the lump under the blanket in the truck bed and then back to the open road behind him. The street was wide and open, clear of any debris that could block his path.

"Block my path back. Last chance." He said.

His life back in Frisco before the revolution had been bad. He worked so hard and was so tired but what did he have to show for it?

"What do you have to show for your new life? Other than blood on your hands?" Another gunshot rang out somewhere, followed by a scream. The blanket in the truck bed shifted but the boy didn't wake up.

Things would get better. If he kept moving, things would get better.

"Moving where?"

He thought of Sandy again, the terrified look in her face. The way she pleaded with him. How she'd buried her face in his chest and cried. How she needed him to do this. He could keep moving and be fine either way; forward or back things would get better. They had to get better, they sure as hell couldn't get worse. But what would happen to Sandy if he went away? If he turned his back on her and left her on her own. What would happen to her? He had failed part of the mission after all, those people were still alive. They were still going to come for her.

Another gunshot. He stared at the open road again. The street was still empty. Still his and his alone.

"Last chance."

Icarus started the truck again, and drove up the street to Sandy's Tower.

7

No more ropes were coming to him, but Johnny Boy stayed in the dark. "Not yet," he told himself, "not yet. Something is here somewhere." Johnny Boy stayed in the darkness, and waited.

Miles away Cook stood with Miranda, Isabelle, and Ramon in a small salvage yard staring at the three small vans she had purchased. They weren't much to look at. Each one was leaning a bit on axles that must've been bent. The windshields were all cracked. Several tires were flat. Two of the vans seemed to be missing their exhaust pipes. All three cars looked like they were made out of rust rather than metal. They were however still in one piece (more or less) and that was a victory in and of itself. Cook felt a certain level of pride in herself for even finding them. The rest of the former caravan members didn't share her pride. The three of them stared at the old vans with uncertainty and mild disgust.

"We gonna have ta fix them up." She said. "But they'll do." The three young adults nodded but still weren't eager.

Andy was gone, he'd won a motorbike from the old man who ran the salvage yard over a game of cards. Cook had absolutely no idea how he had managed to do it and Andy was gone long before she had a chance to ask. It didn't change her job though. These vans were no replacement for the caravan but they would do for a time and when Andy came back with Johnny Boy they would need to be ready to go. Something told Cook that when they came back, a hasty exit would be needed.

Isabelle moved very slowly throughout the entire clean up of the vans. She kept replaying how she had run out of the diner when Johnny Boy had looked at her.

In the darkness, a rope had finally come to Johnny Boy. It was short, very short, Johnny Boy could see both ends of it. However, the thing that struck him the most was that the rope was white. Pure white seeming to push away some of the darkness around him. Johnny Boy reached out and grabbed it tightly.

He was sinking into the ground now, falling through floor after floor of a large building. Dropping deeper and deeper, the rooms growing darker and darker until he finally stopped in a large open room that must've been a basement.

"Or a garage." Johnny Boy thought.

Johnny Boy could see something in the shadows of this basement/garage level. Something big. Its shape was like a giant medal tank with huge wheels and there were several small trailers linked to-

"THE CARAVAN!" Johnny Boy wanted to run to it but he couldn't move. He was sure of it though, he was looking at the caravan. He was seeing the same caravan that had been destroyed. His second home.

"This is what I needed to see." Johnny Boy realized and with that thought, he finally woke up.

11

Johnny Boy woke up with a throbbing headache. The ropes were chaffing his arms and pressing so tightly on his chest that for a moment he couldn't draw a breath. The ropes cut into the tender flesh of the burns on his back and he could feel dried blood on the side of his head. A small film of crust was forming on his eyes, and his arms felt completely numb.

"How long was I gone?" He thought.

Something fuzzy was blocking his vision.

"A blanket."

Johnny Boy shook his body around until he finally got the blanket off his face. He was blinded by the mid-day sun, then his eyes adjusted and he could see the building tops looming over him.

"Frisco. I'm back in Frisco. Son of a- I've been gone for at least two whole days."

He tried to sit up and the ropes tightened their grip on him. His back flared up in pain and his breathing became even more strained. He fell back on the truck bed in pain and the ropes loosened a bit.

"Finally awake huh?" Johnny Boy looked up. Icarus was looking at him through the rear window of the truck bed. He didn't have the manic look on his face that he had right before he knocked Johnny Boy out. He seemed older now, very tired, but also very focused. "Was beginning to worry."

Icarus turned away and Johnny Boy began wondering. His mind ran a mile a minute, trying to figure out why. Wondering why Icarus had brought him back to Frisco.

"Maybe they're gonna execute me for the murder of the Queen. Or maybe all the other dead." Johnny Boy was talking to himself in a very low whisper. "But that can't be it. They never would've let the caravan leave if they had even suspected us."

There was a bump as the truck ran over something.

Probably just a speed bump.

Then the truck bumped again, this time though it was just the right side that lifted and this time the bump felt less sturdy. Like the thing they were running over was much softer.

I pray that was a speed bump.

Then the truck stopped and a man Johnny Boy had never seen before was coming over and looking at him. His face was very square shaped; flat top haircut, firm jaw, and a long rifle slung over his shoulder. Another man, his hair long and his face more oval shaped, leaned into the driver side window of the truck.

"I'm back." Icarus said to Oval shaped head. "Tell Lady Sandy I have the one she wanted."

Lady Sandy. Sandy? Johnny Boy's face must've taken on a look of bizarre wonder. Square shaped head was giving him a very strange look in return. Johnny Boy didn't want to believe it; the same Sandy he had been traveling? The one he had worked with? The same one that-

That disappeared after the show.

"Where's Lucas?" Oval shaped head was asking Icarus.

"Dead." Icarus said. His voice was mild, almost disinterested. Johnny Boy looked at Icarus's profile through the rear window. Icarus looked empty, like something in him had died.

Johnny Boy wondered if he had looked like that when he lost his "life."

12

Two more guards came up to the truck and pulled Johnny Boy out, causing the ropes to tighten again. Another jab of pain shot through his tender back but any screaming he would've done was cut off as the ropes crushed into his chest. He hunched over as the guards pulled him back onto his feet. He had to walk with his face hung low, struggling to take deep breaths, the ropes tightening and then loosening with each step he took.

He was being led to a building, the tallest one, the one that stood over the city like a viscous demon king, its shadow already starting to stretch over the other rooftops. The front glass doors were laced with gold, and another pair of guards were standing on each side. They pulled the door open and Johnny Boy was led into an enormous room. The carpet was a bizarre blend of purple and gold that kind of glowed in the light of the chandeliers that hung from the ceiling. A desk sat on the side wall and another guard was standing behind it. Something about the man sitting behind the desk with a rifle slung over his shoulder with a tattered black t-shirt and blue jeans, struck Johnny Boy as funny but he couldn't take in enough breath to laugh. The crushing ropes made the desire to laugh fade very quickly.

There were three elevators against the back wall and Icarus led the way as the guards pulled Johnny Boy into the middle one. Someone, Johnny Boy was too curled up in pain to notice who, pressed the button marked 105. There was a small jerk in the floor and then the elevator began climbing. If Johnny Boy had been able to look up he would've seen the numbers over the doorway counting as the elevator climbed, but of course he couldn't look up. He didn't even dare to try straightening up. The ropes were still digging into his burnt back and he could feel the tears in the corners of his eyes. He blinked them away and took a few deep breaths. He was beginning to feel better, beginning to breath more easily when one of the guards apparently noticed and jerked his ropes. Johnny Boy bit back a scream of pain and then gagged out another choked breath of air.

The elevator came to a stop, Icarus, stepped out and Johnny Boy was pushed out after him.

The hall was empty except for a set of double doors on the far end of the long hallway they had just stepped out onto. Johnny Boy could see two more guards standing on either side of the doors.

"I can go alone from here." Icarus said. The two escorting guards looked hesitant and Icarus tugged hard on Johnny Boy's ropes.

Johnny Boy fell to his knees in agonizing pain. His breathing stopped completely and his eyes widened until they were nearly falling out of his face. He opened and closed his mouth like a dying fish and then fell on his face. Icarus leaned down with him, pulling on the ropes. Johnny Boy's vision began to dull and he was sure that he was about to black out again.

Only I won't just go away this time. Johnny Boy was thinking. *This time I'll die and nothing will pull me back.*

Then Icarus let go of the ropes and Johnny boy could breath again. He laid on the floor letting in big pools of air, stopping only long enough to cough.

The two guards, satisfied that Icarus could indeed handle Johnny Boy alone, stayed in the elevator and let it close. Now it was just Johnny Boy and his kidnapper (who wasn't much older than him) alone in the long hallway. Once the sound of the elevator began Icarus started walking. Johnny Boy followed after him without being told. He knew that if he moved to slow, Icarus would grab the ropes again. He gritted his teeth against the pain that was biting into his back and chest. If there was a trick that Johnny Boy had learned from Rita for a situation like this, he couldn't think of it. The pain was so great though, that he wasn't really able to think of much of anything other than the ropes around him. He looked over at Icarus, twisting his head as well as he could to try and look into his face.

"Why-" Johnny Boy gasped out. He wanted to say 'why did you bring me here? Why did you attack the caravan?" but he couldn't get anymore of the words out. No response came from Icarus though.

The guards at the other end of the hall opened the double doors for them. Neither of these guard even glanced at the choking, hunched over boy, who was tied up and clearly suffering with every step he took. Icarus reached out gripped the ropes and yanked Johnny Boy into the room, paying no mind to the choked scream of pain that Johnny Boy let out.

13

The first thing Johnny boy could see when he finally came out of the small fog of pain, was Sandy standing before him in a long flowing white dress. The second thing he saw was the red pendant of Rita's dangling from its chain in Sandy's hand. The pendant was glowing brightly and Johnny Boy could feel what little strength he still had in him fall away. He could practically hear Rita laughing.

"Got ya now boy. Oh I got ya now. Ain't no runnin this time."

Icarus fell to his knees in front of Sandy and Johnny Boy could see the amusement in her eyes. The gown gave her an almost angelic look but Johnny boy could see it plainly, there was nothing angelic about her. Now that he was looking at her again for the first time in nearly a month he was wondering how he could not have seen what she was when they were working in the kitchen on the caravan together. This woman had such a sadistic little gleam in her eyes. Icarus couldn't see this, mainly because he was bowing so low that his head was practically touching the thick carpet.

"I found him Sandy," Icarus said, "I found him and I brought him back." Sandy walked up to him and placed her free hand under his chin. She pulled him up, and he stood. He was finally eye to eye with her and the sheer level of devotion that Johnny Boy saw in his face was so bizarre that for a moment Johnny Boy completely forgot about the jewel dangling from Sandy's hand. He also didn't notice that for the first time in nearly a month, Rita was beginning to talk in his head again.

"Ya think ya can just run out on our deal boy? Ya gonna pay ya end whether ya want ta or not."

Johnny Boy squeezed his eyes shut and tried to block her out. It was hard, and he knew that if Sandy put that jewel around his neck it would be impossible. Before, when Johnny Boy had taken his life back, that jewel hadn't mattered. Rita had free range of Johnny Boy while his life was gone, but now she couldn't connect to him anymore and that meant she was pumping everything she had into that damned pendant. She would do a lot more than just talk into his head this time. She'd wipe his mind clean, take him over completely.

Johnny Boy tried to crawl, to do anything, and the ropes tightened around him again. He whimpered and coughed and gagged on the carpet.

Neither Sandy nor Icarus seemed to care.

"I brought him back." Icarus said again. "Just like you asked." Sandy stroked Icarus's cheek with her free hand.

"Thank you so much Icarus." Sandy said. "And the other ones? Did you take care of them?" Icarus's face dropped and Sandy's lost its pleasant smile. "You didn't kill them?"

"I tried but-" Icarus began and Sandy slapped him hard across the face. He stared at her wide-eyed.

"DON'T YOU CARE WHAT HAPPENS TO ME!" She screamed. Her face twisted into an expression of savage rage that made Johnny Boy cringe. It was a lot like the expression Rita sometimes got. "DID YOU FORGET WHAT THOSE PEOPLE WILL DO TO ME!"

"I'm sorry." Icarus said. He was on his knees again and crawling toward her feet. "I tried but-"

"I NEEDED YOU TO DO THIS! I TRUSTED YOU!" Tears were

building in Sandy's eyes and now her rage was falling into something that might have passed for fear. It looked fake to Johnny Boy. "They're gonna come for me and kill me."

"NO! No they won't Sandy." Icarus ran to her and wrapped his arms around one of her legs. His face was still pointed at the carpet. "I promise you. I'm going back out right now. I just need a few people and will get them. I won't bother being subtle I'll just charge at them and kill them."

Sandy dropped to her knees and buried her head into the nape of Icarus's neck. The red jewel was now resting on Icarus's shoulder and glowing in Johnny Boy's face.

"Betta count the seconds ya still got boy!" Rita's voice echoed in Johnny Boy's head. *"Its all gonna be black real soon."*

"Icarus." Sandy sobbed. "Will you really do this for me?"

"Of course Sandy. We'll go right now and we'll be on top of them in two days at most. I know where they are, and they can't be far. I destroyed the caravan."

Something flashed in Sandy's eyes at that. Johnny Boy couldn't tell what it was though.

"Take as many people as you need." Sandy said through her sobbing. "And please come back to me. I need you by my side Icarus." She pulled away from Icarus for a moment, looked into his eyes, and then kissed him. She kissed him deeply, it looked to Johnny Boy like she was trying to shove her tongue all the way down his throat, and when she pulled back Icarus seemed to be hypnotized. His face hung slack and his look of devotion was even stronger than before.

"I'll be back as soon as I can." He stood up and squared his shoulders. Then with a confidence and lightness of heart that was missing from him earlier, Icarus turned and walked for the doors.

"Please be safe Icarus." Sandy said. She was biting her lip and holding her hands to her chest wringing them together. Icarus nodded and then he was gone.

Sandy tears dried up the instant the doors were closed again and her face fell back into rage.

"Simple fucking order," she said through gritted teeth, "how hard is it to kill four useless people, a fat Cook, and an old fart. Useless!" Sandy turned her face down to Johnny Boy and then to the pendant. "Oh well," she shrugged, "deals a deal I guess."

Sandy took a step toward Johnny Boy and he backed away as best he could, this time not noticing the pain in his back or the sudden lack of air in his chest. He was nearly to the wall when Sandy swung her foot out and kicked him in the side of his face. His head swung right and slammed into the wall. There were bright flashes of light across his eyes as Sandy bent down beside him. The flashes were fading just as she looped the chain of the pendant around his neck. The pendant fell and landed lightly on his chest.

"I just woke up." Johnny Boy thought as the world went black again.

14

In the oasis, a place well beyond the range of most people's worlds, two people screamed out. One was an old woman in a shack far outside of the small farm village. She was screaming out victory.

The other was a young woman about twenty-seven. She lived in an enormous farm house, built for at least a dozen people, and she lived in it alone. She was screaming with all her might, screaming in fear and agony for her little brother. Screaming and begging that he could hear her.

15

Andy was nearing the city, about three hours out, when he saw the trucks passing by. Two trucks both with a lot of men in the truck beds, all of them with rifles. Icarus was driving the lead truck and suddenly there was a chill running down Andy's back.

Without thinking, trusting things to instinct, Andy swung the motorcycle around and headed back the way he had come. After the trucks.

16

Johnny Boy was gone to the dark place again. This time though he couldn't see any ropes, and he was sure that none of them were coming. He was also sure that he wasn't getting out of here. This time he was stuck here for good. Rita had him and she was pumping everything she had into him. Using every bit of force that she had to push him as far away from himself as she could.

She had done this to him before hadn't she? Johnny Boy was pretty sure of it. That she had pushed him to the darkness herself when he had first agreed to make that delivery. Was that how he ended up in the woods where Andy found him? He was pretty sure it was. Why though? Was it just to test how solid her control over him was? To see just how much power she had?

"No." Johnny Boy thought. *She knew how much power she had over me. She knew that ever since she first used her magic on me to make me do what she wanted. When she made me-"*

Made him what? He couldn't remember. It was a blank but she had made him do something. Something bad. Had she made him do something bad to the small carriage he had been traveling on when he left the oasis? He hoped not, he couldn't remember much about the other people on the caravan but there had been other people on the caravan. He really hoped she hadn't made him do anything.

"Doesn't matter now. I'm going to be here forever. I'ts not my body anymore."

Then, for just a minute he thought he heard something. A voice very small, very distant.

"Jawnee!"

It was so low it sounded like a whisper. But Johnny Boy knew who it was. It was somebody screaming. A woman screaming. A woman he knew screaming.

"Little Jawnee!"

Suruo. His sister. His only surviving family. Suruo was calling him.

"Little Jawnee!"

Where was she calling from? The voice was so distant it felt like it was coming from all around him in the black. He didn't know what to do, where to reach out. He couldn't speak. He had never been able to speak in the black, regardless of how he got there. He couldn't respond but he could move (in a sense) if he knew where to move.

"Little Jawnee! Little Jawnee!"

He pulled. He chose a direction at random and pushed with all his might. Nothing.

"Please Little Jawnee!"

Now there was desperation in the voice, and Johnny Boy was now very sure that it was starting to fade. That his last connection to the world around him was fading away. He was going to be stuck here forever while Rita used his body to do whatever she wanted. He pushed again, his hope fading quickly, and this time the voice got a little louder.

"Can you hear me Little Jawnee! Please! Say something! Give me a sign! Anything! Please!"

"I can hear you sister!" Johnny Boy tried to say, but nothing came out. He could hear her loud and clear though. He could hear her getting louder as he pulled himself a little more. He could smell something too. Something that smelled like burning. He could feel heat around him too. He was coming back, and he was coming back to fire. That was fine with him. He would come back to fire if he had to. He would be back at least and then he could figure out what to do.

Suddenly he was being pushed away. He pulled himself forward again and could almost feel the wall that was blocking him. Could almost hear Rita's cursing voice as he was pushed away again.

When everything was said and done, he was just not strong enough to face Rita. Even with his elder sister's help, Johnny Boy was nothing but a potential tool to Rita. He was no challenge to her.

There was no chance of him breaking through.

CHAPTER 14
FACE OFF

1

Once Sandy put the pendant around Johnny Boy's neck. She watched in silent wonder as his shoulder went limp. The next moment, the ropes holding him glowed red and disappeared. He slumped over for a moment and then staggered to his feet; swaying left and right as he tried to gain his balance. He opened his eyes, and the two black balls that Sandy had known were gone. In there place were deep gray eyes with thick red veins. This wasn't Johnny Boy, this was Rita.

"Happy now." Sandy said. She could feel her flesh crawling but she kept her voice mild.

"Very." Rita/Johnny Boy said. It was like listening to two people say the exact same thing at the exact same time. It was even more unsettling when they started walking around the room. Johnny Boy's entire body seemed to spasm with every step, like something inside was desperately trying to keep from moving and trying to move at the same time. Rita's eyes rolled around in Johnny Boy's head, taking in everything they saw in the room. Then they turned on Sandy, and she suddenly wished she had been in reach of something she could throw or swing. There was something in those eyes that Sandy didn't like. "Ya did this much right ah give ya that Sandy. Took ya sweet time."

"Deals a deal." Sandy said. There was a large clock sitting on the dresser near the huge bed. It was thick and probably strong enough to crack this Rita/Johnny Boy Thing's skull if she had to. Sandy walked toward it, keeping her steps light and her expression calm. Rita's eyes were focused on her and a twisted little smile was playing in the corners of what used to be Johnny Boy's mouth.

"Dats definitely true." Rita/Johnny Boy said. She/he/it moved in step with Sandy staying about four feet away, keeping hers/his/its knees slightly bent. "Ah agreed to let ya use mah pendant didn't ah?"

"You did. I trust you'll keep your end of the deal." Sandy was right next to the clock now and she laid her hand on the dresser. Trailing her fingers across it trying to look as uninterested as possible until her fingers trailed up onto the clock. She let her hand rest on it and curled her fingers around it. Just in case, she didn't think she would need to, hoped she wouldn't, but just in case.

"Ah course ah am. Just need a minute ta finish what ah'm doin here."

"What are 'ya doin' there?"

"Just finishin a deal ah made with this one."

Rita/Johnny Boy turned it's (yeah Sandy was sure 'it' was the right word) back on her. There was a bright red light on the back wall as the pendant started glowing and then it spun around to face her again.

Sandy dropped to the ground as the dresser behind her exploded in a blast of red light. Another flash of red and Sandy rolled to her right, the gown wrapping around her legs. The spot she had just been in exploded and she could see the room in the floor below her. The floorboards were beginning to burn and the carpet had small flames in it. Another red flash and Sandy dove under the bed. The floor behind her exploded, another red flash, and then the bed was in the air and burning bits of wood were flying over her head.

Sandy looked over at the burnt remains of the drawer and she could see the clock sitting on the floor, just at the edge of the hole that led to the floor below.

There was another flash of light and Sandy was thrown into the air as the ground beneath her blew up. She flew up and slammed into the ceiling. The world grew hazy and she fell down and banged her head on the floor. The small flames from the carpet were beginning to grow and pretty soon the entire room was going to be engulfed in fire.

She wondered why her guards weren't kicking the door down. Weren't rushing in and filling the Rita/Johnny Boy thing with bullets. Then it clicked in her head. She had told Icarus to take as many guards as he needed and he snatched up the first two he found right away. There was no one outside, and the few guards downstairs (assuming Icarus hadn't taken all of them) would never make it up here in enough time to help her.

Fine. She would kill it on her own.

Another red flash and Sandy rolled right. The blast sent up another cluster of wood, some of it stabbed into Sandy's left arm.

She paid no attention and climbed to her feet. The gown snagged and then tore and she force her legs apart enough to support her weight. Then she dove for the clock. A red flash, then a section of the wall over her head was gone.

"Ya a spry little thang." It was laughing and now it sounded more like Rita than Johnny Boy. "Ah'll give ya that much."

Another flash as Sandy rested her hand on the clock. She could feel its heft and she was reassured now that she could kill it if she could get close. She wasn't running. To hell with that. She wouldn't run after all that she had done to earn her power. This was all hers by right and she was going to have it.

There was another blast of light but nothing came after it. The Rita/Johnny Boy thing froze for a minute and its face was twisted into rage.

"Get back ya little brat! Ya ain't getting out again!" It hissed and now it was completely Rita.

Sandy didn't hesitate. She lunged at it and swung the clock upward in a huge arc. It saw her coming and leaned back at the last minute. The clock slammed hard into the side of the pendant but missed it's head. There was a dull flash as the pendant cracked. Sandy was thrown back as the thing howled in anger. Rita was cursing and Johnny Boy was grunting. The body spasmed and the crack in the crystal grew bigger.

2

There was a loud sound in Johnny Boy's ears. The sound of something huge cracking. It filled his ears in the black. He tried to cover his ears but of course he couldn't. He didn't actually have ears to cover in this place.

"Little Jawnee!"

Johnny Boy pulled himself again and once again he hit a wall. But something was different now. The wall didn't push him back. Now it actually bent against his pressure. He pulled harder and this time he could almost feel himself moving through the wall that was blocking him.

"Almost there Little Jawnee! I can feel ya! You're almost there!"

One last pull. The wall began to crack around him and now the sound of cracking turned into the sound of something shattering. The feeling of heat around him was even stronger. Now he knew he really was in a fire. He could see the flames and feel the heat, but he was back.

"Push now Little Jawnee! Push as hard as you can and you might have a chance! And don't forget what you saw!"

He was back in Sandy's huge bedroom but sections of it seemed to have been blown apart. The pain in his back wasn't as sharp and he could breath normally again. It took him a minute to realize that the ropes were gone. Splintered pieces of wood were everywhere and everything was on fire. The rug and all the blown pieces of wood were covered in huge flames that were quickly filling up the room with thick black smoke.

The pendant was on the ground, the flames were slowly surrounding it. He could still hear Rita's voice but now it was coming directly from the pendant instead of his head.

"Ya little bastard! Ya think ya can run forever! I'll find ya again ya hear me! I'll find ya and I'll rip ya apart! I'll make ya wish ya were dead. I'll make ya beg me ta kill ya, ya little bastard fuck!"

The flames engulfed the pendant and it shattered. Rita's voice faded and Johnny Boy was sure that this time, it was for good.

3

Back in the oasis two people screamed again. The old woman screamed in pain and frustration as the red pendant she had been holding exploded in her hand.

In the large house the young woman screamed and cheered. She cried in joy and tears streamed down her cheeks. He made it out, her baby brother, her little Jawnee had made it out. She fell to her knees by her bed and laid her head on the mattress. She didn't want to fall asleep but she had been calling out to him for so long. He wouldn't need her help now though she was sure of that. Things weren't over yet but

"You push now little Jawnee." She said. "You push out just as hard as ya pulled yourself up."

With those words she climbed onto the mattress and fell asleep. Her baby brother would be alright. She was sure of it.

4

Johnny Boy was so wrapped up in watching the pendant explode that he almost didn't notice the movement at his side until Sandy was right on top of him. The big black clock was directly over her head and she swung it down with all the strength in her arms. Johnny Boy had only a second to react and he did the only thing he could think of.

He pushed.

He thought about the feeling he had gotten when he pulled through the darkness and he did the exact opposite. He pushed at Sandy as hard as he could.

Sandy flew backward like something had yanked at her hair. She didn't fly far but she did let go of the clock, which hit the ground with such force that Johnny Boy was sure it would've cracked his head open. Sandy was getting up again and this time Johnny Boy pushed harder. She flew back again, she slammed into the wall hard and when she hit the ground again she didn't get back up. The flames caught hold of her gown and it began to burn. Without thinking Johnny Boy ran toward her and beat the flames out of her dress.

"What the hell are you thinking?" He asked himself. He backed away from her, coughing in the rising smoke, and then ran out of the room.

He had forgotten about the two guards that had been standing at the door. He remembered just as he slammed through the double doors, and he was sure that they would turn their rifles on him and kill him the second he was in the hall. But when he staggered into the long hallway, there was no one there. The guards had left, which seemed odd, and Johnny Boy was alone. The elevators on the other end of the hall were far and his body was still sore (especially his back) but if he had managed to do it while tied up and barely able to breath, then he could do it now. He ran as fast as he could, trying not to wince as the burn on his back flared up, and reached the elevators. It hadn't been as far as his exhausted mind made it look. He hit the elevator button and waited.

He had to get back to them, back to Isabelle and the others, before Icarus got there. That was why the guards were gone, Icarus had taken them. Sandy had told Icarus to take as many as he needed hadn't she?

"The garage." Johnny Boy was saying. "I have to get to the garage." The caravan wasn't going to be down there, he knew that. But he had seen an image hadn't he. Maybe it was something else, maybe something he was going to need to have in order to save the caravan (a big truck with huge guns in it hopefully) was down there. "Gotta get down there."

The elevator finally arrived with a light ding sound. The golden plated doors opened and Johnny Boy stepped in. He hit the big button marked "G" and leaned against the back wall, breathing heavily and waiting for the pain in his back to fade.

5

Sandy crawled out of the burning room with the hem of her gown on fire again. She paid it no mind until she was back on her feet, and then she batted at the flames until they went out. Her hair was wild and tousled from being thrown around and the large splinters of wood from the explosion had torn open the skin on her arms. She was bleeding badly but she wasn't paying any mind to that either. She could see the elevator door at the end of the hall closing and she ran for it as fast as she could. She had no chance of catching it and it was already well on its way back to the ground level when she hit the button.

By the time the second of the three elevators reached her floor, she was pulling that larger splinter of wood out of her arm and howling in pain as she did. She stepped in, throwing a long bloody piece of wood onto the hall carpet. Her fingers went straight for the "1" and froze just before hitting it.

She thought about the carriage in the garage, about the little caravan.

She hit the "G."

6

Johnny Boy didn't hesitate in the darkness as Sandy had. He felt no fear down here at all, only the sense of urgency that he had felt when he left the burning room. He ran through the pockets of shadow and light that covered the garage floor, looking for something he could use. Anything he could use. The second elevator dinged as the car hit the ground but he didn't pay any attention to it. He was running as fast as he could, enjoying the slight burn in his chest from his panting (enjoying that he could breath at all). His eyes shot from one pocket of light to another until they fell upon-

"THE CARAVAN!"

Johnny Boy ran up to it, amazement in his eyes. It dulled only a little as he realized what he was looking at.

It wasn't the caravan, but rather a smaller version of it. More curved and elaborately designed then the simple box shape of Andy's but it was the same concept; a big trailer pulling several smaller ones. Only about

183

four cars behind the main trailer instead of twenty but it was still the same. It was still a caravan. It was still a way out.

Johnny Boy reached for the door, suddenly sure that it would be locked. He climbed up the two stairs on the side of the main trailer, gripped the door handle, and pulled. The door didn't move and he could hear a light clunk sound. Sure enough, the door was locked.

Johnny Boy cursed as loud as he could in his native language. There weren't many curse words in his native language but there were a few, and his older brothers had taken the time to teach him all of them. Now he spit them out in a blast of sound that made someone behind him gasp. He spun around to see Sandy standing behind him. The fear in her eyes was replaced with anger and she jumped at him. Johnny Boy pushed out and Sandy flew back, slamming hard into one of the concrete pillars that filled the garage. She went limp on the ground again and Johnny Boy ran past her back toward the elevators.

There was a doorway leading to the stairs next to the elevators and Johnny Boy flew into it without even considering the elevators. The keys could be anywhere in this building but he was going to hope and pray they were at that desk he had seen on the first floor when he was dragged in. He took the steps two at a time, his breath coming out in long heavy gust now. He stopped at the door with a big black "1" painted on it. There were still guards out there, there had to be they couldn't ALL be gone. He creaked the door open slowly and it opened to the far end of the room. He could just barely make out the desk on the opposite side, but he could only see a corner of it, and he couldn't see anything else in the room. He creaked the door open a little more.

BANG

A section of the door was suddenly gone as a bullet sailed through it and into the wall of the stairway. Johnny Boy ducked back as gunfire fell onto the door. It didn't hold against the gunfire for even a minute. The door was ripped apart by the bullets while Johnny Boy watched in silent horror. That could've been him. After only five or six seconds, the door was little more than a few splintered pieces of wood. Johnny Boy could hear the sound of fast approaching footsteps in the room. He braced himself on his knees, ready to run, as the first of the guards appeared in the doorway.

Johnny Boy pushed him back and the guard was thrown so hard into the room that Johnny Boy could hear some of the guard's bones break.

More footsteps were coming and Johnny Boy dove into the doorway.

Without giving anyone a chance, Johnny Boy pushed focusing on nothing in the room at all but just pushing out as hard as he could. Everything in the room was thrown nearly four feet back. The guards who had been taking aim to fire flew into the air. Their guns bent in on themselves. The desk was shattered in half as its top half flew backward. The chandeliers in the ceiling came undone and slammed to the ground.

Johnny Boy's head went hazy and a gray curtain fell over his eyes. He fell to his knees and felt something running out of his ears. He touched his ears and when he pulled there was blood on his fingertips. He let his head hang for a minute, trying to will the gray curtain away. It faded and he got back to his feet.

"Never doing that again." Johnny Boy said. The keys that had been behind the desk now lay on the floor in several piles scattered all over the floor. Most of the keys were small silver keys with numbers on them. Johnny Boy assumed those to be room keys. One key though was long and red. It's handle had small red and green flowers on it. He stepped over one of the guards who was groaning and curled into a ball, and reached out for the key. There was a sound of something being picked up behind him and he spun around.

Sandy had picked up one of the bent guns and brought it down on Johnny Boy's face. It connected with a sharp *klank* sound and Johnny Boy could feel one of his teeth come loose. She brought it back into the air and Johnny Boy tried to push out again. The gray curtain fell back over his eyes but Sandy was thrown back. She only flew a few inches before hitting the ground with a light *thump*. She got right back up and swung the gun again. Johnny Boy rolled right and the gun slammed down on his back instead of his head. The burn lit up worse than anytime before and he screamed. Sandy was bringing up the gun again and Johnny Boy pushed at the gun. It was knocked out of her hand, and fell about two feet behind her. The gray curtain was a lot thicker now and Johnny Boy fought it back. The key was less than two feet away from him and he grabbed it. Sandy dove on top of him wrapping her hands around his throat and letting out an almost feral scream of rage.

No matter how angry she was or how aggressive she fought, Sandy was only about half the weight of Johnny Boy. He ignored the pain in his back as best as he could and threw her off him. She hit the shattered remains of the desk and rolled onto the floor. Johnny Boy looked down at the big red and green key in his hand, it looked about the right size to him. Andy had shown him the large gray key that was used on the old caravan and it looked about the same.

"If not I'll have to come back here again." He said softly. "**Bur-shef-tord** I'm tired." Sandy was crawling back to her feet.

"This is my fucking world!" She growled at him. "You won't ruin it! I'll kill you before I let you take it from me!"

"You can have it," Johnny Boy groaned without looking up at her, "I don't want anything to do with you."

"Liar! This is your fault, if it wasn't for you that Rita bitch wouldn't have done any of this!"

That was true in a way and Johnny Boy knew it. Sandy had picked up a large chunk of wood and was getting ready to charge at him and this time Johnny Boy didn't bother trying to push her. The curtain was finally beginning to fade and he didn't want it coming back. He reached down and picked up the bent gun. His sisters and brothers had always told him never to hit women but he was sure that this was a valid exception to the rule.

He ducked under Sandy's swing and brought the gun into Sandy's stomach. Her eyes bulged as she fell to her knees and Johnny boy turned and ran back for the stairway. She cursed out after him but he couldn't care less. He had already told her, she could have her little world, he truly didn't care. Maybe later, away from the constant life-threatening events, he might care about what type of horrors she performed. For now it was everything he could do to keep himself moving. He'd spent so much time running and fighting in the last few hours and for all the weight he had lost over the last few months he was still out of shape. He was tired and he wanted to get back to the others. He had to warn them about what was coming after them, maybe he could stop Icarus before he arrived, but he would have to leave now.

Sandy wasn't as content to let him leave though. She jumped on his back and this time she was clawing at the back of his shirt. He could feel her nails against his burned back and it hurt like hell. He flung her over his shoulder and she slammed into the ground hard. He could hear her let out a woofing sound as the breath left her and he stepped over her. He was down the stairs and back into the garage by the time she crawled back onto her feet. She chased after him, screaming and cursing, he stopped moving and turned to face her. Not wanting to risk her actually sinking her nails into his back. That would hurt him enough to shift the balance of this fight. Sandy stopped at the doorway though, and he could see something that resembled rational thought creeping back into her eyes.

Johnny Boy prayed she was finally getting it through her head that charging him wouldn't do any good. It seemed like that was exactly what was happening when she turned and ran back into the stairway. He didn't bother waiting to see if she was coming back down. He spun and moved toward the mini-caravan at a light jog.

He just didn't think he had enough energy to run anymore. Then there was a sudden blast of gunfire from the first floor and Johnny Boy discovered that he could still run. He had to rest his hands on his knees and catch his breath when he reached the caravan.

He was worried he had the wrong key. Of course he was. How good was his luck lately after all? But the key slid into the lock perfectly and when he turned the lock came undone. He pulled the door open and climbed inside.

The drivers section was separated from the small sitting area in the main carriage by a small doorway. The two seats in front of the enormous driver side window were covered in black leather that felt wonderful to the touch. As Johnny Boy sat on it and leaned back he sank a little ways in and there wasn't a bit of pain in his back. The dash board was a pearl color that glowed even in the low light of the garage. There wasn't a sign that this seat had ever been sat on, or that the caravan had been used at all. It fact, Johnny Boy realized that it was very likely this thing had never been used before. That made another fear run through his mind.

"What if there isn't any gas in it? What'll I do then?"

He stuck the key in the ignition and prayed. He had never been very religious so he prayed to his family. He prayed to his sisters. His head pressed against the steering wheel (which was much smaller than the one in the old caravan) and prayed.

"Suroa. Becca. If you're still watching me, please help me. *Ketoruahsishio*. Give me a direction."

He turned the key and the engine roared to life. His eyes fell on the little gas meter and he could practically feel his fear evaporate as the needle went up and rested on the F. With a sign of relief he shifted the huge thing into gear and started to turn the huge wheel. The caravan jerked and began the slow, laborious, process of turning toward the large steel gate that blocked the exit. It was still down but he was sure that he could tear straight through it. This thing wasn't as big as the old caravan but this thing was big enough. It would break straight through the fence without trouble. He pressed hard on the gas and felt the caravan begin its slow acceleration until it was flying along at a steady speed. It wasn't until he nearly hit a pillar that came flying out of the partial darkness, that he even thought to turn on the headlights. There was no switch under the wheel (where the headlights had been on the old caravan) and he felt around with one hand while trying to keep the caravan steady with the other. He found a switch over his head and flicked it without looking up. The headlights kicked just in time for him to catch sight of another pillar. He veered around it and gave a sigh of relief when he didn't hear it slam into one of the trailers.

He saw the gate ahead and pressed down even harder on the gas. The engine roared again. Johnny Boy closed his eyes as the gate flew at him, and the caravan tore through the gate without effort. The perfect paint job was probably scratched to hell, but he was out and on the open road again.

There was a small gathering of guards running toward the tower. They had probably been drawn by all the gunfire. He didn't want to run them over but he would be damned if he was going to slow down.

There was a small chain over his right shoulder, he pulled down on it and sure enough the horn blew. It didn't give out a normal blast but rather the sound of a dozen horns in a musical note. It would be interesting to see Andy's reaction to that.

If Andy was still alive when-

The guards dove out of the way as the caravan roared past them. It hit the downhill slope and sped up even more. The trailers were accelerating behind him and he knew what would happen if he tried to turn the caravan at this speed. It would tip over. If he slowed down now, the trailers behind would keep going and slam into each other. The bottom of the hill was coming up fast and Johnny Boy swerved the car left and tried to swing the car in a large right arc.

The car swerved and he could feel it starting to lean right. If he tried to turn left again the weight would shift. He held his breath and gripped the wheel so tight that his knuckles went several shades brighter. The car straightened and he could feel it level off again. The bridge was straight ahead. He hit the gas again, and drove out of town.

Sandy had a brief thought just before she charged after Johnny Boy in the garage. She remembered something she had seen and had dismissed in her rage.

The wounded guards that were scattered across the main floor had been rolling around and groaning. A lot of them had been clutching their stomachs in pain, like something inside them had been twisted. It wasn't them she thought about, it was their guns. Each one of the automatic rifles that she had seen had been twisted beyond use. When Johnny Boy tossed her off his back and she had slammed into the remains of the large desk, she had seen one underneath one of the guards. One rifle barrel that wasn't twisted or bent at all. It had been thrown out of the guard's hands but it was perfectly fine other wise. Perfectly usable.

She spun back around and ran back up the stairs to get it. She didn't have Johnny Boy's extra-weight to hold her down and she was able to get up the stairs much faster than he could've hoped to. She ran across the room, stepping down hard on one guards' crotch, and pulled the gun out from under another guard. She was right, it was perfectly fine. The strap snagged on the guards' arm and Sandy let out a viscous roar of irritation before pulling the trigger and unloading several bullets into the unfortunate guy. She yanked on the strap and it came loose. She was back down the stairs and running under the lights when she heard the caravan starting.

She could see the last trailer disappearing ahead of her and she broke into a run. She sprang for the back of the trailer and grabbed the edge of the trailer. She hoisted herself up and held on for dear life as the caravan broke through the gate. She nearly dropped the rifle but managed to hold on to it.

The caravan roared over the bridge and back onto the open roads. Johnny Boy gave it another wide arc and turned the caravan to the east. A few hours later, the city was disappearing from his rear window. He could still see the smoke rising from one of the high windows of Sandy's Tower.

CHAPTER 15
PART OF THE FAMILY

1

Nearly four days after Johnny Boy lost sight of the city he came upon an overturned truck. There were three bodies scattered across the street and a lot of blood in the grass. They were more of Sandy's guards and he hoped that whatever happened to them had ended his problems. It was still a long way to the small little town he had left the others in.

He would've driven right past the overturned truck without a second look if not for the large, gray haired, figure laying next to an overturned motorcycle. His breathing stopped and he slammed on the breaks not caring about the way the back trailers bumped into each other when he did. He killed the engine and took the key out before leaping out of the main trailer and running toward the figure.

"ANDY!"

Andy lifted his head and Johnny Boy was sure he was going to faint. Andy's face was smeared with blood from a huge gash on his forehead. His right arm was bent at an unnatural angle and the lower part of his shirt was soaking wet and a very deep scarlet.

"johnny boy." Andy said. His voice was very low and it came between deep shuddering breaths. "you all right."

"Yeah I'm fine. Don't talk all right." Johnny Boy was trying to beat back the panic that was building up in him. He was failing and in a few minutes he was going to be so panic stricken that he wouldn't be able to think straight.

"couldn't get im all. Nother truck still on the move. You gotta," Andy took a deep breath, "you gotta stop im. Keep movin and look out for each other."

"Stop talking like you aren't coming with us." Johnny Boy said. He tore open the wet section of Andy's shirt and winced. There was a large cut in his side and blood was everywhere. It didn't look like anything

vital had been hit, but Johnny Boy didn't know that for sure. He needed-
"Wait here." Johnny Boy realized immediately how stupid that request
was. "I'm gonna find a first aid kit."

"Seein things." Another deep breath. "Could swear I was looking at
my caravan."

If there was a first aid kit it would be somewhere in the main trailer.
Under the driver seat maybe, hopefully. He climbed back up and stuck his
head under the seat. Nothing. Just the steel of the wall that separated the
driving section from the seating section. Johnny Boy climbed into the
trailer and through the door into the sitting area.

This area looked very comfortable. A large red couch, two huge red
chairs, and a large brown coffee table that sat on a thick red and blue
carpet. The walls were painted in pink with gold trim. Johnny Boy paid it
no attention and looked around frantically for something, anything, that
might have looked like it would have a first aid kit in it. There was a huge
golden chest sitting against one wall. There was no lock on it and Johnny
Boy flipped the lid open. The inside was empty and brilliantly polished.
He had been right in his earlier idea, this caravan had never actually been
used before. A closet was on the opposite wall and he ran to it next. It
was a small closet and just as empty as the chest except for something
sitting on a high shelf in it. He reached up, feeling around for whatever it
was he saw and his hands fell upon a plastic handle. He pulled it off the
shelf and was yanked down to the floor by its weight when it came free of
the shelf. It was a black case, very heavy, and with a large red cross on
the front.

"Thank you." Johnny Boy whispered. He lifted it up and could feel
his arms howling. The bag was in a beautiful leather case with golden
latches and handles but it was so heavy. "Fashion over common sense."
He could carry it though. He had to. Andy needed it. He didn't carry it
back to the driver's seat, instead he went to the double doors that opened
to other trailers and kicked it open.

He hadn't taken two step out when a hail of gun fire erupted around
him. On instinct he dropped to the ground, dropping the case. It nearly hit
the concrete road underneath but Johnny Boy caught it with one hand and
managed to pull it back up. Another hail of gun fire and Johnny Boy dove
back into the trailer.

"YOU'RE DEAD YOU BASTARD! YOU HEAR ME! YOU ARE
FUCKING DEAD!"

Sandy. Johnny Boy groaned in both fear and irritation. She just wouldn't stop. She was like a revenge crazed demon. She was coming. He could hear her footsteps and he thought he might be able to push her again. His head was clearer, but if he wanted to stop her (to kill her? Yes. Yes he meant to kill her this time.) then he would have to push hard. What if this time he blacked out instead of just feeling like he was going to? Andy was dying not twelve feet away. He had to deal with her without pushing. He ran behind the doorway and held the case high over his head. His arms were trembling a bit but they kept the case over his head. Sandy came running in and he brought the case down on her head.

There was a sort of *wonk* sound and she dropped like a stone onto the ground. The rifle clattered to the floor next to her and Johnny Boy snatched it up. He was going to sling it over his shoulder but the strap was undone. Sandy laid at his feet, eyes closed and he contemplated shooting her. That was what he needed to do anyway wasn't it? He had already told himself that he meant to kill her. Telling himself that he would and actually doing it however, were two different things. He had never killed anyone before.

Not intentionally little Jawnee but-

Instead of shooting her, Johnny Boy pulled her out of the trailer and dragged her onto the road, next to the overturned truck and the dead guards. He noticed that there were bullet holes all over the truck, fuel was leaking out of the ruptured fuel tank and running into the grass. He left her there, went back to the trailer, got the first aid case, and dragged it back to Andy.

Andy was still breathing. It was slow and raspy, but he was still breathing. Johnny Boy dragged the case to him and opened it. There was mostly just bandages inside but there was also a bottle of disinfectant. Johnny Boy knew enough to use that first. There was a small piece of cloth inside the case and he poured some of the disinfectant on it. Then he pressed it against the wound on Andy's side.

Andy let out a scream of pain that made Johnny boy jumped back. Johnny Boy sighed in relief. If he could scream in pain than maybe he could still be saved. Johnny Boy didn't quite understand that train of thought but it still made sense to him in a strange way.

He spent a good twenty minutes doing everything he could to clean and bandage Andy. When he was done Andy looked a little better. His face and chest were covered in bandages that weren't laid particularly well but he wasn't a bloody mess anymore and his breathing seemed to have grown a bit stronger. Johnny Boy tucked himself under Andy's right arm and lifted him up. He had to leave the first aid case and the rifle behind to carry Andy back to the caravan. It was difficult helping Andy up into the main trailer. Two times Andy nearly fell on top of him but he eventually did manage to get him into the trailer and laid him on the couch.

"Am I dead?" Andy asked as he laid across the couch. "Cause I think I'm on the caravan."

"You're not dead Captain Andy." Johnny Boy said. Johnny Boy couldn't remember the last time he used Andy's title. "Just rest."

"Others. Rest of the caravan...don't let them...can't lose anyone else..."

"We won't. Go to sleep."

Andy drifted off to sleep and Johnny Boy ran back outside to get the case and the rifle. He threw a quick glance at the overturned truck to make sure Sandy wasn't getting back up.

She wasn't there. His heart beat hard in his chest as he thought of Andy asleep and defenseless in that caravan. He dropped the case and readied the rifle. A shot rang out and the dirt next to Johnny Boy kicked up. He caught sight of something, Sandy, behind the truck. Without thinking Johnny boy took aim, completely forgetting his moral confusion about killing Sandy, and fired. The windshield of the truck shattered and the figure disappeared completely. Johnny Boy moved without even thinking, he ran for the truck with the rifle in hand (anyone who knew about handling guns would've noticed that he did nothing to try and cover himself) and stopped as the figure rose up. He fired again and this time the figure flew back. He stood waiting, the gun pointed at the truck, his knees feeling like two steel pipes in his legs. He wanted to duck down so his head wouldn't be sticking over the truck in plain sight, but he couldn't seem to move his legs at all. Much less bend them.

Forty seconds passed (to Johnny boy it felt like an eternity) and there was no movement or sound coming from the other side of the truck. Johnny Boy took a step toward the truck and leaned over to look, sure that he was going to see Sandy waiting with her rifle at the ready and that would be the end.

Sandy was there but she was laying on her back, eyes staring at the sky, and a small red hole directly between her eyes. Johnny Boy stared at her for a minute, his hands trembling, and then he ran back to the caravan. He felt like he was getting ready to throw up, but he pushed it away. He had to get moving, he was taking too long.

Three minutes later, the caravan was roaring down the road again.

2

The vans were running. That was something of a miracle given that only Cook and Ramon had any real mechanical skills and Cook's were pretty basic. They had managed it though, gotten two of the three vans running perfectly and Cook was sure that by the next night the third van would be running too.

Ramon and Cook were both sitting in the shade of one of the vans, talking about the parts they would still need to search for in order to get the last van ready. Miranda and Isabelle were sitting next to each other in the shade of another van and talking quietly. Isabelle's face still looked sunken and she seemed older but at least she was talking. For a while it had seemed like a reversal of the lake; where Isabelle had been moving around all the time and Miranda had been sitting silent.

"Ya think Andy's found him yet?" Ramon asked as he flipped a small pipe around in his hand. "Think he's on his way back right now?"

"I think so." Cook said. "That's good too cause I can't shake this feeling that we need to be movin on soon."

"What do you mean?" Ramon stopped spinning the pipe and looked at her. He looked haggard too, but nowhere near as bad as Isabelle. Cook could feel a wave of sadness run inside her. These were good kids. They didn't deserve all of this.

"I mean that it ain't gonna be safe to stay here much longer. So we need to get these things ready."

"How do ya-"

Cook wasn't looking at him anymore. Something had turned her attention to the west side of town.

3

Icarus still had a group of maybe five guards. It was enough. It was more than enough to take care of four people. The old man was dead on the highway behind him. With him dead the only real problem was that huge bitch that had stepped on Icarus before. He would deal with her and let the rest of the group deal with the three kids.

The truck tore through the city Icarus standing up in the truck bed searching for his targets. The people in town were all running into their houses, locking their doors, and drawing their blinds. That was smart of them, Icarus's patience was so thin now that he would've shot everyone in his path if he had to. He didn't want to but he was beyond worrying about the consequences. Besides, what was a few more dead when you'd seen all this chaos anyway?

The town was small and he had swept through it very fast without catching sight of any familiar faces. There was no one left on the streets either. He should have snatched someone up and pumped them for information. He shifted his attention to houses, wondering which one to break into first. Which family was he going to terrorize for information.

"Can you really-" that Anti-Sandy voice in his head began and he fought it off. Of course he could. It was Sandy's will after all and he would not fail her again. He would kill them, bring some proof back to Sandy (a head maybe) and then it would be over. If that meant that he had to scare a family or two then that's what he would do. If they told him what he wanted to know then he wouldn't have to do any permanent dam-

Icarus's eyes caught sight of the huge piles of garbage on the eastern end of town. The salvage yard. It was worth a shot.

"Yeah!" That Anti-Sandy side of him screamed out. *"Go check the yard, hell you'll see that they kept moving east anyway."* Icarus pushed the voice away again, but he didn't stop looking at the salvage yard.

It was worth a shot anyway.

4

The caravan was tearing down the concrete as fast as it could possibly move. If Johnny Boy tried to turn it at this speed it would definitely tip over. But he was making good time. He would be back to the others by sunset if he kept moving. If he just kept moving. Every so often Andy would groan but Johnny Boy couldn't stop to check on him. He just had to put it on faith that Andy was just having nightmares or feeling the pain from his wounds. He hoped that Andy's wounds weren't getting infected.

The road forked up ahead. The left road lead up to the lake where everything had been going so well. He took the right fork.

Isabelle and Miranda saw Icarus standing up in the truck bed long before he saw them. Miranda was screaming for Cook and Ramon as Isabelle climbed into the van they had been sitting under.

"Get in that van Miranda!" Cook was screaming. "Me an Ramon are gonna draw them off! You head west and meet up with Andy understand!?"

"What?" Miranda didn't even want to imagine losing anyone else.

Isabelle was screaming for Miranda. In the heat of the moment, Isabelle's sunken look had faded away. She wasn't her old self again but it was still in there somewhere. Miranda was backing toward the reved up van but she wasn't moving nearly fast enough.

"Go Miranda!" Ramon was screaming as he climbed into passenger seat of Cook's van. They didn't have anything to fight with but the one rifle that Ramon had been carrying when the caravan blew up. One boy with a rifle versus what looked like five (maybe six) very large men with rifles. Miranda didn't want to leave. "Go!"

Miranda climbed into Isabelle's van. Isabelle was slamming on the gas before Miranda could close her door. They flew down the street and gunfire rang out ahead of them. The windshield exploded in a shower of glass and both girls ducked, putting their arms over the back of their heads. The van veered a little to the left and slammed into a bench. The bench was crushed underneath the wheels and the van nearly overbalanced. Isabelle stuck her head back up as the van flew past the truck and managed to keep the van moving. Another blast of gunfire rang out and Isabelle could hear it hit the side of the van. Bullets holes appeared in the side of the rear doors but neither Isabelle nor Miranda was hit. Isabelle turned her attention back to the town road and slammed her foot down on the gas. The van jerked and an unpleasant *klunk* sound came from somewhere underneath the girls' feet. One of those bullets had apparently hit something.

The van was still moving though and it was nearing the edge of town when they heard gunfire again, this time very distant. Cook and Ramon had engaged the truck.

The *klunk* sound came from the van again.

"What is that?" Miranda asked. Her face had gone very pale.

"I don't know!" Isabelle shouted back. Her hands were gripping the wheels so tightly that her knuckles had gone as white as Miranda's face. "I don't know!"

"We need to go back!" Miranda said as she reached out and gripped Isabelle's shoulder much too tightly. "We have to help them!"

"HOW!" Isabelle screamed. She wanted to turn back, of course she did, but they couldn't possibly help. The van would be ripped apart with gunfire before they got anywhere near the truck. Isabelle just kept staring out of the shattered windshield, looking at the road ahead. She had never felt like she did at that moment. So very desperate to escape and save what little bit of her old life was left that she was nearly psychotic with horror. She wanted her old life back. She wanted the old days of dancing back. She wanted the old man Curtis, and sweet Jessie, and even that pain in the ass Nathan back. She wanted her nights of slightly drunk good humor with the other girls back. She wanted the overly fatherly nagging of Andy back. She wanted her caravan back.

And Johnny Boy. She wanted things back to the way they had been when Johnny Boy was first learning her language. She wanted him back to. More than anything else though, she wanted the caravan.

Then she saw it. The caravan roaring toward her from the other end of the road. Her mouth dropped open and her iron grip on the steering wheel loosened. She could feel Miranda's grip on her shoulder fall away as Miranda saw it too. There home, there "life", was barreling down the road. Then a brief glint of setting sunlight reflected off it and they both blinked. When they looked again they could tell it wasn't their caravan. It was much smaller, a completely different color, and rounded in the edges. It felt more like a very elaborate carriage. Even with all those differences though, they thought the same thing.

It is the caravan. Home. It is the caravan.

The caravan didn't slow and flew past them with enough force that the van was pushed away a bit and Isabelle gripped the wheel tightly in fear. She had only an instant to see that Johnny Boy was the one driving the caravan.

6

Johnny Boy barely noticed the van that he had nearly run off the road. He didn't notice that Isabelle was driving it at all. He had caught sight of the truck as it began to accelerate toward the salvage yard, and then all thinking had completely flown from his mind. He got an image, horrible in its clarity, of everyone else from the caravan laying dead. Bullets between their eyes just like Sandy laying somewhere on the road behind him. He had bent down his head pressing against the windshield the steering wheel in his hands seemed to be vibrating even more than it had been when he first hit the maximum speed of the caravan. He had never bothered to take note of just how fast he was going, but he knew he was going way too fast. That the caravan hadn't tipped over already, or blown a tire, or its fan belt, or lost one of the trailers, or anyone of a thousand other things that could've gone wrong going that fast for that long, was nothing short of a miracle. The salvage yard came into view very fast.

Johnny Boy had just a split second to see Ramon and Cook hiding behind one of two large vans with one rifle between them. The truck was parked a few feet away from the vans, Icarus and two guards behind it, and two more crouched in the truck bed. The sound of gunfire rang through Johnny Boy's ears for a split second (he would have nightmares over that sound for years to come) then he closed his eyes and braced for impact.

He could hear a scream of surprise, some man was swearing, and then the caravan slammed into the truck.

7

Icarus had just enough time to turn around and see the caravan flying at him. He rolled right as it tore into the truck. One of the other guards was crushed immediately. The other rolled away. The two in the truck bed were thrown into the air. They all lost their rifles and Icarus could see the boy from behind the van (Icarus was pretty sure his name was Ramon) come running out and snatch one of the rifles up. Icarus reached for his rifle but he had no chance. There was a loud *boom* sound and Icarus was blown right. He hit the edge of a small incline in the ground and slid down onto the road. He could feel the blood flowing out of his side, and he could feel the lower part of his body already growing cold.

There was the sound of gunfire above him as Ramon and Cook took advantage of his guards' momentary defenselessness. Icarus found that he couldn't really care about them anymore, things seemed to be fading away. The Anti-Sandy part of his mind whispered to him, sounding as distant as he was beginning to feel.

"Should've taken the road."

Icarus craned his head up a bit and looked at the street. The road led out of town, toward the east. He could see the path clearly. Open to anyone who saw fit to take it.

"Should've taken the road."

"Yeah," he said in a voice that was little more than a whisper. "I should've."

He fell silent, and died.

8

Johnny Boy fell out of the driver's compartment and landed on his knees in the dirt of the salvage yard. His hands were trembling and his heart was beating so fast that it felt like it was going to pop out of his chest. Cook and Ramon were looking at him in stunned silence; their eyes shifting from him to the caravan. He didn't get what was so amazing about the caravan at the moment. It seemed completely irrelevant next to the suicidal drive he had just taken. It seemed irrelevant next to the new pile of bodies to add to the ever growing pile that he seemed responsible for.

Before he could truly start in on his self-loathing though a thought crossed his mind. The person that had been laying battered and bloody in the road. He turned his attention to Cook and Ramon.

"Andy!" He shouted. "Andy's in the front trailer. He's really hurt!"

Cook and Ramon ran past him and into the main trailer. He watched them go and tried to stand up to follow them. His knees shook and he fell back to the ground. It still didn't feel right. He had saved them, the last people who felt like his family. Why didn't it feel right?

"Cause they won't take me back." He thought. *"I'm still different and dangerous to them. They still won't look at me."* He was still trembling and now he was pretty sure it had nothing to do with how dangerous the run had been.

The van he had nearly ran off the road came to a screeching halt. He looked at it, at the bullet holes that decorated its side and the shattered windshield. His eyes widened when he saw Isabelle and Miranda climbing out of the van. Miranda's eyes fell on the caravan and her mouth dropped as she stared at it. Isabelle stared at Johnny Boy. There was no fear in her face, but no warmth either. Johnny Boy stared back and his trembling stopped.

EPILOGUE

The people in town wanted the group out immediately. Johnny Boy couldn't blame them. The caravan seemed to have drawn a great deal of danger to this tiny little town. The fact that no one in the town was hurt seemed little more than blind luck. Cook was fairly pissed that they had to leave behind two of the three vans, but they weren't needed now that the group had a new caravan and they wouldn't have much resale value with shattered windshields and bullet holes all over them. They left them behind and Cook drove behind the caravan to the next town where she sold it and used the money to buy supplies for her new kitchen. She bitched and moaned about how small it was but she loved it and it showed on her face.

Miranda looked at the new caravan like some type of magical creature. Like Johnny Boy had brought the old one back from the dead and cleaned it up. She wandered around it like a curious little child whenever they stopped and when she looked at Johnny Boy there was a look of genuine gratitude. Johnny Boy found that same look in Ramon's eyes, and even Andy's eyes. Isabelle he saw very little of.

He had talked to Andy one night while he was driving the caravan southeast, he liked the slightly smaller main trailer and told Johnny Boy so.

"You did good ya know." Andy told him. "You saved all of us and you got us moving."

Johnny Boy hadn't said anything to that. He hadn't wanted to take any credit. It was his fault they had been in all that danger anyway as far as he was concerned.

"Why did you come after me?" Johnny Boy asked. Andy looked at him in confusion. "You'd be better off without me wouldn't you?"

Andy smiled kindly to him, it was a look that Johnny Boy wasn't used to seeing on Andy and something in it made him stop feeling sorry for himself. If only for a moment.

"You're part of the caravan Johnny Boy," Andy said, "If there's one thing this whole thing has taught me, you never leave behind a member of the caravan. A member of the family."

Johnny Boy hadn't been able to say anything to that. For all his fear, for all his worry, he couldn't bring himself to even consider leaving again after hearing that. Part of the caravan, part of the family. He left feeling uncertain. He walked the entire way to the opposite end of the trailer then stopped. Isabelle was sitting on the edge of the caravan walkway in front of his room.

"Hi." She said. She still sounded tired but there was some warmth in her voice again. She smiled at him and he smiled back. Both of their smiles were very nervous.

She stood and stretched, she must've been waiting a while. She walked to him and stopped barely an inch away from him. She wouldn't meet his eyes.

"I'm sorry." She said. She looked at him and smiled a little more openly. Her eyes took the slight droop that they always seemed to take when she looked at him. "I'm so sorry for...for hurting you. And I'm glad you're back."

He smiled at her and took her hand in his. She held his hand tight but neither of them moved any closer to each other. He couldn't bring himself to try and kiss her. There was a certainty that she would pull away. Instead he held her hand and said-

"Its good to be home."

She leaned in and kissed the corner of his mouth.

"Welcome home Johnny Boy."

THE END

THE FORTUNE TELLER

COMING SOON